# MOONLIGHT INN

## A COZY READ WITH A TOUCH OF MAGIC AND ROMANCE

### MOONLIGHT SPRINGS
### BOOK FIVE

## LULA WARD

Leanna McMann never asked for the gift that is ruining her life. Every touch floods her with visions of an object's past and, more alarmingly, its future. Desperate for control, she turns to the Moonlight Inn and Verena's guidance, where the walls themselves seem to hum with secrets.

Joe Hall, the quiet craftsman restoring the inn's antiques, understands better than most how stories linger in wood and stone. Together, he and Leanna uncover visions tied to the legendary Amber Stone, a powerful relic whose disappearance has left the town vulnerable to dangerous fractures in time. But they are not the only ones searching. A ruthless developer is racing to claim the stone first, and Leanna's unstable gift may be the only thing standing in his way.

As Joe and Leanna's bond deepens, she must decide whether to hide from her ability or embrace it fully before the past, present, and future of Moonlight Springs collapse into chaos.

Blending heartfelt romance with the

shimmer of magical realism and small-town charm, *Moonlight Inn* is a story of courage, connection, and second chances. Perfect for readers who believe love and destiny can be found in the most unexpected places.

*Have you ever stayed at an old inn where you could almost feel all the history? I have, and we make a point to try to stay at them when we travel. This book is dedicated to all the old inns still welcoming guests.*

# CHAPTER 1

The rumble of the bus engine finally quieted as the brakes hissed to a stop. Leanne McMann pulled her hands deeper into her leather gloves and pressed her back against the worn seat. Through the window, Moonlight Springs unfolded. Quaint shops lined the main street, their painted signs advertising handmade chocolates and artisan pottery. She looked at the doorknobs on storefronts. The wooden benches. The iron railings that everyone grabbed when the sidewalk iced over. Thirty years of strangers touching everything.

She stayed in her seat an extra moment.

"End of the line, miss." The bus driver's voice carried the patient tone of someone who'd said those words a thousand times before.

Leanne nodded and stood carefully, keeping her elbows close to her sides as she navigated the narrow aisle. The noise had started to fade somewhere around hour two of the ride. By the time they crossed into the valley, her head had gone quiet. No echoes of strangers' memories bleeding through car doors and handrails. No grocery lists, arguments, and first kisses, all fighting to get in.

She stepped onto the sidewalk and breathed deeply. The crisp air smelled of pine and river water and hinted that winter was just around the corner.

The bus pulled away, leaving her alone on the corner by Riverside Boardwalk. Moonlight Inn waited at the top of Moonlight Way, a short walk through the historic district. She'd made this walk hundreds of times as a teenager. Back then, she'd run it without thinking. Now she stood on the corner, looking at every surface between here and there.

She started walking, her boots scuffing against the old wooden boardwalk. She passed a bakery where the scent of cinnamon rolls made her mouth water, then a bookstore with stacks of novels visible through mullioned windows. Everything looked inviting and warm.

"Welcome to paradise," she said under her breath.

A woman emerged from the bakery carrying a white box tied with string. She smiled at Leanne, the kind of automatic friendliness small towns were famous for.

Leanne looked away and sidestepped, giving the woman five feet of clearance. The smile faltered, then vanished.

*Five minutes. New record for becoming the town weirdo.*

This was going to go well.

She turned onto Moonlight Way and slowly climbed toward the inn. The road was definitely steeper now than when she'd left over thirty years ago. Was that possible? She paused to catch her breath before continuing, one hand braced against her knee, winded by a hill she used to sprint up for fun.

Moonlight Inn appeared around the next bend. She stopped walking. The familiar building rose from terraced gardens, managing to look both elegant and welcoming. She passed by the garden maze, and her lips lifted in a smile at the memory of getting lost in it on purpose when she was young. The hedges had grown taller, but the pattern looked the same.

She stopped and looked up at the inn. It looked beautiful.

It looked terrifying.

It was old. Very old. And old meant layers upon layers of human experience soaked into every board and stone. Maybe she should rethink this decision on returning to Moonlight Springs…

She stopped at the garden gate. The brass latch was old, polished by thousands of thumbs over a century. Even from two feet away, the latch hummed with accumulated touch. Decades of guests arriving with hope, exhaustion, and secrets.

"Just a gate latch," she told herself. "It's not going to kill you."

But her hands stayed in her pockets. She could stand here until someone let her in. She'd done worse. She'd once spent two hours in a parking lot because she couldn't make herself touch a coffee shop door.

"Okay, McMann. You can't live in the garden like a stray cat."

She pulled out her phone to call Verena, then remembered it had run out of power during the bus ride. The screen remained stubbornly black.

"Perfect. Just perfect."

She slipped her hands in her pockets and nudged the gate open with the toe of her boot. It swung inward with a well-oiled silence.

*Coward*, a voice in her head sneered. *You came all this way to hide?*

She wasn't hiding. She was managing. There was a difference.

Probably.

She climbed the porch steps. The front door was massive oak with a brass handle that looked shaped to fit a human palm perfectly. She stood before it, her heart hammering a frantic rhythm against her ribs.

She raised her gloved hand. She could open it like this. Keep the barrier. Stay safe.

But if she went in there numb, if she walked into that house blind, she'd never know. She needed to know what was waiting for her inside. Was it just old memories? Or was what she'd sensed in her nightmares real?

She bit her lip, the taste of iron sharp on her tongue. Slowly, she peeled the glove off her right hand. Her skin looked pale, almost translucent in the sunlight. Naked.

She reached out.

The moment her skin made contact with the brass, the world split open.

*A young woman in a white dress rushing through the door, tears streaming down her face. The same door opening for a man in a military uniform, his jaw set hard. Children running through, shrieking with laughter. Couples walking hand in hand. A woman in 1940s clothing clutching a telegram. A young man in bell-bottom jeans arguing with someone out of view. Decades of arrivals and departures stacked on top of each other.*

And underneath it all, the door itself seemed to pulse with energy. Energy that had nothing to do with the people who'd touched it.

*The visions shifted, accelerated. She saw the inn not as it was now, but with windows dark and broken. Paint peeling in long strips. Gardens overgrown and wild. The building shimmered. Went translucent. Started to fade.*

The final image sucked the breath right out of her. The inn reduced to nothing but a foundation and a few standing walls. Rubble where the gardens had been. And in the center of the destruction, a stone that pulsed with amber light, then went dark forever.

"No!" She yanked her hand back, stumbling. She caught her heel on a loose board and scrambled for balance, clamping her hand against her chest as if she'd been burned.

The afternoon sun snapped back into focus. The birds were singing. The inn was whole.

"Well, that's one way to make an entrance."

Leanne spun around.

Verena stood in the now-open doorway, tall and graceful with silver-streaked hair twisted into a casual knot and brown eyes that crinkled at the corners. She looked so much the same. She still wore the moonstone pendant around her neck, and it caught in the afternoon sunlight.

"Oh. Verena." Thirty years of birthday cards and occasional phone calls hadn't prepared her for this.

Verena smiled. She opened her arms, a familiar gesture from a lifetime ago. Leanne flinched, a tiny, involuntary movement.

Verena stopped instantly. Her arms lowered slowly to her sides. "Some things don't change, do they?" Her voice was soft. It held no pity, only recognition. She'd seen that look before, decades ago, when Verena had found her crying in the garden maze after touching the wrong antique.

"You got taller," Leanne managed. The joke fell flat even to her own ears.

A small laugh escaped Verena. "Or you got shorter. Come in."

Verena held the door open. Leanne slipped past her without touching her or the doorframe. The air inside was warm. A grandfather clock ticked softly in the corner. For anyone else, it would be a haven. For her, each surface hummed with a quiet history. She kept her gloved hands deep in her coat pockets.

"Your room is at the top. It's quiet there." Verena led the way toward the wide staircase.

The wooden banister glowed with the patina of age. Leanne walked closer to the wall instead, her shoulder nearly brushing the wallpaper. Each step on the creaking stairs was deliberate. She kept her hands in her pockets.

The room at the end of the hall was simple. A comfortable bed was covered with a thick quilt patterned with blue and white stars. A single armchair sat near the window. The furniture looked new. The air felt different here. Cleaner.

"Most of this is new. I thought you'd be more comfortable." Verena leaned against the doorframe.

She walked to the large window. It looked out

over the terraced gardens and the town below, with Shadow Mountain rising dark and majestic in the distance. The view was vast and beautifully impersonal. A landscape didn't hold memories. It just was.

She turned back to Verena and took a shaky breath. "The doorknob. When I touched it, I saw..." Her voice faltered. She couldn't bring herself to describe the chaos, the layers of pain and joy. She focused on the final, terrifying image. "I saw the inn. Destroyed. There was just rubble and a glowing amber stone that went dark."

She turned from the window. She expected to see shock on her old friend's face. Instead, Verena just nodded slowly, her expression serious.

"The disturbances are getting stronger." Verena crossed her arms. "I've felt them too."

"Disturbances?"

"The Amber Stone waking up."

She shook her head in confusion. "The Amber Stone?"

"That's a story for when you're more rested. I can see the trip exhausted you. We'll talk more in the morning."

"No, tell me now."

"Let's just say the stone is calling to you. It wants to be found."

"A *stone* is calling me? How do we find it?"

"The clues are here. Somewhere..." Verena

gestured vaguely to the rest of the house. "They are hidden in the oldest pieces of furniture. The ones that hold the strongest memories."

Her hands went cold inside her gloves. "The oldest pieces?"

"There's a man here. A restorer working on the old furniture. He's got a feel for things. History. I don't know how else to put it. I believe you're supposed to work with him."

Leanne stared at her, the impossible request hanging in the air between them. "Work with him? How?"

"He works with his hands, Leanne. And to find the stone, he'll need you to do the same."

# CHAPTER 2

Leanne unpacked her small suitcase with the door firmly closed. Each item found its place in the room's new dresser, a task she could accomplish without removing her gloves. The simple act of organizing her few belongings gave her something to do besides think about Verena's impossible request.

Work with a furniture restorer. Touch the oldest pieces in the inn and deliberately seek out the very thing she'd spent years avoiding.

She sank onto the edge of the bed and pressed her gloved hands against her knees. Through the window, the sun was setting behind Shadow Mountain, tossing streaks of amber and rose across the sky. The color reminded her of the stone from her vision, pulsing with light before going dark.

A soft knock interrupted her spiraling thoughts.

"Leanne? I've made tea. Come down when you're ready." Verena's voice carried through the door, warm and patient.

She stood and checked her reflection in the small mirror above the dresser. The woman looking back at her had tired eyes and hair that needed washing after the long bus ride. She looked older than her years.

"You came here for answers. Time to start asking questions," she told her reflection.

The hallway was quiet as she made her way back downstairs. The grandfather clock still ticked its steady rhythm. A fire crackled somewhere nearby. The inn felt peaceful in the gathering dusk, like it was settling in for the night.

She found Verena in a small parlor off the main hall. A fire burned in the stone fireplace, and two armchairs sat angled toward the warmth. A tea service waited on a low table between them, steam rising from the pot.

"Chamomile," Verena said, gesturing to the empty chair.

She lowered herself into the chair, grateful it was upholstered in what looked like relatively new fabric. Less history to seep through.

Verena poured tea into two delicate cups painted with tiny flowers. She handed one to Leanne, who accepted it by the handle, careful to keep her gloved fingers away from any surface Verena's bare hands had touched.

They sat in silence for a moment, sipping tea and watching the fire. She counted the ticks of the grandfather clock. Fourteen. Fifteen. Sixteen.

She finally broke the silence. "I had to come back. I had no one else to turn to." She paused and looked directly at her friend. "And you were the first person I thought of. Someone who could... help me. I can't keep doing this. It's getting stronger. It's overwhelming me."

"You did the right thing, coming home."

"I wasn't sure you'd want to see me since I left so suddenly all those years ago."

Verena smiled gently. "I was angry when you left. Not at you specifically. Just angry at the situation. At your gift. At the universe for making you choose between staying in Moonlight Springs and maintaining your sanity."

"I'm sorry."

"Don't be." Verena turned to look at her, face half in shadow from the fire. "You did what you had to do. I understood that, even if I hated it at the time."

"Still. I left you here alone."

"And Gary had left before you. I felt very... abandoned." Verena's mouth curved in a sad smile.

"I've always felt guilty for leaving you like that. But I... I had to."

"I know. And there was something keeping me here. This place. This responsibility. The magic that runs through Moonlight Springs, through everything here.

"And Gary left because he didn't understand."

"Oh, he kind of understood. He just didn't—or couldn't—believe in the magic. That was the problem. He asked me to choose anyway. Choose him or choose this. So I chose."

Leanne heard the echo of her own impossible choice in Verena's words. Stay in a place that overwhelmed her senses every moment of every day, or leave behind everyone and everything she loved. Some choices weren't really choices at all.

"I know that was hard. I should have been there for you."

Verena set down her cup and leaned back in her chair. "Those first few months after you left were the loneliest of my life. Gary was gone. You were gone. The inn felt enormous and empty. The magic felt heavier somehow, like it knew I was alone and decided to test whether I was strong enough to handle it."

"But you were."

"Was I?" Verena's laugh held no humor. "I'm still here, if that's what you mean. But strong? I don't know. Some days, I think I was just too stubborn to fail. Too afraid of what would happen to this place if I walked away."

The fire popped, sending a small shower of sparks up the chimney. Leanne watched them dance and disappear. She thought about all the years she'd spent in the city, insulated from human contact, carefully constructing a life where she could survive without truly living. And here was Verena, who'd chosen the opposite. She'd shouldered an enormous burden alone because someone had to.

"I'm sorry," she said again. The words felt inadequate, but she meant them.

"I told you, don't be." Verena reached across the space between their chairs as if to touch Leanne's hand, then seemed to remember and pulled back. "We all make choices, don't we? And they shape everything that comes after."

"Do they?" She pulled her hands into her lap, wrapping them around each other even through the layers of leather. "Or are we just fooling ourselves? Maybe we're all just walking down paths that were set the moment we were born. And choice? It's just an illusion we cling to so we don't feel quite so helpless."

Verena studied her for a long moment. "When did you get so philosophical?"

"I've had a lot of time alone with my thoughts."

"Too much time, maybe. Leanne, I need you to understand something. The visions you saw when you touched the doorknob? Those aren't inevitable.

The future isn't written in stone, amber, or otherwise."

"Then why show it to me?"

"Because it's a warning. A possibility." Verena's intensity filled the small room. "The Amber Stone of Time doesn't just show the past. It shows what might happen. What you saw, the inn falling apart, that's not set. It's a warning of what might happen if the stone isn't found and if it isn't protected by someone who understands its power."

Uneasiness crept through her. "You think I'm supposed to protect it."

"I think it's calling to you for a reason."

"But I can't even touch a doorknob without falling apart. How am I supposed to handle something as powerful as what I saw?"

"Maybe that's exactly why it chose you." Verena sat back. "You've spent your whole life overwhelmed by the past contained in objects. You know better than anyone how powerful those echoes can be. Who better to guard it?"

"Or who better to be destroyed by it?" She stared at the fire rather than at Verena.

"That's the risk, yes. But running from it won't make it go away. The disturbances are getting stronger every day. People are experiencing moments that haven't happened yet or reliving memories that aren't their own. Time is beginning to fold in on itself."

"And you think I can stop that?"

"I think you're the only one who can."

The fire crackled in the silence that followed. She wanted to argue, to list all the reasons this was… wrong. She couldn't do it. She was broken. She'd been broken for over thirty years. You didn't hand someone like her the keys to something as fundamental as time itself.

But she'd seen the vision. The inn reduced to rubble. The stone going dark. And underneath all her fear, she'd felt something else in that moment of contact with the doorknob. A pull. A recognition.

The stone was calling her home. And she hated that she believed that.

"Tell me about the furniture restorer," she said finally.

Verena's shoulders relaxed, as if she'd been holding her breath waiting for Leanne's decision. "His name is Joe Hall. He's been working here for about three weeks, going through all the antique pieces one by one, cleaning them, repairing them, and bringing them back to life."

"And you think he can help me?"

"I think you can help each other." Verena picked up the teapot and refilled both their cups. "He has a gift for understanding the history in wood and the stories that live in the grain and the joints. He works with his hands the way you read with yours."

"That's not the same thing at all."

"Isn't it?" Verena smiled. "Both of you have spent your lives connected to the past through physical objects. He just chose to embrace it while you ran from it."

The words stung because they were true. "When do I meet him?"

"Tomorrow."

Leanne took a long sip of tea. It helped, a little. Tomorrow, she would meet a stranger and touch furniture that would flood her with visions she couldn't control. And tomorrow she would take the first step toward either saving this place or confirming that she really was as broken as she'd always believed.

"We do all make choices," she said quietly, echoing Verena's earlier words. "And they shape the future."

"Yes." Verena raised her teacup in a small salute. "Here's to hoping we make the right ones this time."

# CHAPTER 3

The next morning, Leanne stood at the top of the grand staircase, leather gloves firmly in place. She'd slept surprisingly well last night, lulled by the distant sound of the river and the comforting weight of the thankfully-not-antique quilt Verena had insisted she use.

No visions. No chaotic flood of memories from strangers long dead. Just sleep.

She could get used to that.

But now, standing here in the daylight with hours stretching ahead before Verena returned from her morning errands, curiosity itched beneath her skin. Moonlight Inn was brimming with history. Every piece of furniture, every decorative object, every doorknob held stories waiting to be discovered.

Or rather, waiting to assault her consciousness whether she wanted them to or not.

"Just exploring. Looking, not touching. We can manage that."

She moved down the stairs slowly, trailing her gloved hand along the banister. Even through the leather, the faint hum of time pressed against her palm. Decades of hands sliding along this same path and countless guests ascending to their rooms after long days. The gloves muffled the sensation to something almost pleasant, like overhearing a conversation from another room rather than having someone shout directly in her ear.

She reached the bottom of the stairs, and there, tucked beside the staircase, was a door she remembered from her childhood. It stood slightly ajar, revealing floor-to-ceiling bookshelves. The library.

Her heart lifted despite her caution. She'd always loved books. They didn't trigger her abilities unless they'd been particularly beloved or traumatic to their owners. Most books carried nothing more than a whisper of turning pages and quiet reading. Bookstores were one of her few safe pleasures.

The door swung silently open under her push.

The library was infinitely cozy. How many hours had she and Verena hung out here, all those years ago, talking and reading? The same two armchairs she remembered flanked a reading lamp. Tall windows let in streams of morning sunlight. The books themselves looked old, their spines cracked and faded in that particular way that spoke of genuine use rather than decorative neglect.

And there, positioned beneath the largest window, stood an antique writing desk that stopped her mid-step. She didn't remember it from before.

It was a masterpiece. Rich mahogany, if she wasn't mistaken, with intricate carvings along the legs and drawer fronts. Floral and geometric patterns mixed in a style that suggested late 19th-century craftsmanship. The desktop showed the gentle wear of decades of use, and the brass hardware had developed a soft patina that only authentic age could provide.

She circled it, hands firmly at her sides. This was why she'd loved her work as a historical researcher and appraiser. Before her abilities had escalated to unbearable levels, she'd been able to use them carefully and selectively to authenticate pieces and uncover their origins. Back then, her curse had purpose.

The desk pulled at her. Not dangerous. Just loud. This piece had stories to tell.

A sound from behind made her spin around.

A man knelt on the floor in the corner near one of the bookshelves, his back to her. He wore well-worn jeans and a blue flannel shirt with the sleeves rolled to his elbows. A canvas tool bag sat open beside him, with various implements spread across a drop cloth. He lifted a piece of carved wood trim, examining it with the kind of focused attention usually reserved for precious gems.

Brown hair grayed at the temples. When he tilted his head to better catch the light, she caught a glimpse of his profile and weathered features that suggested someone who spent time working with his hands rather than sitting behind a desk.

He must have sensed her presence because he turned, those eyes meeting hers with mild surprise.

"Morning." Steady, warm, unhurried. "Didn't hear you come in."

"I didn't mean to disturb you. I can leave if you're working."

"No need. You must be Verena's friend. She mentioned you'd be staying for a while."

"Leanne." She kept her gloved hands tucked firmly into her jacket pockets. "Leanne McMann."

"Joe Hall." He didn't offer to shake hands, which she appreciated more than he could know. Instead, he pointed to the trim piece and the bookshelf behind him. "I'm restoring some of the woodwork. Verena's been after me for months to get to this room."

"Oh, Verena mentioned you. You're restoring? You're a craftsman?" So this was the man Verena insisted she was supposed to work with.

"Furniture restorer, specifically." Something

flickered across his face with a brief tightening around his eyes before settling back into that patient calm. "I specialize in antiques and bring old pieces back to their original condition without erasing their history."

Without erasing their history. If only she could interact with antiques that way. If only she could appreciate their past without being consumed by it.

"That desk." She nodded toward the writing desk. "Is that one of your projects?"

He turned to look at it. His shoulders straightened. His eyes sharpened with interest. "It is. Verena acquired it last year from an estate sale. Beautiful piece, probably 1880s based on the construction and style. But it needs work. The veneer's lifting in places, and one of the drawer runners is cracked."

He crossed to the desk and ran his hand over its surface the way she used to touch things, back when touching was still allowed. Back when her gift was more controllable.

"The craftsmanship is incredible. See how the grain flows continuously through the pattern? Whoever made this understood wood at an intimate level. They worked with it, not against it."

She drifted forward, pulled by his enthusiasm and her own fascination with the piece. She stopped an arm's length away, just close enough to see the details he described but far enough that she wouldn't accidentally brush against anything.

"The carvings. They're not just decorative, are they? There's a story in the pattern."

He glanced at her, eyebrows raised. "You have a good eye. See here?" He traced a series of intertwined roses and thorns. "This repeats on all four legs but with subtle variations."

"Like each corner tells a different part of the same story." She leaned closer, mesmerized despite her caution. "A life story carved into the wood."

"Exactly." His voice warmed. "Most people just see pretty flowers. But whoever commissioned this desk wanted something deeper. They wanted their story preserved."

Preserved. That word again. Her fingers tingled inside her gloves. The desk's pull strengthened, more insistent than before. Not threatening. Inviting. It wanted her to know its history. Wanted her to see.

"How do you know when a piece has a story worth preserving?"

He was quiet for a moment, considering. His hand hovered over the desktop, and she noticed his fingers were scarred and calloused. Working hands. Hands that created and mended.

"You can feel it," he said finally. "The way it's built, the wear patterns. Every scratch tells you something. Who used it. How much they cared. This one was loved."

Step back. Leave the library and find somewhere safe, modern, and devoid of history. Remember why she wore gloves in the first place.

Instead, her hand reached toward the desk.

"The detail here is extraordinary." She was drawn to a particularly intricate carving along the desk's edge. Roses and thorns twisted together in a pattern that seemed almost alive. Her gloved finger hovered an inch above the surface. "I've never seen anything quite like it."

"Neither have I." He moved to stand beside her, close enough that the scent of sawdust and aftershave reached her. "That's what makes restoration work so rewarding. Every piece is unique."

Her finger drifted closer to the wood. Just a better look. Just to appreciate the craftsmanship up close.

Her glove caught on a splinter of lifting veneer.

The vision slammed into her.

A different room. Wallpaper covered the walls in a pattern of blue morning glories. Oil lamps provided the light instead of electric fixtures. And at the desk sat a woman in a high-collared dress, her dark hair swept up in the style of another century.

The woman's hand shook as she dipped her pen in ink. Tears streaked her face, dropping onto the paper. But she kept writing, desperate and determined.

*My dearest Thomas,*

*If you are reading this, then I have failed. Failed to convince Father, failed to make him see reason, failed to save us both from this fate he has chosen. By the time this reaches you, I will be married to a man I do not love.*

Leanne absorbed the woman's anguish as though it were her own. The weight of obligation. The crushing knowledge that love alone was not enough. The desk soaked up every tear, every tremor of the woman's hand, every desperate scratch of the nib across paper.

*But I need you to know this truth, even if I can never speak it aloud. You are my heart. You were always my heart. And though I will wear another man's ring and bear another man's name, that truth will never change.*

*If there is another life beyond this one, find me there. I will be waiting.*

*Forever yours, Elizabeth*

The woman folded the letter with shaking hands. Then, with a furtive glance toward the closed door, she pressed a hidden catch on the side of the desk. A small compartment sprang open, invisible unless you knew exactly where to look.

She tucked the letter inside and closed it again. Her fingers lingered on the wood as though saying goodbye to more than just furniture.

The vision released Leanne abruptly. She stumbled backward, gasping for air. Verena's library swam back into focus.

And Joe, his hand hovering near her elbow, his eyes wide with concern.

"Steady there. Are you all right? You went white as a sheet."

She yanked her arm back by instinct, then felt immediately guilty when hurt flashed across Joe's features. He released her instantly, holding both hands up in a gesture of peace.

"Sorry." Her voice came out rough, throat scraped raw by Elizabeth's grief. "I'm fine. Just... dizzy for a second."

"You should sit down. Can I get you some water?"

"No. No, I'm okay." She pressed her gloved palms against her temples, trying to ground herself in the present. The vision clung to her. Elizabeth's anguish still tasted like salt on her tongue. "I just... that desk. There's something..."

She trailed off. How did she explain her... *gift*... to a stranger? How did she make someone understand that she had just lived a moment from over a hundred years ago and felt a dead woman's heartbreak as intimately as her own memories?

But Joe was looking at the desk now, head tilted. "Something about the desk?"

"It's going to sound crazy." She forced herself to breathe slowly and evenly. The vision was fading, settling into memory rather than overwhelming her present. This was why she hated her gift. Hated the inability to control when and how the past invaded her consciousness. "But I saw something. A woman writing a letter there. Elizabeth. She was saying goodbye to someone named Thomas. She hid it in a secret compartment."

His eyebrows rose, but he didn't laugh or roll his eyes. Instead, he gave the desk that same careful attention he'd given the carved trim. "You saw this? Just now?"

"I know how it sounds… I have this *thing*. This ability, I guess. When I touch old objects, sometimes I see their history. Not always, but often enough that I can't…" She gestured helplessly at her gloves. "That I can't risk it most of the time."

Silence stretched between them. She braced herself for the skepticism, the polite dismissal, the careful backing away that people always did when they realized she was different. Broken.

Instead, he moved to the desk and knelt beside it. His fingers traced along the carved edge where she'd touched it, searching.

"A hidden compartment. Is that what you saw? She hid the letter in a secret compartment?"

"You believe me?"

He shrugged. "Verena mentioned you might be… sensitive. And I've been working in this town long enough to know that strange things happen here. Things that don't have easy explanations."

Methodically, he pressed various points along

the desk's frame, testing, searching. His movements held the confidence of someone who understood how furniture was constructed and where hidden mechanisms might be concealed.

"There. On the side, about two inches down from the top. She pressed right... there."

His finger found the catch. Something clicked softly.

A small drawer popped open, so cunningly concealed that it looked like nothing more than decorative molding. Joe stared at it for a long moment, then looked up at Leanne, mouth slightly open.

"Well, I'll be."

She sank into the nearest armchair, not trusting herself to stand. The compartment was real. Which meant the vision had been real. And meant Elizabeth had been real. "Is there..."

Joe reached carefully into the compartment and withdrew a folded piece of paper, yellowed and brittle with age. He held it like it might crumble to dust. "A letter. There's actually a letter."

He carried it to her and held it out, then seemed to think better of it. "You probably shouldn't..."

"No. I definitely shouldn't."

He set the letter on the small table between the armchairs instead. They both stared at it, this impossible piece of evidence that Leanne's curse was also somehow a gift.

"How long have you been able to do this?" He took the other armchair, keeping a respectful distance but leaning forward.

"Since I was a child. It started small. Just feelings, impressions. But it got stronger as I got older. More detailed. More overwhelming."

"And you can't control it?"

"Not really." A bitter laugh escaped her lips. "Touching something old is like opening a door. Sometimes I just peek through. Sometimes the whole past comes flooding in, and I can't shut it out. That's why the gloves. Why I avoid antiques and old buildings and anywhere with too much history."

"And yet you came to Moonlight Inn, full of history and antiques."

"I needed…" She let out a small sigh. "I needed Verena."

He accepted her explanation, and his gaze moved from her gloved hands to the letter on the table, then to the desk with its hidden compartment.

"So, what you described. The woman writing the letter. Could you see details? The room, what she was wearing?"

She closed her eyes. Elizabeth's anguish washed over her again. "Everything. She wore a high-collared dress, dark blue or maybe gray. Her hair was up. The wallpaper had morning glories. And she was crying because she loved Thomas but had to marry someone else."

"That's incredible. Do you know how valuable that kind of ability would be for historical research? For authentication?"

"That's what I used to do." The admission slipped out before she could stop it. "I was a historical researcher and appraiser. I could verify where an antique came from and detect forgeries. For a while, I thought maybe my curse had a purpose. But then it got stronger. More invasive. I'd shake someone's hand and see their grandmother's death. I'd touch a doorknob and live through decades of arguments and affairs. It became too much."

She met his eyes, expecting pity. Instead, his expression was steady. Open.

"So you ran away."

"I isolated myself. There's a difference. Running implies I was going toward something. I was just trying to escape everything."

He nodded slowly, looked at the letter again, then back at her. "What if you didn't have to? Escape, I mean. What if there was a way to control it instead?"

"If there was, I'd have found it by now."

"Maybe. Or maybe you just needed the right catalyst. Verena said you came back to Moonlight Springs for a reason. That things are intensifying and changing."

"I don't want change. I want to be fixed."

"Maybe they're the same thing."

The quiet words stopped her.

He leaned back in the chair. "I fix broken things. Furniture, mostly. And you know what I've learned? Sometimes you can't restore something to its original condition. Sometimes the damage is part of its story now. But that doesn't mean it's ruined. It just means it's different."

"That's a nice metaphor, but I'm not a broken chair you can sand down and refinish."

"No." His mouth curved in a small, sad smile. "You're a person with an extraordinary ability that you never asked for. And I'm just a carpenter who thinks *maybe* you're looking at this wrong."

"How should I be looking at it?"

He got up and moved to the desk. "This desk has been around for nearly 150 years. It's held Elizabeth's grief, and who knows what other moments of joy and sorrow. All that history is embedded in the wood, and you can access it. You can tell Elizabeth's story when no one else can. That's not a curse. That's a gift."

"A gift that isolates me from everyone and everything."

He turned to face her. "Only because you're trying to shut it out instead of learning to work with it. What if you had help? My help. What if there was a way to channel it, focus it, and use it deliberately instead of just being overwhelmed by it?"

She wanted to argue. Wanted to explain all the ways she'd tried and failed to control her abilities over the years. All the techniques, therapies, and coping mechanisms that had ultimately proved useless.

But somewhere deep inside, beneath layers of fear and resignation, a tiny spark of hope flickered to life. "Even if that were possible, why would you want to help me? You just met me."

"Because Verena asked me to." He flashed her a smile, a real one this time, that crinkled the corners of his eyes.

Leanne laughed. "Verena is impossible to say no to, isn't she?"

He nodded. "That she is."

# CHAPTER 4

The afternoon air bit at Leanne's cheeks as she and Verena made their way down the winding path from the inn toward town. Maple trees lined the walkway, their mostly bare branches clicking together in the breeze. A few stubborn leaves still clung on, brilliant red-orange against the gray sky.

Leanne kept her gloved hands tucked into her jacket pockets. The leather gloves were soft and worn, practically a second skin after all these years. She'd tried cotton once, silk another time, but always came back to these. They were her armor, thin as it was.

"I forgot how beautiful this walk is." The comment felt safe, neutral. Better than the dozen questions racing through her mind.

Verena glanced at her with that knowing look

she'd mastered. The same one she'd used when they were teenagers and Leanne had tried to pretend everything was fine. Some things never changed.

"You've been gone too long. This town has missed you."

Moonlight Springs had gotten along just fine without her. Better, probably. No awkward explanations about why she couldn't shake hands or why she flinched away from casual touches. No pitying looks when people remembered what she was.

A psychic. A freak. A woman whose own mother had learned to announce herself before entering a room, just in case.

They reached the stone steps leading to Moonlight Way. Leanne counted them without meaning to. Thirty-two. The same number as thirty years ago. Her boots scraped against the worn treads, and she wondered how many thousands of feet had traveled this path. How many memories were embedded in these stones.

She pushed the thought away before her fingers could itch with curiosity.

The town square opened up before them, and Leanne stopped walking. "Oh," she whispered.

Moonlight Springs hadn't just survived in her absence. It had thrived. The square bustled with afternoon activity. A farmer's market occupied one corner, with vendor stalls arranged in neat rows. A freshly painted gazebo sat in the center, surrounded by benches where couples sat close together and an old man fed pigeons. Shop windows glowed with warm light despite the overcast day.

She spotted a clothing store that hadn't existed before and a cafe with outdoor seating, with tables occupied by people wrapped in scarves and nursing steaming mugs.

"There's a lot that's new here in town. Ivy reopened her Nana's bakery. You remember Sweet Memories Bakery, don't you? And Maura, Francine's granddaughter, reopened Starlight Antiques."

"I guess it's nice that some places still exist, even if they have new owners."

"And we have new places too. Not only this cafe and that clothing store…" Verena pointed to the new businesses. "And down on the boardwalk, there is a new bookstore and a gallery. I'll have to introduce you to the owners. Hazel owns Enchanted Bookshop, and Quincy opened Crystal River Gallery."

"I guess it's inevitable that things change."

"Some things change." Verena paused. "Most things, actually. But not the important ones."

Leanne started to say something, but her friend was already moving forward. They continued down the sidewalk. She kept her hands firmly in her pockets, her elbows close to her body. Someone brushed past her shoulder, and she tensed, but it was just fabric on fabric. Safe. No visions of where that coat had been, who had worn it before, or what sorrows or joys had soaked into its fibers.

They reached a bench near the gazebo. Verena sat, patting the space beside her. Leanne remained standing for a moment, studying the structure. It was older than she remembered, or maybe she was just noticing details she'd been too young to see before.

She sat down, maintaining a careful distance between herself and Verena. The metal bench was cold through her jeans. At least it was new enough not to scream its history at her. Small mercies.

Verena angled slightly on the bench so she could look directly at Leanne. "Okay, I think it's time we talked. I mentioned the Amber Stone, but there are actually six stones that protect the town."

Leanne opened her mouth to ask another question, but the air changed.

It happened so fast she didn't have time to understand what she was feeling. A pressure built behind her eyes, sharp and sudden. The autumn afternoon seemed to brighten, colors intensifying until they hurt.

Then the world split.

Not literally, but close enough that her vision doubled, tripled, fractured into overlapping images that made her stomach lurch.

The town square was still there. The farmer's market, the people in modern clothes, the cars parked along the street. But superimposed over it, translucent but growing more solid with each passing second, was something else.

The same square, but different. The gazebo looked newer. The buildings surrounding the square wore different facades. Gas lamps lined the streets instead of electric lights. And the people—

She gripped the bench, her gloved fingers digging into the wood.

The people flickered in and out of existence. Men in dark suits and bowler hats. Women in long dresses with bustles and elaborate hats. They walked through the same space as the modern residents, two groups occupying one location, neither aware of the other.

A woman in a green Victorian dress walked straight through a man buying apples at the farmer's market. He stumbled, looking around in confusion. The vendor steadied him, concern creasing her face.

"What—" The man shook his head. "I felt cold. Like someone walked over my grave."

More people were reacting now. A child pointed at empty air, insisting she saw a horse and carriage. Her mother pulled her close, frowning. Two teenagers near the library stopped mid-conversation, their heads swiveling as if trying to track something invisible.

The Victorian scene grew stronger. Leanne could hear it now, voices calling out in old-fashioned cadences. The clip-clop of horses' hooves on cobblestones. Music from somewhere, a brass band playing a waltz.

A banner stretched across the square in that other time, its words wavering but readable: "Harvest Festival 1889."

"Leanne." Verena's hand hovered near her arm but didn't touch. "Stay with me. Focus on my voice."

The disturbance lasted less than a minute, but it felt like an eternity. The Victorian festival scene flickered like a faulty projection, then began to fade. The sounds diminished. The translucent figures grew thinner, more ghostlike, until finally, they winked out entirely.

The modern world remained, but everyone in it looked shaken. People clustered together, talking in urgent, worried voices. A few sat on benches, heads in their hands. The child who'd seen the horse and carriage was crying.

Leanne looked down and found her hands shaking. She stared at the gloves. For once, she wished she had touched something, anything, to explain what had just happened. At least her visions came with context, with history she could understand, even if she couldn't control it.

She turned to Verena. "Okay. I'm not sure what just happened, but please tell me that wasn't the town's ghost-themed historical reenactment group getting a little too into character. Because if so, their budget is out of control."

Verena's lips curved into a small smile. "No, it wasn't that."

"I think you need to explain what's going on. This has something to do with the Amber Stone, doesn't it? Tell me about the stone. All of it. Not the edited version you gave me last night when I was half-dead from exhaustion."

Verena's expression shifted with a look that came from bearing something too long alone.

"It's actually six stones. Six protections. They were hidden throughout Moonlight Springs generations ago, when the town's magic needed to be preserved and protected. Each stone has a purpose. Amethyst for protection. Sapphire for memories. Ruby for stories. Emerald for visions. Amber for time. Opal for unity."

"And they're actually real." She heard the skepticism in her own voice, even as she knew it was ridiculous. She touched objects and saw their pasts. Who was she to doubt magic?

"They're real. We've found four. The women who found them each had abilities similar to yours.

Different gifts, but all connected to something greater than themselves."

"And now time is breaking." She said it flatly, a statement rather than a question.

"Yes."

"This has been happening more frequently," Verena said quietly. "It started about a month ago. Small things at first. A flicker here, a shadow there. But they're getting worse. Lasting longer. Affecting more people."

"The Amber Stone."

"Yes."

Leanne stood. She needed to move, to walk, to do something other than sit still while her mind raced. She paced in front of the bench, her boots scuffing against the pavement. "The visions I've been having. They're not random. They're warnings."

"They're the stone calling to you."

She stopped walking. She turned to face Verena, and for the first time since arriving in Moonlight Springs, she let herself really look at her old friend. The silver threads in Verena's dark hair. The fine lines around her eyes. The moonstone pendant that she'd been wearing since the night Gary left her, resting against her collarbone.

"Why me? I can't even control what I have. I've spent thirty years running from this ability, learning to avoid it. You want me to suddenly embrace it?

Use it? Find some magical stone that controls time itself?"

Verena stood too. She moved slowly and deliberately, keeping space between them, respecting boundaries the way she always had, even when they were teenagers and Leanne had first started wearing gloves.

"The others asked the same question," Verena said. "Maura, when she could see protective wards around buildings. Ivy, when her pastries started triggering time slips. Hazel, when she found herself literally pulled into stories. Quincy, when her paintings began predicting the future. They all thought their gifts were curses. They all learned otherwise."

"This is different."

"How?"

She gestured at the square, where people were still recovering from the disturbance in time. "Because I'm not special. I'm just broken. And now you're telling me that my broken brain is somehow the key to saving this town from whatever that was?"

"It's not the visions that broke you, Leanne."

She wanted to argue, to defend herself, to list all the very valid reasons she'd learned to be afraid. The boyfriends who'd fled when she'd accidentally seen their darkest secrets. The job opportunities she'd lost when employers discovered she couldn't handle certain tasks. The simple, devastating loneliness of never being able to accept a hug.

But standing in the town square, surrounded by confused residents trying to process what they'd just witnessed, Leanne couldn't form the words.

"The Amber Stone controls, well, not time exactly. More like how time all fits together," Verena continued. "Past, present, future. All intertwined. And your ability connects you directly to that web. You see the past in objects, yes. But the visions you've been having? Those are different. Those show you what could happen if the stone remains lost and unguarded."

"The inn in ruins."

"Yes."

"The whole town, maybe."

Verena nodded.

She counted to four on the inhale, held for four, and exhaled for four. The therapist who'd taught her that technique had charged two hundred dollars an hour. At least something stuck.

"You said I'm supposed to be its Guardian." The word felt foreign in her mouth. Guardian. Like she was someone noble, someone chosen. Not a woman who'd spent three decades hiding from her own hands.

"The stone doesn't call to just anyone. It recognizes something in you. A connection. The ability to understand its power because you share a piece of it."

A gust of wind swept through the square. Leanne watched leaves skitter across the pavement, chasing each other in circles. "What happens if I can't find it?" she finally asked.

"Then this keeps happening. Gets worse. Eventually, the town won't snap back to normal afterward. It'll just... stay broken. Every era happening at once, all the time."

"That's not ominous at all. Just a town-wide case of perpetual jet lag. With ghosts. Got it."

Verena's lips twitched. Almost a smile. "I've always appreciated your sense of humor."

"It's either that or screaming."

"I've found humor to be more productive."

They stood together in silence for a moment. Around them, the town continued its attempt to return to normal. The farmers' market was packing up early, vendors clearly eager to leave. The outdoor cafe had emptied. Even the pigeons seemed unsettled, flapping away from the square.

"Tell me about the others," Leanne said finally. "The women who found the other stones. How did they do it?"

Verena's expression softened. "They learned to trust. Their abilities, certainly. But more importantly, they learned to trust other people. Each of them had someone. A partner who could handle knowing about all this. Someone to hold onto when it got strange. The stones aren't meant to be found alone."

"And I have Joe." She said his name carefully, testing how it felt.

"Joe understands history in ways most people don't. His hands have touched thousands of objects, restored them, and brought them back to life. He knows how to listen to what old things have to say."

"Without losing his mind in the process."

"He could teach you to do the same."

Leanne wanted to believe that. Believe the small spark of hope Joe had kindled yesterday. The way he'd found that hidden compartment, validating her vision instead of dismissing it. The way his hands had moved over the desk, reverent and sure.

She shoved that last thought away. This wasn't about attraction or connection or any of the things she'd long ago accepted she couldn't have. This was about survival. The town's, and maybe her own.

"Where do we start?" she asked.

"With the inn's oldest piece. The grandfather clock in the entrance hall. It's been there since the inn was built. If any object knows the stone's location, it's that clock."

"Of course it is," she muttered. She'd walked past that clock a dozen times already, carefully avoiding even looking at it too directly. It practically hummed with accumulated time. She could feel its hundred-plus years of ticking from across the room.

They walked back toward the inn together. The path seemed steeper now, or maybe Leanne was just dragging her feet. The trees rattled overhead, their clicking branches like a countdown.

"Leanne," Verena said as they climbed the stone steps. "You asked why you. Why now?"

"And?"

"Because you're the only one strong enough to bear it. Your gift, properly channeled, becomes strength. The stone knows that. I know that. Eventually, you'll know it too."

*Strong enough?* The woman who considers successfully navigating a grocery store without touching a single stray shopping cart a major victory is strong enough to wrangle time itself? The universe really needed to re-evaluate its hiring practices.

# CHAPTER 5

The morning light fell across the butcher block counter where Verena kneaded bread dough. The rhythmic motion soothed her, the way it always had. Her hands pressed into the soft dough, folded it over, pressed again. Simple. Grounding. Nothing magical about flour and water and yeast, except perhaps the everyday miracle of transformation.

She'd been awake since before dawn, unable to sleep after yesterday's disturbance in the town square. The vision of that Victorian harvest festival overlaying the present had shaken even her, though she'd kept her composure for Leanne's sake. The Amber Stone was calling out more desperately now, its absence creating larger and larger rifts in time.

The kitchen smelled of rising dough and the lavender tea steeping on the counter. She had set out two cups on instinct. She was fairly certain Gary would be stopping by. That instinct had sharpened over the years, though she still couldn't tell if it was magic or simply the muscle memory of caring for someone she'd known most of her life.

The back door opened without a knock. Only one person entered her kitchen that way.

"Morning, Vee."

Gary's voice was a little deeper now with age but still able to make her heart skip a beat. But she ignored that.

"Help yourself to tea." She nodded toward the counter without looking up from her dough. "Lavender. Should help with that tension you're carrying in your shoulders."

"How do you know I'm tense?" He moved to the counter, his footsteps familiar on her kitchen floor.

"Sheriff, you've been tense since you pinned that badge on." She finally glanced up at him, allowing herself a small smile. "Also, you're doing that thing where you roll your neck like it might actually help."

He laughed and stopped mid-roll. "Caught."

He poured tea into both cups and brought one to her, setting it carefully within reach. He knew better than to interrupt her kneading. She'd taught him that over forty years ago, back when her hair was still brown, and neither had so much as a trace of silver.

He leaned against the counter beside her

workspace, close enough that she caught the clean scent of his soap and cedar, maybe. Or pine. Something that reminded her of the forests surrounding the town and the long walks they used to take before everything got complicated.

"Had another incident last night." He sipped his tea, his eyes on her hands working the dough. "Mrs. Baker called about strange music coming from her attic. When I got there, she said she could hear a big band playing, clear as day. By the time I arrived, it had stopped."

Verena's hands stilled for a moment before resuming their rhythm. "The 1940s. Her house was a boarding house back then. They used to host dances in that attic every Saturday night."

"That's what she said too." Gary's voice held a question he wasn't quite asking. "Said her grandmother told her stories about it."

"The past is getting louder." She shaped the dough into a smooth ball and placed it in an oiled bowl, covering it with a clean cloth. She wiped her hands on her apron, finally turning to face him fully. "The time disturbances are increasing."

"Is that what we're calling them? Time disturbances?" The corner of his mouth quirked up. "Sounds very scientific."

"Would you prefer weird time hiccups?"

"Actually, yes. More honest." He set down his cup, and his expression grew serious. "Vee, people are getting scared. I've had a dozen calls in three days. Yesterday's incident in the square terrified half the town. I need to tell them something."

She met his eyes, those steady hazel eyes that had always seen too much. "Tell them we're working on it."

"Are you?"

"Yes."

"Does this have to do with Leanne? She's back in town, right?" He paused. "I saw you two in the square right before the disturbance hit."

Verena moved to the sink and washed the flour from her hands. The water ran warm over her fingers. She could feel Gary's gaze on her back, patient but persistent. He'd always been good at waiting her out.

"You remember Leanne."

"Of course, I do. You two were inseparable when you were younger. But she left town, right?"

She dried her hands slowly. "She left town about thirty years ago."

"And she's back now because?"

"Because she needs my help. And… the town needs hers." She turned, leaning against the sink. The morning light fell behind Gary, softening his edges. "She has certain abilities that might help with our current situation."

"Abilities." He didn't make it a question, but his eyebrows rose slightly.

"She can touch things and see their history. Their past." She picked up her tea, warming her hands on the cup even though the kitchen was perfectly comfortable. "It's not an easy gift to carry."

He absorbed this the way he absorbed most things about Moonlight Springs' particular strangeness. With a slow nod and no judgment. "And you think she can help stop these time disturbances?"

"I think she might be the only one who can. But it's going to be difficult for her. She's spent most of her life running from her abilities. Now I'm asking her to run toward them."

"Sounds familiar." His voice held gentle teasing, but his eyes were serious. "Someone else I know spent a long time running from things."

"I never ran."

"No. You dug in your heels and stayed put." He moved closer, just a step, but it felt like more. "Even when it cost you."

"I made the choice I had to make."

"I know." He reached out slowly, giving her time to move away if she wanted. When she didn't, his hand covered hers on the cup. "I finally understand why. Doesn't mean I don't wish things had been different."

"Gary." She didn't pull away, but she didn't lean

in either. Forty years had taught her caution. "We can't—"

"I'm not asking for anything." His thumb brushed across her knuckles, a whisper of touch that shouldn't have undone her but did. "Just acknowledging what's here. What's always been here."

Before she could respond, footsteps sounded in the hallway leading to the kitchen. They sprang apart, or rather, Gary stepped back smoothly while Verena turned to the stove with her tea like she'd been there all along.

Leanne appeared in the doorway, already gloved despite the early hour, her arms wrapped around herself. She stopped short when she saw Gary, and her eyes widened.

"Oh. I'm sorry, I didn't realize—" She started to back away.

"Leanne." Gary's face shifted into a smile of recognition. "Good to see you."

"Gary Daniels." Leanne's voice held surprise interlaced with caution. "You're here. In Moonlight Springs."

"Got back a few months ago." He moved toward the door, giving Leanne space to enter or retreat as she chose. "Took the sheriff position. Figured it was time to come home."

"Sheriff." Leanne glanced between Gary and Verena. "That's quite a change."

"Life's full of them." He paused at the doorway, his eyes finding Verena's. "I should get to the station. Thanks for the tea."

"Anytime."

He nodded to Leanne. "Good to see you back in town. Hope you're staying awhile."

"We'll see."

Gary left through the back door, and silence filled the kitchen in his wake. Leanne remained in the doorway, her posture stiff, her gloved hands tucked into her cardigan pockets.

Verena busied herself at the stove, pulling down a third cup. "Tea?"

"Gary Daniels is back. The man who broke your heart." Leanne moved into the kitchen slowly, like she was navigating a room full of fragile objects. "The man who left forty years ago and swore he'd never set foot in this town again."

"People change their minds." Verena poured hot water over fresh tea leaves, watching them steep. "Time has a way of shifting perspectives."

"Verena." Leanne stopped on the other side of the butcher block island, putting solid wood between them. "What's going on? And don't give me one of your cryptic non-answers. I just saw the way you two looked at each other."

Verena set the teapot down. Her friend had always been observant, even before her abilities had sharpened that skill to a supernatural edge. There was no deflecting Leanne when she'd made up her mind to push.

"He came back a few months ago." She handed the fresh cup across the island, making sure Leanne could take it without their hands touching. "The sheriff position was open. He applied."

"Just like that? Out of nowhere?"

"Yes, just like that. I was as surprised to see him as you just were."

"And everything that happened all those years ago? How he broke your heart?"

"It was a long time ago."

"Not that long ago that you've forgotten." Leanne's voice softened. "I saw your face just now, Vee. That's not all just ancient history."

She moved to the window, looking out at her garden. The maze of hedges stretched toward the old oak grove, their shapes familiar and comforting. She'd walked those paths thousands of times, often alone, always aware of the choice she'd made all those years ago.

"When he left, I thought I'd made peace with it." She spoke to the window, to the garden, to the ghosts of past decisions. "I chose this town and the inn. My responsibilities here. He wanted to see the world. We wanted different things."

"And now?"

"Now he's back, and I don't know what we want." Verena had built her life on certainty, on knowing her purpose and fulfilling it without complaint. Uncertainty wasn't something she handled well. "I don't know if we get a second chance at this. I don't know if we should even try."

Leanne was quiet for a long moment, her tea steaming between her gloved hands. "Does he know? About all of this? The stones and the magic?"

"Some of it. Not all." She turned back to face her friend. "It's complicated."

"Love usually is." Leanne's mouth slanted into a wry smile. "Though I'm probably not the best person to give relationship advice, considering I've spent three decades avoiding human contact."

"You're here now."

"Because… I felt this impossibly strong pull to return. Not because I'm brave."

"You came back. That counts."

"Or foolish."

"Often the same thing." Verena smiled. "Though I prefer to call it optimistic stubbornness."

Leanne laughed, a real laugh that softened the tension in her shoulders. "Optimistic stubbornness?"

"Better than catastrophically poor judgment, which is what my mother would have said."

They sipped their tea in comfortable silence, the kind that only existed between people who'd known each other since childhood.

"So." Leanne set down her cup. "So Gary's back, and the town's falling apart. Busy week. Did I miss anything?"

"That about covers it."

"And people say small towns are boring."

She smiled. "Those people have clearly never been to Moonlight Springs."

"Fair point." Leanne straightened her shoulders, the gesture small but significant. "All right. Where do we start today?"

"The grandfather clock in the main hall." Verena rinsed her cup in the sink, buying herself a moment. "Been here since the inn first opened. It's the oldest piece in the inn."

"Of course it is. Why would we start with something easy, like a doorknob or a spoon?"

"Where's the challenge in that?"

"Challenge. Right. I'll go look at it, but I'm not going to touch it."

"First, I think you should talk to Joe. See if he can help you."

"He'll probably think I'm nuts." Leanne frowned.

"And yet, when you think about it, you feel like you should go talk to him, don't you?"

Leanne let out a long sigh. "Yeah, I think I should."

"If you don't find him in the library, look out

back in the old workshop. He's been working out there quite a bit."

Leanne moved toward the doorway, then paused. "And Verena? About Gary? Don't overthink it."

She left before Verena could respond, her footsteps fading down the hallway toward the main rooms.

Verena stood alone in her kitchen, surrounded by the scents of rising bread and lavender tea. Her hand drifted to the moonstone pendant at her throat.

The bread would need punching down in an hour. The guests would want breakfast soon. The inn required her attention, as it always had, as it always would. And after that, she might figure out what to do about Gary. Or she might not. The bread wouldn't wait either way.

Leanne tucked her gloved hands deeper into her cardigan pockets and followed the worn stone walkway behind Moonlight Inn toward a cedar-shingled building nestled between two ancient oaks.

The workshop door stood open despite the morning coolness. She paused at the threshold, letting her eyes adjust to the dimmer interior. Sunlight filtered through high windows. The space smelled of sawdust and linseed oil, of cedar and walnut, maybe. Or cherry. The scents layered over each other like pages in a book, each one telling its own story.

Joe stood at a workbench near the far wall, his attention focused on a chair back he was sanding. He moved with the same deliberate patience she'd noticed yesterday in the library. Each stroke of sandpaper followed the grain, careful and precise. His flannel sleeves were rolled to his elbows, revealing forearms dusted with fine wood particles that caught the light.

She cleared her throat.

Joe looked up, his brown eyes registering surprise before settling into something more guarded. He set down the sandpaper and wiped his hands on a rag hanging from his belt.

"Morning."

"Morning. Verena said I might find you here." She stayed in the doorway, one foot still on the stone path outside. Easier to retreat if this went badly.

"Something I can help you with?"

Direct. No small talk. She appreciated that, even as her stomach twisted with nerves. She forced herself to step fully inside, though she kept her hands firmly in her pockets. "Actually, yes. I need to ask you something. Something that's going to sound strange."

"Stranger than a woman who can read a desk's memories?" One corner of his mouth lifted slightly. Not quite a smile, but close enough to ease some of her tension.

"Fair point." Leanne moved closer, navigating around a half-finished sideboard and a stack of reclaimed wood. "You might have heard there was a bit of a… ah… time disturbance in town yesterday."

Joe picked up the rag again, folding it with more attention than the task required. "Verena mentioned some strange things have been happening. Said you might be able to help."

"I might. If I can find what's causing it." She stopped a few feet from his workbench, close enough to see the grain in the wood he'd been sanding but not close enough to accidentally brush against anything. "There's a stone. The Amber Stone of Time. It's been lost for generations, and without it, the town's magic is destabilizing. The visions I'm having are connected to it. My… *gift*… might be able to track it through the objects here at the inn."

Joe set down the rag. His jaw worked slightly, a muscle jumping near his temple.

"Town magic, huh?"

She nodded.

"So you want to touch more furniture." He said it like it was a normal comment to make to a person.

"Not exactly." She pulled her hands from her pockets, holding them up. The soft leather gloves looked almost delicate in the dusty light. "I need to touch the right furniture. The oldest pieces. The ones that have soaked up the most history. And I need someone who understands those pieces, who knows how they were made and how they've survived. Someone who can help me make sense of what I see."

"That's a tall order."

"I know."

He turned back to the chair, running his thumb along the curve of the wood. The gesture looked unconscious, automatic. The way some people twisted their hair when they were thinking. He looked up then, directly into her eyes. "What happened yesterday, with the desk. That was real."

It wasn't quite a question, but Leanne answered anyway. "The letter was real. Elizabeth was real. All of it happened exactly as I saw it."

"And you've been dealing with this your whole life."

"Since I was eight and touched my grandmother's wedding ring." The memory still burned. The rush of joy and terror as her grandmother had gone into labor, alone in a farmhouse during a blizzard. "It's gotten stronger over the years. More intense. Harder to control."

"That why you left town?"

The question was harder to answer than he probably intended. Leanne wrapped her arms around her middle, a poor substitute for the hug she'd probably never be able to accept.

"Part of it. Moonlight Springs has a lot of history. Every building and every object carries decades or centuries of memories. It was too much. I thought if I went somewhere newer, somewhere with less past, it might be easier."

"Was it?"

She managed a thin smile. "For a while. Turns out even new places have old things."

His gaze was steady, assessing but not unkind. "What do you need from me?"

"Your expertise. Your knowledge. And maybe your hands. Sometimes I need someone to move objects, position them, and hold them steady while I try to read them. I can't always do it myself without getting overwhelmed."

"You want me to be your assistant in all this."

"I want you to be my partner." She hurried to clarify. "In finding the stone. Verena seems to think we need to work together. That your understanding of these pieces and my ability to read them might be the key."

He picked up a chisel from the workbench, testing its edge with his thumb. Not hard enough to cut, just feeling the sharpness. When he spoke, his voice was measured. "I work with wood. With solid, physical things I can see and touch and fix. These stones and visions. That's not my world."

"I know."

"But you're asking me to step into it anyway."

"I'm asking you to help save the town." She pulled her gloves tighter. "Yesterday's disturbance in the square was just the beginning. They're getting worse. More frequent. Eventually, past and present might blur so badly that neither one exists anymore. Everything Moonlight Springs has been, everything it could be, just collapses into chaos. I think that's what I saw when I first got here and touched the doorknob to the inn."

The chisel stilled in Joe's hand. "That's what you saw?"

"Mostly." She didn't want to describe the rest. The ruins and the darkness. The terrible silence where the town's heartbeat should have been. "I've never seen anything that far forward before. My gift usually shows me the past, sometimes glimpses of things happening in the present. But that vision was the future. And it was clear. That doesn't happen unless something is very, very wrong."

Joe set down the chisel and crossed his arms. Not defensive, exactly. More like he was literally holding himself together while he processed. "What if I can't help? What if I don't know enough, or we can't figure out where this stone is?"

"Then we try anyway. Because the alternative is doing nothing and watching the town fall apart."

Silence stretched between them, broken only by the distant sound of birds in the garden and the creak of the old building settling. She waited.

Finally, Joe exhaled and uncrossed his arms. "Okay, I'll help. My family lived here years ago. My grandparents and great-grandparents. I've been here myself for over twenty-five years. This town is my home." He moved to a shelf on the far wall, scanning the tools arranged there. "I'll help, but I need to understand what I'm working with. What you're working with."

"What do you mean?"

He selected something from the shelf and turned back. He held a wood plane, the kind used for smoothing rough lumber. The tool had a warm patina, its wooden body dark with age and countless applications of oil. The metal blade gleamed despite obvious wear.

"This belonged to my great-grandfather. He was a finish carpenter and built half the trim work in the original houses around here." He moved closer, holding the plane carefully. "If your gift works the way you described, you should be able to read it. Tell me what you see."

"You want to test me."

"I want to understand. There's a difference. And maybe you need to see that not every vision has to be overwhelming. You said yesterday's experience with the desk was powerful but clear. Focused. Maybe that's because you were working with me. With someone who understood the object you were reading."

"Or maybe it was a fluke." But even as she said it, hope flickered in her chest. Small, but present.

"Only one way to find out."

She stared at the plane. It looked innocent enough in Joe's steady hands. Just a tool, well-used and well-loved. But she knew better. Every object carried its history in invisible layers, waiting for her touch to peel them back.

She flexed her gloved fingers. The leather felt thinner than usual, less protective. Her usual barriers seemed suddenly inadequate.

"I'll need to remove my gloves."

"Figured as much."

"If it's bad and I can't control it, I might drop the plane."

"I'll be right here." His voice carried the same patient steadiness he'd used when sanding the chair. "And this old thing has survived worse than a fall. Built to last."

She nodded, not trusting her voice. She worked the first glove off slowly, peeling the leather back from her wrist. The cool air hit her skin like a shock. She'd worn gloves for so long that bare hands felt almost obscene. Vulnerable.

The second glove joined the first, tucked into her jacket pocket.

Her hands looked pale in the workshop light. Small and fragile compared to Joe's work-roughened ones. These hands had betrayed her a thousand times, showing her things she never wanted to see and connecting her to traumas and sorrows that weren't hers to carry.

But they were the only hands she had.

"Ready when you are." He held the plane steady, not pushing but not retreating either.

She reached out. Her fingers trembled slightly as they approached the smooth wooden body of the plane. At the last second, she almost pulled back. Almost put her gloves back on and walked away from all of this.

Instead, she touched the wood.

*The vision came immediately, but not like the usual assault. This time, it flowed like warm water, gentle and clear. She saw a workshop, older than this one but similar in spirit. A man stood at a bench, his hands guiding this same plane across a length of golden pine. Wood shavings curled away from the blade, perfect spirals that fell like ribbons at his feet.*

*Charles Hall. The name came with the image, along with a sense of who he was. Careful. Precise. Proud of his work but humble about his skill. He was crafting window trim for the Miller house, third one that month. Good, steady work. Good, steady pay to support his young family.*

*She felt his satisfaction as the plane revealed the wood's true beauty beneath the rough surface. Felt his quiet joy in the simple act of creation. There was no trauma here, no sorrow or fear. Just honest work and honest pride.*

*The vision shifted. Charles was older now, teaching a boy to use the plane. He guided small hands on the tool, showing him how to read the grain, how to let the wood tell him which direction to cut.*

*"Always respect what you're working with," Charles said. His voice echoed across the decades, warm and patient. "Wood has memory. It knows what it was and what it wants to become. Your job is just to help it get there."*

The workshop faded. She found herself back in the present, her hand still resting on the plane in Joe's grip. Her cheeks were wet.

She was crying.

Not from pain or fear, but from the sheer unexpected beauty of what she'd witnessed. The vision had been gentle. Warm. Almost welcoming.

"You all right?" His eyes searched her face.

She lifted her hand from the plane and wiped at her face with her palm. "Your great-grandfather, Charles. He was a good man."

"You saw him?"

"I saw him working. Teaching. He loved this plane. Loved what it could do." She laughed, the sound watery but genuine. "He told this boy he was teaching that wood has memory. That it knows what it wants to become."

Joe's expression shifted, something unreadable crossing his features. "My grandfather used to say that. Said it was the most important lesson he ever learned."

"It's true. I felt it." She looked down at her bare hands, still trembling slightly but no longer from fear. "That vision was different. Clear. Focused. Not overwhelming at all."

"Because you knew I was here? Holding the other end?"

"Maybe." She met his eyes. "Or maybe because the object itself carried good memories. Love and pride instead of pain."

"Not everything old has trauma attached to it."

"No. Not everything does." The realization settled over her.

Joe set the plane back on the workbench, treating it with even more care than before. When he turned back to her, his expression had shifted from guarded to certainty.

"I'll help you. With the furniture, with finding this stone. Whatever you need." He picked up the rag again, worrying it between his fingers. "But I've got one condition."

"What's that?"

"We do this carefully. You don't push yourself past what you can handle. And if a vision starts going bad, you pull back. I don't care if we're halfway to finding the stone. Your safety comes first."

The protectiveness in his voice surprised her. They barely knew each other and had shared maybe an hour of actual conversation. But he looked at her like she mattered. Like her well-being was worth protecting.

She hadn't felt that from anyone in longer than she could remember.

"Deal." She extended her still-bare hand toward him. "Partners?"

He looked at her hand, then at her face. "You sure? Skin contact might give you another vision."

Her hand stayed steady despite her racing heart. "I know, but some risks are worth taking."

His calloused palm met hers in a firm shake. The contact sent a faint tingle through her fingers, but no vision came. Just the warmth of human touch, simple and uncomplicated.

It was the first time in thirty years she'd shaken someone's hand without fear.

When Joe released her, she found herself smiling. Actually smiling, wide enough that her cheeks ached from the unfamiliar stretch.

"So." She pulled her gloves back on. "Where do we start?"

Joe moved to a cabinet on the far wall and retrieved a leather-bound notebook. He flipped through pages covered in neat handwriting and careful sketches.

"Verena asked me to catalog the inn's oldest pieces when I started working here. I've documented everything over a hundred years old." He ran his finger down a list. "The grandfather clock in the main hall is the oldest, but there's also the dining room table, the mirror in the upstairs hallway, and about two dozen smaller pieces scattered throughout the rooms."

"Verena said I should start with the clock."

He nodded and closed the notebook. "Give me ten minutes to clean up here, and we'll head inside together."

"Together." She tested the word, finding it fit better than she'd expected. "I like the sound of that."

"Yeah." Joe's mouth lifted in that almost-smile again. "Me too."

# CHAPTER 7

The grandfather clock stood in the main hall like a silent protector. Leanne paused in front of it. Eight feet of dark walnut rose before her, its brass pendulum swinging in steady rhythm. The clock face showed delicate hand-painted moon phases, each one precise and luminous even after all these years.

"This is the oldest piece in the inn's collection." Joe moved beside her. "Built in 1847 by a clockmaker, Samuel Morrison. He carved every detail by hand. He's said to be related to James Morrison who worked on the metalwork on the fountain in Crescent Park."

Leanne studied the intricate scrollwork along the clock's sides. Her gloved fingers hovered near the wood, not quite touching. "Let me guess. He was deeply in love with someone, poured his heart into this piece, and she died tragically before he could give it to her."

"Actually, they married and had six children." Joe's mouth curved with amusement. "Sometimes things work out."

"Well, that's refreshing." She pulled her hands back and tucked them into her pockets. "Though significantly less dramatic."

"Ready?"

No. She would never be ready. But the town square, flickering between past and present yesterday, had made one thing clear. Ready or not, time was running out.

Leanne tugged off one glove. She reached toward the clock's case, her fingertips trembling slightly.

The wood felt smooth and cool. Then the vision slammed into her.

*Hands moving across wood, the whisper of a plane shaving away curls that fell like snow. Pride in every stroke. A woman's laugh, bright and clear. Children running through a workshop. The tick-tick-tick of gears finding their rhythm for the first time.*

She pulled back, gasping. The visions had been quick, fragmented. Happy. Her heart hammered in a syncopated rhythm.

"You okay?" Joe's hand moved toward her shoulder, then stopped. Checking himself. Respecting her boundaries.

"Yes. Just… it was good. Mostly." She flexed her fingers, trying to ground herself in the present. "I saw the clockmaker. His family. But nothing about the stone."

He studied the clock with the calm focus she was beginning to recognize. "Start with what you know. Rule things out. That's how I work anyway."

She tugged her glove back on. "You make it sound so logical."

"Isn't it?"

"Joe, I see memories when I touch things. Logic left the building a long time ago."

He chuckled quietly. She found herself smiling back.

They moved through the inn's main floor, cataloging pieces. A carved sideboard from 1862. A hall tree with brass hooks. Each vision came and went like waves, leaving her breathless but functional.

In the library, Verena had set out a collection of smaller items on a cloth-covered table. A domed glass display held several pocket watches. On a nearby shelf, a child's wooden top sat next to a worn book and a tarnished silver letter opener.

"I borrowed these from Cole from the history museum. These came from the town's founding families." Verena appeared in the doorway carrying a tea tray. Steam rose from three cups, fragrant with chamomile. "I thought they might be worth examining."

Leanne approached the table slowly. The watches glinted in the afternoon light. She reached for the largest one, a heavy piece with an ornate cover.

The moment her bare fingers touched the metal, time fractured.

*A man in a dark suit checking the watch. Anxiety spiking through him. A train platform. Steam and smoke. Someone he loved leaving, the watch ticking away precious seconds. Years passing. The watch changing hands. A boy winding it with careful fingers. A woman tucking it away in a drawer. Darkness. Then Verena's hands, gentle and sure, placing it under glass.*

"It belonged to one of the town's founders." She set the watch down, her hand shaking. "He used it to time the trains. He lost someone. A daughter, maybe? She left on a train and never came back."

Verena nodded slowly. "There's a story about the Swanson family. George Swanson's eldest daughter married a man from Boston against her father's wishes. He kept that watch until the day he died, hoping she'd return."

"Did she?"

"No." Verena poured tea, the domestic ritual oddly soothing. "But her granddaughter did, sixty years later. Sometimes the stories take longer than one lifetime to resolve."

She picked up her teacup, grateful for something warm to hold. This porcelain cup was newer, free of history's clinging fingers.

Joe examined the child's top. "What about this?"

"You can touch that one." Leanne managed a smile. "Give me a break for a minute."

He spun the top on the table. It whirled in tight circles, its painted stripes blurring together. Watching it spin steadied her.

"I used to make toys." Joe's voice was soft and quiet. "Before I focused on restoration."

"Why'd you stop?"

His hand stopped the top's spinning and he shrugged. "Sometimes it's better to restore things others have made."

Verena watched them both. She sipped her tea and said nothing, letting the moment settle.

Leanne reached for the top. The wood felt worn smooth by small hands, warm from Joe's touch. The vision came gentler this time.

*A little girl laughing. Her father's hands guiding hers as she learned to spin the top. Birthday candles. The top passed down, generation to generation. Joy layered over joy, four generations deep.*

"Happy memories. A lot of love in that piece." She set it down carefully.

"The Langley family donated it last year." Verena refilled their cups. "Four generations played with that top."

"Still nothing about the stone, though." Frustration crept into Leanne's voice. "What if I can't find it? What if my visions are just random noise and I'm supposed to see something I keep missing?"

"You're doing exactly what you need to do. Building your understanding piece by piece."

The front door opened with a creak of old hinges. Footsteps crossed the hardwood floor, confident and quick.

"Hello? Anyone there?"

Verena's expression shifted, her warmth sliding behind something more guarded. "We have company."

A man appeared in the library doorway. He wore an expensive suit that looked out of place in the cozy room, his smile too white and too practiced. She didn't like the way his gaze inventoried the room before it landed on the people in it.

"Ms. Harrison, there you are." He extended his hand. "I've been hoping to speak with you."

Verena didn't take his hand. "Mr. Denton, I don't believe we have anything more to discuss."

"Well, you know I'm prepared to make you an extremely generous offer for this property." Denton's gaze swept the room, lingering on the antiques. "A place like this, so full of outdated charm, must be quite a burden to maintain."

"It's not a burden." Verena's voice stayed pleasant, but Leanne heard steel underneath. "It's my home."

"Of course, of course." Denton moved further into the room, circling like a shark before stopping by an antique chair and resting a hand on its back. "But surely you've considered the future? This building requires constant upkeep. The historic designation limits what you can do with it. I could take that burden off your hands and preserve its legacy in a modern, profitable way."

Leanne's jaw clenched. The way he said the word *preserve* made it sound like he meant *demolish*.

"These pieces, for instance." Denton gestured toward the table of artifacts. "Lovely items, but they'd be much better appreciated in a proper museum setting. I have connections with several institutions that would pay handsomely."

"They're not for sale." Verena's words came out flat and final.

"Everything's for sale at the right price." Denton picked up the silver letter opener, turning it over in his hands.

Leanne took in a sharp breath. She watched his fingers on the tarnished silver, saw the calculating gleam in his eyes. He wasn't admiring the craftsmanship. He was appraising and calculating value.

"Mr. Denton." Joe moved forward, his size

suddenly apparent. He wasn't a large man, but something in his posture and the set of his shoulders made him seem bigger. "The lady said it's not for sale."

Denton set down the letter opener. His smile never wavered, but his eyes went cold. "Of course. My apologies. I get carried away when I see potential." He pulled a business card from his jacket. "My offer stands, Ms. Harrison. When you're ready to discuss the future in realistic terms, give me a call."

He placed the card on the table and left. The front door closed behind him with a soft click that felt too much like a threat.

Leanne waited until his footsteps faded completely. Then she moved to the chair near where Denton had been standing. Where he'd rested his hand. A leather wingback, burgundy with brass studs. Old. Very old.

"Leanne, you don't have to." Verena stepped forward.

"Yes, I do." She pulled off both gloves and pressed her palms flat against the leather.

The vision hit like a punch to the gut.

*Cold. So cold. Ambition sharp as broken glass. Six stones glowing in darkness. Power. Control. The stones scattered, lost, and a burning need to find them, claim them, use them. History rewritten. Bloodlines corrected. Wrongs righted through force. The Amber Stone pulsing with stolen time.*

Leanne jerked away, stumbling backward. Joe caught her before she fell, his hands catching her around her waist. As soon as she was steady, he quickly let go.

"What did you see?" His voice came from far away, filtered through the ringing in her ears.

She blinked, forcing the present back into focus. Joe's concerned face. Verena's sharp attention. The cozy library with its books and warm light.

"He knows. About the stones. He's looking for them. The Amber Stone specifically." The words scraped out of her throat.

Verena nodded slowly. "I'm certain he does."

"I saw it in his thoughts, his plans. He doesn't want to buy the inn for development." Her hands shook as she pulled her gloves back on, needing the barrier, the protection. "He wants access to its history. To whatever clues might lead him to the stone."

"Why would a developer care about magical artifacts?" Joe frowned.

"I don't know." Leanne's mind raced, trying to make sense of the fragmented images. "But it's not just curiosity. It's an obsession. He believes the stones should belong to him. That he has some kind of claim on them."

Verena picked up Denton's business card, her mouth pressed into a thin line. "He's been looking for the stones for quite a while. He's trying to buy up historical properties around town, tear them down, and build some kind of modern destination town. And he did everything in his power to thwart the other Guardians."

"Can you see where the stone is?" Joe stayed close. "In your visions?"

"No. I see what was, what people felt when they touched things. Denton doesn't know where it is either." Leanne moved to the window, staring at the bare branches on the trees. "But he has resources and money, doesn't he? People working for him? We have me touching old furniture and hoping for clues."

"You have more than that." Verena joined her at the window. "You have the town's history in your hands, Leanne. Every object here connects to the people who built Moonlight Springs. Those connections are stronger than money."

"Are they strong enough?"

"They'll have to be."

Outside, a black car pulled away. Denton, leaving. But he'd be back. Leanne knew it as surely as she knew the sun would set.

Joe began carefully covering the artifacts with cloth, protecting them. "We need to narrow our search. Focus on items connected directly to the town's founding."

"The grandfather clock." Leanne turned from

the window. "It's the oldest piece, but I didn't see anything about the stone."

"Because you were touching the case." Joe's eyes lit with sudden understanding. "What about the mechanism inside? The works would have been handled more and held more meaning for the clockmaker."

Verena smiled. "That's why I asked you to help, Joe. You understand these pieces in ways the rest of us don't."

"Can we open it?" Leanne looked between them. "Without damaging anything?"

"That depends." Joe headed for the door. "On whether Verena trusts me with her oldest treasure."

"I trust you. Both of you."

They returned to the main hall where the grandfather clock stood, keeping its steady time. Joe retrieved tools from his workshop while Leanne studied the clock face, watching the moon phases cycle through their eternal dance.

The pendulum swung. Back and forth. Back and forth. Marking seconds into minutes into hours into years. Time flowing forward, always forward, unless something stopped it.

Unless *someone* stopped it.

She pressed her gloved hand against the clock's case. She couldn't read it through the leather, but she felt its age anyway. Its patient presence. This clock had witnessed generations of life in Moonlight

Springs. Births and deaths. Weddings. Celebrations and sorrow. It had stood here while the town grew and changed around it.

If the Amber Stone controlled time, what would happen if someone like Denton got his hands on it?

She thought of the town square flickering yesterday, past and present colliding. Of Verena's worried face and Joe's careful hands restoring beauty to broken things.

Some things, once broken, couldn't be fixed.

Joe returned with a wooden box of tools. He set it down with care, then looked at her. "Ready?"

She pulled off her gloves and tucked them in her pocket. Her bare hands flexed, nervous and ready all at once.

"Ready."

Joe opened the clock's front panel. The mechanism gleamed inside, brass gears and wheels fitted together like an intricate puzzle. The smell of old oil and metal filled the air.

The works were beautiful. Samuel Morrison had touched every piece, adjusted every gear, breathed life into metal and time.

"These gears here." Joe pointed to the largest wheel. "This would have been the heart of it. Where he spent the most time getting it exactly right."

Her hand moved forward. Stopped. Moved again.

"Take your time." Joe stepped back, giving her space.

Verena appeared in the hallway, watching quietly.

Leanne's fingertips brushed the central gear. Cool metal. Smooth edges. Then the vision bloomed behind her eyes.

*Workshop light falling across brass. Samuel's hands, patient and sure, fitting each piece into place. Pride swelling in his chest. But something else. A memory within his memory. His own father showing him a glowing amber stone, hidden in—*

The vision shattered into fragments. Moonlight on water. The riverwalk. The fountain in Crescent Park. Images flickering too fast to catch, shifting through decades like shuffled cards.

She pulled back, gasping.

"What did you see?" Joe moved closer.

She shook her head, trying to hold onto the fading images. "I'm not sure… it doesn't make any sense. Just… fragments." She leaned against the wall, steadying herself as exhaustion surged through her.

Verena stepped forward. "I think it's time for you to take a break. Let the visions sort themselves out. Why don't you head up to your room to rest, and I'll bring you a little snack?"

She nodded gratefully. "Taking a break sounds

like a good plan. Maybe if I rest, I'll be able to sort out what these visions mean."

# CHAPTER 8

Joe closed the door to his workshop in town and stood in the quiet space, letting the familiar scents of wood and varnish settle his thoughts. The afternoon light poured through the windows, spilling onto the chair he'd been working on before Leanne had come to request his help.

And he'd said yes. The question was, why? Why had he agreed to help her? He wasn't even sure he believed in all these visions and magical stones. Only… it was real. He could tell Leanne was having actual visions of things that had happened in the past. And maybe things that might happen in the future? It was all just so confusing.

He walked over to the workbench. His great-grandfather's plane still sat on it where Leanne had set it down.

He picked it up, running his thumb along the

smooth walnut handle worn to a burnished glow by generations of hands. His hands. His father's hands. His grandfather's and great-grandfather's hands before that. The metal blade gleamed clean and sharp, cared for across a century of use.

She had seen it. Not just held it or felt some vague impression. Leanne had watched his great-grandfather at work, had felt his pride and love for the craft as clearly as if she'd stood beside him in that long-ago workshop.

He set the plane down carefully.

His family had told stories about Charles Hall, about the man's skill and dedication, about how he'd built half the fine furniture in Moonlight Springs back in the day. Joe had grown up hearing those tales and had learned his craft, trying to live up to that legacy.

But Leanne hadn't heard stories. She had witnessed the truth of them, had touched the past itself.

And she was terrified of it.

He moved to the oak chair he'd been restoring, the one with the damaged leg he'd been slowly coaxing back to stability. The wood felt solid under his palm. He reached for his sandpaper and began working the grain, letting the repetitive motion calm his nerves.

The woman was brave. Terrified, yes, but she'd agreed to deliberately touch that grandfather clock, to open herself to whatever visions it might hold. She wore gloves like armor and flinched from contact, but she was still here. Still trying.

Most people would have run.

The sandpaper whispered against wood. Fine dust gathered on the floor, pale gold in the afternoon sunlight. He focused on the chair, the gentle give of damaged wood slowly accepting repair, and the patience required to restore something broken to wholeness.

*Don't force it. Work with the grain. Let the wood tell you what it needs.*

The lessons his father had taught him. The same lessons that were passed down through generations.

His hand stilled on the chair.

For a moment, he wasn't in his workshop at all. He was standing in a different space, watching flames crawl up wooden beams, hearing the crack and roar of fire consuming everything he'd built. Smoke filled his lungs. Heat seared his face. The smell of burning wood, acrid and wrong, so different from the sweet scent of sawdust and shavings.

Joe jerked back from the chair. He pressed his palms flat against the workbench until the memory loosened its grip. The workshop was intact. No flames. No smoke. Just clean wood and afternoon light and the faint tick of the wall clock marking steady, reliable time.

He breathed in slowly. Sawdust. Oil. The damp smell of the approaching winter days drifting through the open window.

His gaze found the plane again.

It had survived. When everything else had burned, when he'd lost his tools and his materials and the piece he'd been so proud of, this plane had survived. Safe. Untouched. A connection to everything that came before, preserved while his own work turned to ash.

Joe picked it up again, needing the comfort of its weight in his hand.

He'd been so young then. So full of ambition and creative fire, eager to make his mark not just as a restorer but as a craftsman in his own right. He'd wanted to build something original, something that would carry his name into the future the way his great-grandfather's work had carried the Hall name through the past.

That had been before.

Before the fire. Before the fear. Before he'd learned that some things you created could be destroyed, and the loss could break you in ways no amount of careful restoration could fix.

He set the plane down and picked up the sandpaper again, returning to the chair. The motion soothed him, gave his hands purpose. This he could do. Take something damaged and make it whole.

Work with what already existed, honor its history, and preserve its story.

Creating something new meant risking its loss. Restoration meant saving what was already there. The distinction mattered, even if he couldn't always explain why.

Even if, on quiet nights alone in his apartment, he sometimes woke with his hands itching to design something original and feel raw wood take shape under his tools into a form that existed first in his imagination.

He pushed the thought away like he always did.

The chair's leg was responding well to treatment. Another few days of careful work, and it would be stable again, ready to support weight and serve its purpose for another generation or two. There was satisfaction in that. Deep, quiet satisfaction that didn't come with the risk of devastating loss.

He straightened, rolling his shoulders to ease the tension gathering between his shoulder blades.

Leanne's face flickered through his mind. The way she'd looked when she'd touched his plane, her eyes distant and full of wonder, seeing across a century into his family's past. The way she'd pulled back after, exhausted but steady, determined despite her fear.

The way she wore those gloves like shields.

She was trapped. As surely as he was trapped by

his own old promises and older fears, Leanne was imprisoned by her gift. She spent her life avoiding touch, avoiding the kind of contact most people took for granted.

And yet she'd come here. She'd agreed to help. She was facing the thing that terrified her most because Verena asked and because the town needed it.

His hands curled into fists. He got up and moved to the window, staring out at the bare branches and the last leaves scurrying across the yard in the breeze.

What would it be like, he wondered, to live your entire life afraid of touch?

To know that every handshake, every casual brush of contact, every hug or held hand would slam you into someone else's memories? To have your gift feel like a curse instead of a blessing?

He thought of his own craft. Imagine if every time he touched wood, instead of reading its grain and moisture and story through practiced skill, he was overwhelmed by chaotic visions he couldn't control. Imagine if the thing he loved most became a source of pain and fear.

Imagine cutting yourself off from it entirely, just to survive.

Leanne hadn't cut herself off from her gift, though. She'd simply never learned to channel it or work with it, instead of being worked by it. She'd spent decades in fear when what she needed was understanding. Control. Maybe even acceptance.

Both of them were trapped by the past. She was drowning in too much of it, unable to escape the flood of memories. He was hiding from it, refusing to create anything new because of what he'd lost years ago.

She needed to learn to control her gift. He needed to learn to let go of his fear.

He turned back to the workshop, his gaze moving across the familiar space. His tools hung in neat rows on the wall, each one exactly where it belonged. Wood was stacked and organized by species and age. The workbench was clean, maintained with the same care he brought to every restoration project.

This space was his sanctuary. His place of safety and purpose. But maybe it had also become his prison, the walls he'd built to keep himself from risking anything that mattered.

The plane caught his eye again, sitting patiently on the workbench where it had rested for over a hundred years of use.

His great-grandfather had created pieces that lasted generations. Had built furniture that became family heirlooms, that held memories and stories and meaning. Had taken risks with his craft, tried new techniques, pushed himself to grow.

Had Charles Hall ever been afraid? Had he ever lost something that made him want to quit?

Joe didn't know. The family stories didn't include those parts, if they'd existed at all.

But he knew that his great-grandfather had kept creating. Had kept building. Had passed his skills and his tools down through his son to his grandson to Joe himself, a legacy of craftsmanship that spanned a century.

And Joe had let that legacy stop with him.

The thought surfaced before he could stop it. He pushed it away, but it didn't go far.

He'd become so focused on preservation that he'd forgotten creation was part of the legacy too. His great-grandfather hadn't just restored other people's work. He'd made new things, had taken raw materials and transformed them into furniture that would outlast him by generations.

Joe had lost that part of himself in the fire. Had set it down and walked away and never picked it up again, too afraid of what might happen if he did.

Just like Leanne had pulled away from connection, from touch, from the possibility of control over her gift.

They were both hiding, both trapped. Fear had been making their choices for years.

He moved back to the chair and ran his hand over the repaired leg, feeling the smooth wood under his palm. The piece was beautiful in its own right, well-made by skilled hands over a century ago. Restoring it was good work, important work.

But it wasn't the only work he was capable of.

The thought scared him. It also thrilled him in a way nothing had for years.

He picked up the plane one more time, holding it with both hands, feeling its balance and heft. It had survived the fire that destroyed so much else.

Maybe that meant something. Maybe survival wasn't about hiding from risk. Maybe it was about continuing forward despite what you'd lost, honoring the past by building a future worth having.

Maybe helping Leanne learn to control her gift, face her fear, and find strength in what terrified her would help him remember how to face his own fears too.

He set the plane down gently and returned to the chair. But something had shifted inside him, some small crack in the walls he'd built so carefully around himself.

Leanne needed him. Not just his knowledge of the inn's antiques or his understanding of historical pieces. She needed someone who understood what it meant to be trapped by your own past and knew how isolation could feel like safety even when it was slowly suffocating you. And maybe he needed her too.

He picked up the sandpaper and got back to work. The chair wasn't going to fix itself.

# CHAPTER 9

The morning air held a crisp edge that made Leanne's breath visible in small puffs. She stood outside the Moonlight Inn's entrance, waiting for Joe to arrive with his truck. Her gloved hands fidgeted with the strap of her messenger bag, and she forced herself to stop. The nervous gesture made her feel like a teenager waiting for a first date rather than a grown woman about to chase down ghostly visions in a public park.

At least if this were a date, she could bail with a fake headache. The town's stability didn't offer that option.

Joe's pickup rolled into the circular drive at precisely eight o'clock. Punctual. She appreciated that about him. In her experience, people who respected wood and craftsmanship tended to respect time as well. The irony of that thought, given her current mission to find a literal time stone, wasn't lost on her.

He stepped out of the truck wearing his usual work attire of worn jeans, a flannel shirt in deep green, and boots that had seen plenty of use. His silver hair caught the morning light, and when he smiled at her, the corners of his eyes crinkled in a way that made her stomach do an unexpected flip.

"Ready to go hunt some historical ghosts?" he asked.

"As ready as I'll ever be to deliberately trigger a psychic episode in a public space." She walked toward the passenger side. "What could possibly go wrong?"

Joe held the door open for her. "Well, according to Verena's list of recent incidents, we could accidentally summon a Victorian garden party, a 1940s big band concert, or possibly the town's founding ceremony. So there's variety, at least."

She climbed into the truck. "Your optimism is noted. And concerning."

"I've been practicing." He closed her door and walked around to the driver's side. "Figured if I'm going to be your backup on magical missions, I should work on the whole encouraging thing."

"How's that working out?"

"Jury's still out." He started the engine and pointed to the cupholder where a stainless steel travel mug sat. Steam escaped from the small opening in the lid. "Want some?"

"You brought me coffee?"

"Tea, actually. Chamomile with honey. Verena mentioned you preferred it." He pulled out of the drive and headed toward town. "Figured you might need something calming before we dive into whatever happens at the fountain."

She felt a flush of gratitude. She reached for the mug carefully, her gloved fingers wrapping around the smooth metal. "Thank you."

"Don't thank me yet. I have no idea if I got the honey ratio right."

She took a sip. Perfect. The sweetness balanced the floral notes exactly how she liked it. Verena knew how she liked it and had clearly passed that information to Joe. The thoughtfulness made her smile. "It's good."

Joe glanced at her, then back at the road. "Good. Because I made Verena write down the exact proportions. Apparently, I'm not trusted with beverages after the Great Coffee Incident of last Tuesday."

"Do I want to know?"

"Let's just say that Verena's definition of strong coffee and my definition are radically different. She called it motor oil. I called it adequate." He turned onto Main Street, where early morning shopkeepers were opening their doors.

She laughed, surprising herself. "You seem remarkably calm about all this. The visions, the time slips, and the magical stones. Most people would be demanding rational explanations or running for the hills."

"Most people didn't watch their great-grandfather's entire life story play out because you touched a wood plane. After that, I figured I could either accept that the world's stranger than I thought or spend a lot of energy being wrong about reality. The first option seemed more productive."

"That's very pragmatic."

"I'm a furniture restorer. We're practical people." He shrugged. "Plus, I've lived in Moonlight Springs a long time. You don't spend decades in a place without noticing that odd things happen."

She watched the familiar streets slide past. The town had changed since she'd left thirty years ago. New shops occupied old buildings, fresh paint brightened facades, but the bones remained the same. The history ran deep here, layer upon layer of accumulated memories that pressed against her awareness even through her gloves.

"I tried to forget," she said quietly. "After I left. I convinced myself that if I stayed away long enough and avoided places with strong histories, I could pretend the visions weren't real. That I was just sensitive or imaginative or any other explanation that didn't involve actual psychic abilities."

"Did it work?"

"Not even a little bit." She took another sip of tea. "Turns out you can't outrun yourself. You just get really tired from trying."

He pulled into a parking spot near Crescent Park. Through the windshield, she could see the historic fountain at the park's center. Water cascaded down its tiers in a gentle rhythm. Morning sunlight made the droplets sparkle like scattered diamonds.

Beautiful. And absolutely saturated with history.

Her hands started to sweat inside her gloves.

"Hey." His voice drew her attention. "We can take this slow. You're in control here."

"Am I?" She gestured toward the fountain. "Because that thing has been around since the 1800s. That's at least 150 years of memories, impressions, and psychic residue. The vision I had from the grandfather clock practically knocked me unconscious, and I was prepared for that. Out here, with no warning of what I might touch—"

"So we'll be careful." He turned in his seat to face her fully. "You tell me what you need. I'll make sure you don't touch anything accidentally. We'll work together, just like we did with the desk and the clock."

She wanted to believe him. The rational part of her brain pointed out that Joe had been nothing but supportive since they'd met. He'd found Elizabeth's letter exactly where her vision indicated. He'd helped her navigate the clock's memories. He'd shown up this morning with perfectly prepared tea.

The irrational part—or maybe it was the *rational* part—remembered thirty years of isolation and fear and whispered that trusting anyone was dangerous.

She told that part to shut up.

"Okay." She unbuckled her seatbelt. "Let's go."

They walked across the grass together, Joe matching his pace to hers. The park was mostly empty at this hour. An elderly woman walked a small dog near the playground. A jogger circled the perimeter path. Normal morning activity in a normal small town.

Except nothing about Moonlight Springs was normal. Not anymore. Maybe it never had been.

The fountain loomed larger as they approached. Up close, Leanne could see the intricate detail work on it and a dedication plaque near the base. The craftsmanship was exquisite.

It was also triggering every psychic alarm bell in her body.

"The founders dedicated this fountain in the 1800s," Joe said, stopping a few feet away. "According to the historical society, it was supposed to represent the town's prosperity and bright future."

"And Verena said the first stone was found here. Maura found the Amethyst Stone in the fountain's central column a few months ago. There was a hidden compartment inside."

"I admit, I'm still having a hard time with the whole magical stones thing." He waved his hand. "But carry on. I'm here for you."

She studied the fountain's structure. "If one stone was hidden here, maybe there are clues about the others. The founders would have known about all six stones, right? They might have left breadcrumbs."

Joe walked slowly around the fountain's perimeter. "The question is what kind of clues we're looking for."

She closed her eyes and took a deep breath. She'd spent thirty years avoiding her gift, suppressing it, and running from it. But running hadn't worked. The visions had followed her everywhere, breaking through at the worst possible moments. Maybe Joe was right. Maybe the problem wasn't the gift itself but her approach to it.

Instead of bracing against the psychic pressure radiating from the fountain, she tried something new. She relaxed her mental shields just slightly, letting herself feel the edges of the memories without diving fully into them. Like dipping a toe in water instead of jumping into the deep end.

The sensation was overwhelming and subtle all at once. Layers of history pressed against her awareness. She felt more than saw dedication ceremonies and summer picnics, marriage proposals and children's laughter, quiet moments and celebrations. But instead of experiencing each memory as a full vision, she sensed them as impressions she could perceive without drowning in them.

"There's so much here," she whispered. "So many moments."

"Can you sort through them?" He stood close enough that she could feel his presence, something steady to focus on. "Find the relevant ones?"

"I'm trying." She focused on the dedication ceremony, the earliest memory tied to the fountain. The impressions sharpened. Men in formal attire from the 1800s. Women in elaborate dresses. A crowd gathered around the fountain for its unveiling. And there, at the center of the gathering—

"Someone's holding a box." Her eyes were still closed, her attention fixed on the vision. "Wooden, rectangular, about the size of a shoebox. Beautiful craftsmanship. The dovetail joints are hand-cut, with perfect angles. The wood is walnut, I think. Highly polished."

"Can you see who's holding it?"

She pushed deeper into the memory, letting more details filter through. The man holding the box wore an expensive black coat with velvet lapels, a silk vest, and polished boots. His face was weathered but proud.

"An older man has it," she said. "He's presenting it to someone. The mayor, maybe? No, wait. A woman. She's older, dressed simply compared to the others. There's something about her that feels... different."

"Different how?"

She struggled to articulate the sensation. "Like she's more solid than everyone else. More real. The other people in the vision feel like memories, but she feels like..." She grasped for the right word. "Like a marker. A signpost pointing toward something important."

Joe was quiet for a moment. "Verena told me about the Guardians. The ones who protected the stones. Could that be one of them?"

"Maybe." The vision was starting to fragment, the details slipping away like water through her fingers. "They're saying something. The dedication speech. The man is talking about the town's future, about preserving its history for generations to come. He's putting the box—no, he's handing the box to the woman."

"A time capsule." Joe's voice held excitement. "The Pioneer's Time Capsule. It's been a local legend for decades. People assumed it was lost or destroyed."

Leanne's eyes snapped open. The present day

rushed back, colors too bright after the muted tones of the vision. "But where is the box now?"

She walked over to join Joe near the fountain, her legs slightly unsteady. The vision had drained her more than she'd expected. Controlling her gift, even partially, took significant energy. "Let me try something."

Before she could second-guess herself, she pulled off her right glove. Her fingers trembled slightly.

Joe noticed. "You don't have to—"

"Yes, I do." She knelt beside the fountain's base, her ungloved hand hovering above the bronze plaque. "If I'm going to help find this stone, I need to stop being afraid of what I might see."

She pressed her palm flat against the cold metal.

The world tilted.

*She wasn't at the fountain anymore. She was inside the box, experiencing the darkness and confinement from the box's perspective. Time moved strangely here, accelerating and slowing in irregular pulses. Years flashed past in heartbeats, with seasons changing and moments through history.*

*Then the light flooded in. Hands reached. A woman's face, blurry but somehow familiar, peering into the box. The woman picked up the box carefully, reverently. She looked directly at where Leanne's consciousness hovered, as if she could see her across the years.*

*"For the one who comes seeking," the woman said. Her voice echoed strangely. "Follow the threads."*

*Then the vision shifted violently. Leanne watched from*

*above as the same woman carried the box through Moonlight Springs. The streets were different. Cars instead of horses.. The woman walked with purpose, heading toward—*

*The vision fractured. Time slipped, dozens of them cascading over each other like shuffled photographs. The park flickered. The fountain was new, then weathered, then new again. A woman in 1970s bell-bottoms walked through a man in a Victorian coat. She saw the fountain's dedication. She saw the woman with the box. She saw Maura finding the Amethyst Stone. She saw the park as it existed now, this morning, with Joe kneeling beside her.*

*All of it happening at once.*

*Her awareness splintered across decades, unable to find purchase in any single moment. She was everywhere and nowhere, drowning in chaos—*

"Leanne!" Joe's voice cut through the confusion. His hand gripped her shoulder, solid and real. "Come back!"

She gasped, yanking her hand away from the plaque. The present day snapped back into focus with almost physical force. She was kneeling on grass that had been wet with morning dew. Her right hand, still bare, was shaking violently.

Joe crouched beside her, his face tight with worry. "Are you okay? What did you see?"

"The box." Her voice came out rough. "Someone moved it. A woman. I couldn't see her face clearly, but she knew about the stones. She knew someone would come looking."

"Did you see where she took it?"

She closed her eyes, trying to hold onto the fractured images before they dissolved completely. The woman had walked through town, the box tucked under her arm. She'd passed the courthouse, turned at the corner, and headed toward—

But nothing else came to her. The vision faded into darkness. "I just don't see where she took it."

"Nothing that gives you a hint?"

"Nothing." She pulled her glove back on, needing the barrier between herself and the world. She accepted Joe's offered hand and let him help her stand. Her legs felt like overcooked noodles.

They walked back to the truck in silence. Her mind churned through the vision's details, trying to organize the fragments into coherent information. The woman's face had been familiar. That nagged at her. How could she recognize someone from a vision from years ago?

Joe helped her into the truck with a steadying hand on her elbow. Once he was behind the wheel, he didn't start the engine immediately. "That was intense."

"That was nothing." Leanne leaned her head against the cool window glass. "The time slips are getting worse. While I was connected to the fountain, the past and present were bleeding into each other. If we don't find the Amber Stone soon—"

"We will." His certainty made her look at him. "You just narrowed our search to one building. That's progress."

"Progress that ends with us searching the whole town for a box that might not even still exist. The historical society would kill for this kind of adventure. I just want a nap."

Joe started the engine. "How about we compromise? I'll get you back to the inn, you can rest for an hour or so, and then we tackle the Great Box Hunt with reinforcements."

"Reinforcements?"

"We could go to the Historical Museum and talk to Cole Brinkman. He might have some ideas for us. Plus, I make a fantastic search assistant. Very thorough. Excellent attention to detail."

"Is that what your references say?"

"My references say I'm occasionally stubborn and possibly too invested in wood grain patterns, but yes, thorough made the list." He shot her a sideways smile. "Also that I make terrible coffee but adequate tea."

Despite her exhaustion, she smiled. "Adequate tea and thorough searching. What more could a woman ask for?"

"Exactly." He navigated through morning traffic, which in Moonlight Springs meant waiting for Mrs. Holloway to slowly cross Main Street with her shopping bags. "See? We're a great team already."

She watched the town pass by outside her window. Somewhere in the town, a wooden box held clues to the Amber Stone's location. Somewhere in the town's fractured timeline, answers waited to be found. And somewhere inside her, a small seed of hope was taking root.

Maybe she wasn't as broken as she'd always believed. Maybe her gift wasn't a curse but a tool she'd simply never learned to use properly.

One step at a time. Find the box first. Worry about saving the town after lunch.

# CHAPTER 10

The Moonlight Springs Historical Society occupied a Victorian building on Moonlight Way. Leanne paused on the sidewalk, studying the hand-painted sign above the door. Someone had added cheerful yellow stars around the lettering, which seemed at odds with the serious nature of historical preservation.

"Just wondering if I should have worn my academic face." Leanne smiled and gestured at her comfortable jeans and burgundy sweater. "I feel underdressed for archive research."

"You're fine." Joe smiled back at her. "Besides, we're not exactly following traditional research methods."

"True. I doubt many historians include that they consulted a local psychic in their methodology section."

He nodded gravely to hide his smirk. "We'll leave that part out of the official record."

They climbed the granite stairs and pushed through the large wooden door. Inside, the historical society resembled a library that had married an antique shop and never quite sorted out whose belongings were whose. Bookshelves lined every wall, interspersed with display cases containing everything from vintage postcards to what appeared to be an authentic butter churn.

A man looked up from a desk buried under manila folders and leather-bound ledgers. He had dark hair and sharp, intelligent eyes behind wire-rimmed glasses. Recognition sparked in his expression.

"Joe." He stood, moving around the desk with an easy smile. "Haven't seen you in a few weeks. Finally ready to donate that secretary desk you've been restoring?"

"Not quite yet. Still working on the inlay. Cole Brinkman, this is Leanne McMann. She's staying at the inn and helping Verena with some research."

Cole extended his hand automatically, then paused when Leanne didn't reciprocate.

"Sorry." She offered an apologetic smile. "Severe contact dermatitis. Nothing personal."

"No problem at all." Cole dropped his hand without the awkwardness some people showed. "Any friend of Verena's is welcome here. What kind of research are you doing?"

"We're looking into the town's early history," Joe said. "Particularly anything related to the founding families and the original settlement. Photographs would be especially helpful."

"That's a fairly broad topic." Cole moved to a filing cabinet and pulled open a drawer. "Any specific time period or family?"

She exchanged a glance with Joe. They'd discussed this on the walk over. "We're interested in the dedication of the fountain in Crescent Park. The one with the original time capsule."

Cole's expression brightened. "The Pioneer's Time Capsule. That's one of my favorite local mysteries." He pulled out several folders and carried them to a large table by the window. "The capsule was sealed at the fountain's dedication, but it disappeared at some point. No one's sure when or why."

"What do you think happened to it?" She approached the table.

"Theory one is that someone stole it during the Depression when people were desperate. Theory two is that town officials moved it for safekeeping during World War Two and forgot to document where." Cole spread out several photographs, handling them with care. "Theory three is that it never existed and the whole thing was ceremonial folklore."

"You don't believe that last one." Joe came to stand beside her.

"No." Cole grinned. "I've seen too many documented references. It was real. The question is, where did it go?"

He laid out a series of black-and-white photographs showing the fountain at various points in its history. She leaned closer, studying each image. The fountain looked much the same across the decades, though the surrounding park had changed. Trees grew taller. Benches appeared and disappeared. Fashions shifted from long skirts to short hemlines to bell-bottoms.

"May I?" She gestured to one of the photos, a shot from what appeared to be the 1950s.

"Of course. Just try not to touch the image itself. The oils from skin can damage them." Cole indicated the white borders. "Hold them by the edges."

She pulled off one glove, tucking it into her pocket. She picked up the photograph carefully, touching only the border as instructed.

Nothing. Just the smooth feel of photo paper beneath her fingertips.

She moved to the next image, this one from the 1960s, based on the clothing styles. Again, nothing beyond the physical sensation of paper.

Joe watched her with quiet attention. He understood what she was doing, what she was hoping to feel. Or rather, what she was hoping might trigger the visions that now served as their only reliable clues.

"Here's an old one." Cole pulled out a photograph from deeper in the stack. "Town festival, summer of 1922."

She accepted the photo. The moment her fingers touched the border, the world tilted.

*The historical society faded. She stood in summer sunshine with the smell of grilled meat and cotton candy heavy in the air. Children ran past, laughing. A band played on a temporary stage. She recognized the fountain immediately, draped with red, white, and blue bunting.*

*Her vision pulled away from the festival itself, drawn to the edges. There. An older woman in a floral dress moved away from the crowd, heading toward the street. She carried something clutched against her chest. A wooden box.*

*Her consciousness followed the woman up the winding street, past shops and houses that looked simultaneously familiar and strange in their younger incarnations. The woman glanced over her shoulder twice, as if checking whether anyone was watching.*

*She turned onto a narrow path, one Leanne recognized. The steps leading up to the Moonlight Inn. The woman climbed with determination despite her age, breathing hard by the time she reached the top.*

*At the summit, where the path met the inn's gardens, an*

*old stone retaining wall held back the hillside. The woman looked around once more, then knelt. Her fingers found a loose stone in the wall. She pulled it free, creating a dark gap. She slid the wooden box inside, then carefully replaced the stone. She stood, brushed off her dress, and walked toward the inn without looking back.*

The vision released Leanne so suddenly that she swayed.

"Whoa." Joe's hand touched her elbow, steadying her. "I've got you."

She blinked as the historical society swam back into focus. "I saw…"

Cole watched her with concern. "Are you all right? Do you need to sit down?"

"I'm… fine." She carefully set the photograph back on the table. "Just got a little dizzy. Low blood sugar, probably."

Cole still looked worried. "There's a chair right here if you need it." He looked at her skeptically. "You said you saw something?"

"Oh, it was nothing. I was just a bit confused, I guess."

Cole shrugged. "I've learned not to ask too many questions about strange things happening around here."

She managed a smile. "Actually, these photographs are incredibly helpful. Would it be possible to get copies of a few? Particularly this one from 1922?"

"Absolutely. I can scan them and email them to you or print copies if you prefer."

"Email would be great." Leanne gave him her email address.

They spent another twenty minutes looking through the photographs, though Leanne didn't touch any more with her bare skin. She'd gotten what she needed. Finally, they thanked Cole and stepped back out into the afternoon sunshine.

She waited until they'd walked two blocks before speaking. "The stone wall. At the top of the path to the inn."

"You saw it?" Joe matched her pace as they turned onto the street leading uphill.

"A woman hid it there during the 1922 festival. She looked worried someone might see her." Leanne paused at a crosswalk, watching a mother push a stroller past. "The box was small, maybe eight inches long. Dark wood."

"Did you see her face clearly?"

"No, I'm not certain of her age. Older. Floral dress. Hair pulled back." She frowned, trying to recapture the details. "She moved like someone who knew exactly what she was doing. This wasn't impulsive."

They crossed the street and started up the hill toward the inn. The path wound between old houses with neat gardens, the same route Leanne had seen in her vision. She could almost overlay the two images in her mind. Past and present, occupying the same space but separated by decades.

"If she hid it in 1922, it could still be there." Joe sounded cautiously optimistic. "Depending on how well she concealed it."

"Only one way to find out."

The climb grew steeper as they approached the inn. By the time they reached the stone steps, Leanne's calves burned. She really needed to exercise more. Maybe when her life didn't revolve around chasing magical artifacts and learning to control psychic visions, she'd join a gym. Or take up hiking. Or something other than hiding in her apartment, avoiding all human contact.

The thought came with a twist of dark humor. A week ago, the idea of normal activities like gyms had seemed impossibly distant. Now she was actually considering future possibilities beyond mere survival.

"This wall?" Joe approached the stone retaining wall that held back the hillside garden.

"Yes." Leanne studied the structure. Moss grew between many of the stones, and small ferns had taken root in the crevices. The wall looked original to the property, probably built when the inn was constructed. "She was kneeling about here."

She indicated a section of wall near where the path leveled out. Joe crouched and examined the stones. "Several of these look loose." He worked his fingers around one stone, testing. "This whole section probably needs repointing."

"Can you move any of them?"

Joe wiggled another stone. It shifted slightly. He pulled, and it came free in his hands, leaving a dark hollow in the wall. He glanced inside. "I don't see anything."

Her shoulders sagged. Of course, it wouldn't be that easy.

"Wait." He set the stone aside and reached into the gap. "There's something farther back."

He stretched, his arm disappearing into the wall up to his elbow. When he withdrew, his hand emerged covered in dirt and cobwebs, clutching a small wooden box.

Her pulse raced as she leaned closer.

Joe stood, brushing debris from the box with gentle sweeps of his hand. The wood underneath was dark with age, walnut or maybe mahogany. No lock, just a simple hinged lid.

"Should we open it here or take it inside?" Joe looked at her.

"Here. I can't wait." She pulled off both gloves and stuffed them in her pockets. "If there's anything inside I need to read, it's better to do it now."

He carefully lifted the lid.

Empty.

The box contained nothing but decades of

accumulated dust and the brittle remains of what might once have been tissue paper.

Disappointment crashed over her. They'd been so close. She'd seen it, followed the vision, and found the exact hiding place. And someone had gotten here first. But who? She only hoped it wasn't Denton with his obsessive search for the stones.

"I'm sorry." Joe closed the lid gently. "I know you were hoping…"

"It's fine." She heard the brittleness in her own voice. "At least we know we're on the right track. The box existed. Someone did hide it. We just weren't fast enough."

"Maybe." Joe turned the box over in his hands, studying it from all angles. His brow creased in concentration. "But look at this."

He angled the box so sunlight fell across the bottom. She stepped closer.

"The wood is ancient oak." Joe ran his thumb across the grain. "See how tight these growth rings are? This tree was old when it was cut. And the joinery is hand-done, probably mid-nineteenth century."

"So?"

"So this wasn't made in town. This particular oak doesn't grow around here anymore." Joe looked up at her. "Except there is a rumor about where it grows. Somewhere near a hidden spring."

"Ah, another mystery. Great. And a rumored

hidden spring. Can't anything be easy? Even a little bit?"

He opened the box again, tilting it to catch the light. "There's something else. Look at the inside of the lid."

Leanne leaned in closer. At first, she saw only bare wood, slightly lighter than the exterior. Then her eyes adjusted, and she made out faint lines carved into the surface. Not random scratches. Deliberate markings. "What is that?"

"I'm not sure." Joe pointed to a curved line. "I can't make out the details. The carving is too shallow, and there's too much dirt built up in the grooves."

"We could clean it."

"Let me take it to my workshop. I have the right tools and better light." He started to close the lid, then paused. "Unless you want to try reading it first? Your gift might show you what it looked like originally."

She considered. Her talent had limits. She could read memories from objects, but only if those memories were strong enough. Someone deliberately carving into a box might have left an impression, but there were no guarantees.

"Let's try the conventional method first." She pulled her gloves back on. "If we can't make sense of the carving after cleaning, then I'll touch it."

They started down the path together, moving

more carefully now that Joe carried the box. She watched her feet on the uneven stones, grateful for the excuse not to examine her own tangled emotions. Relief that they'd found something. Disappointment that the box was empty. Hope that the carvings might lead somewhere. And underneath it all, a growing awareness of the man beside her.

Joe had been patient with her gift, even encouraging. He'd brought her tea this morning without being asked, steadied her after the vision without making a fuss, and let her lead the investigation while offering support. He saw her as competent, not fragile.

"My workshop is just off Main Street." Joe glanced at her as they reached the bottom of the hill. "Above the hardware store. Fair warning, it's a mess. I wasn't expecting company."

"I grew up in a house with four siblings. Mess doesn't scare me."

They walked through the downtown area, past shops with people coming and going. The smell of fried food drifted out from Crescent Moon Cafe. A florist arranged buckets of daisies and roses outside her door. Normal, everyday life continued around them while they pursued magical stones and temporal disturbances.

The contradiction should have felt jarring. Instead, it reminded her of her childhood in

Moonlight Springs, before her gift had fully manifested. Magic had always existed here, woven into the fabric of ordinary existence. She'd just forgotten how natural that combination could feel.

Joe led her down a narrow alley to a wooden staircase on the side of the hardware store. His workshop occupied the second floor, accessed through a door with peeling green paint.

Inside, sunlight streamed through large windows, illuminating a space that smelled of wood shavings and turpentine. A long workbench dominated one wall, covered with tools arranged in neat rows despite Joe's warning about mess. Several pieces of furniture in various states of restoration occupied the room. A dresser with missing drawer pulls. A chair with new caning half-complete. The secretary desk he'd mentioned to Cole, its veneer gleaming with fresh finish.

"Have a seat anywhere." Joe cleared space on the workbench and set down the box. "This might take a few minutes."

She pulled up a stool and watched as he gathered supplies. A soft brush. Cotton swabs. A bottle of what looked like mineral spirits. He worked carefully, treating the old box like the valuable artifact it was.

"You really love this." She gestured at the workshop, the tools, the furniture. "Restoration."

"I do." Joe dipped a cotton swab in the mineral

spirits and began carefully cleaning the carved lines. "I like the puzzle of it. Figuring out what's missing, what needs to go where."

"But you used to create your own furniture. Verena mentioned it."

Joe's hand paused for just a moment before continuing. "That was a long time ago."

"What changed?"

"I did." He switched to a fresh swab as a carefully controlled look settled on his features. "There was a fire…"

She sat silently, letting him continue.

"It destroyed… well, everything. I'd been so wrapped up in my creations. They were my whole world. Which is kind of silly, isn't it? Making *things* your whole world. So much in life is more important than possessions. But the fire… it taught me a lesson. I almost lost…" A faraway look crossed his face as if he were reliving a memory, then he shook his head. "Anyway, after the fire, I gave up creating new pieces. Restoring old items felt… more productive."

She wondered what he had almost lost, but he didn't seem willing to talk about it, so she didn't ask. He turned back to his work. Gradually, the carved lines emerged more clearly from the wood. She stood and leaned over the box, studying the pattern.

"Can I see it?"

He gave her the box, and she tilted the lid

toward the window, squinting at the carved surface. The symbols emerged from the wood grain like constellations. Stars with delicate points. Crescent moons nested between them.

"What do you make of these?" She pointed, careful not to touch them yet.

He leaned closer, his shoulder nearly brushing hers. "Decorative? Or they could mean something."

"Everything in this town means something. Everything is a mystery." She set the box down. "Can't anyone just carve pretty pictures for fun?"

His lips twitched with a small smile. "Apparently not in Moonlight Springs."

"We should show this to Verena. If anyone knows what celestial doodling signifies, it's her."

"Celestial doodling?" His eyebrows rose.

"I'm workshopping my terminology. Give me time."

"Not sure time is on our side…"

She started to respond, then gasped as something touched her hand.

She looked down. Joe had reached for the pencil at the same moment she'd moved. His fingers rested against her bare knuckles, warm, solid, and real.

She'd forgotten to put her gloves back on.

Her whole body tensed, bracing for the onslaught of vision. Joe's memories would pour into her mind, overwhelming and unstoppable. She'd see his entire history. His childhood, his losses, his private thoughts. Whatever he'd almost lost but wouldn't talk about. Everything he'd never chosen to share.

But the vision didn't come.

Instead, she felt only warmth. The simple, startling sensation of human contact. His skin against hers. The slight calluses on his fingertips from years of working with wood. The gentle pressure of his touch.

It lasted perhaps two seconds before Joe realized and pulled back. "Sorry, I didn't mean to..."

"It's fine." She stared at her own hand, stunned. "I didn't see anything."

"What?"

"No vision. Nothing." She looked up at him, her heart racing for entirely different reasons now. "I just felt you touch me."

His expression shifted, moving from surprise to something softer, more vulnerable. "Is that normal? For your gift?"

"I have no idea." She laughed, the sound shaky. "I've spent thirty years avoiding this exact situation. I don't know what's normal anymore."

They stood there in the sun-filled workshop, the carved box and its mysterious carving temporarily forgotten. Her hand still tingled where Joe had touched her. Not with psychic energy or overwhelming visions, but with the strange, terrifying, wonderful feeling of connection.

"We should probably go see Verena," Joe said finally.

"Right. Yes. Verena." She pulled her gloves back on, though the action felt different now. Not like armor. More like a choice she was making, one she might unmake later.

They gathered their things and headed for the door. But Leanne paused on the threshold, looking back at the workshop bathed in golden afternoon light.

Something had shifted between them in this room. Something that had nothing to do with magical stones or time disturbances.

The wooden box sat on Verena's kitchen table like an accusation. Leanne stared at it from across the room, her gloved hands tucked firmly in her cardigan pockets. The last of the late afternoon light filtering through the inn's windows made the worn wood grain glow with a warmth that should have been comforting. Instead, it filled her with dread.

"Tea?" Verena moved around her kitchen with the ease of someone who'd done this thousands of times. The kettle hummed on the stove, and the scent of fresh bread lingered in the air, probably from whatever she'd been baking at dawn.

"Please." Leanne dragged her attention away from the box. "Something strong. Maybe with a sedative chaser."

Verena's mouth lifted in a small smile as she set three mismatched mugs on the counter. "I'm afraid I'm fresh out of sedatives. You'll have to settle for chamomile with honey."

Joe stood near the table, one hand resting lightly on the back of a chair. He'd been quiet since they arrived, his gaze moving between her and the box with that careful, assessing look he got when examining a particularly challenging restoration project.

The comparison should have annoyed her. Instead, it steadied something fluttering in her chest.

"So." Verena placed the mugs on the table and settled into her chair with the grace of someone who'd earned the right to every creak in her bones. "You found the Pioneer's Time Capsule in my garden wall. That's quite the discovery."

"Empty." Joe pulled out a chair for Leanne, waited until she sat before taking his own seat. "But the inside lid has carvings. Stars and crescent moons."

Verena reached for the box. "May I?"

Leanne nodded.

Verena lifted the lid and studied the interior with the focused attention of someone reading a beloved book. Her fingers traced the carved symbols with a tender, slow stroke. After a long moment, she looked up.

"It's a celestial map." Verena turned the box so they could see. "Each star corresponds to a full moon. See how they're connected in a sequence?"

Joe leaned forward. "A calendar?"

"More like a countdown." Verena's finger moved from one carved moon to the next. "Six moons. Six stones. This marks when each stone was placed, I think. Or perhaps when they need to be found."

The flutter in Leanne's chest became a drumbeat. "How many moons are left on the countdown to the Amber Stone?"

"Three." Verena met her gaze. "The next full moon is in three days."

Of course it was. Because apparently, the universe had a deadline, and she was running out of time to find a magical artifact while learning to control the psychic ability she'd spent three decades trying to suppress. Nothing stressful about that.

Joe pulled out his phone and searched. "11:47 P.M. three nights from now."

"Three days." She heard the edge in her own voice. "That's plenty of time. I'll just touch every antique in Moonlight Springs and sort through centuries of memories until I find the right needle in the psychic haystack. Should be done by lunch tomorrow."

Joe's hand moved across the table. Not touching

her, just resting near enough that she could feel the warmth of his skin through her glove. A reminder that she wasn't alone.

The gesture unknotted some of the tension in her shoulders.

"I know it's asking a lot." Verena's tone carried no judgment, only understanding. "But I think the box itself might give you what you need. Not the wood, which has been touched by many hands over the years, but what's carved inside. Those symbols were made deliberately, with purpose. They might hold a memory of where the stone was hidden."

She looked at the open box. The carved moons seemed to shimmer in the light, though that might have been her imagination. Or her anxiety. Hard to tell the difference anymore.

"You want me to touch it." Not a question.

"Only if you're ready." Verena pushed the box closer. "But I won't lie to you, Leanne. Time is fracturing around us. Yesterday, Hank, the mailman, walked into his backyard and found himself at a barn raising from 1891. He was there for over five minutes before the present snapped back into place."

Joe straightened. "Is he all right?"

"Shaken. Confused. But unharmed." Verena's gaze stayed on Leanne. "For now. The disturbances are getting stronger. Lasting longer. If we don't find the Amber Stone soon..."

She didn't finish. She didn't need to.

Leanne pulled her hands from her pockets. Her fingers found the edge of her right glove. She hesitated. The leather was soft from years of wear, molded perfectly to her hand. A second skin. Her armor.

"I'll need space." Her voice came out steadier than she felt. "If this goes badly, I might..."

"Fall down, scream, or otherwise alarm the neighbors?" Verena's dry tone was so familiar it ached. This was the friend who'd understood her even as a child, who'd never made her feel broken. "I've cleared my evening. Gary knows not to send anyone to the inn unless it's an emergency. You have all the space you need."

Joe shifted his chair closer. "What do you need from me?"

Such a simple question. Such an impossible answer.

*I need you to stay. I need you to catch me if I fall. I need your voice to pull me back if I get lost in someone else's memories.*

But all she said was, "Just be here. That's enough." She peeled off her right glove, feeling the cool air against her palm.

He didn't look away. "I'm not going anywhere."

She believed him. That was the terrifying part.

She flexed her bare fingers, then reached for the box. The wood was smooth under her touch, still warm from Verena's hands. She took a breath, centered herself the way Joe had taught her, and lowered her palm to rest flat against the carved interior.

For a heartbeat, nothing happened.

Then the world exploded into light and time and memory.

*A woman's hands, wrinkled with age, lifting something from the box. The weight of it in her palms. Amber catching the light like captured sunshine. The stone pulsed with a rhythm that matched a heartbeat, and underneath that pulse, Leanne felt the current of time itself, flowing like water, wild and refusing to be contained.*

*The woman carried the stone through the darkness. Moonlight filtered through trees. The woman's breath came hard, her body tired but determined. She whispered words Leanne couldn't quite hear, a prayer or a promise.*

*The stone went into something. Not the ground. Not a wall. Something that felt alive under Leanne's psychic touch, something with grain and growth rings and the memory of roots and leaves.*

*"Something born of the grove, yet crafted by hand." The woman's voice echoed across the decades, clear as if she stood beside Leanne. "Where old magic and new purpose meet."*

*The vision shifted. Leanne saw the inn in the background, its windows glowing warm against the night. She was seeing it from somewhere specific, somewhere important. But where?*

*The images came faster. Too fast. Full moons cycling*

*overhead like a flip book and seasons blurring together with new leaves unfurling on the trees, mixed with bright red leaves blowing in the wind. The ground covered in freshly mown grass, then concealed by fallen snow. She saw the stones pulsing in sequence, saw them calling to each other across distance and time. Saw them failing. Saw the fabric of time itself beginning to tear.*

*She saw Moonlight Springs aging and un-aging, buildings rising and crumbling, people flickering in and out of existence like candle flames.*

*Saw destruction.*

*Saw ending.*

The vision slammed into her with physical force. Her psychic senses, which she'd worked so hard since her return to carefully control, ripped wide open. She felt everything at once. Every moment the box had witnessed. Every hand that had touched it. Every hope and fear and desperate prayer that had soaked into its wood over more than a century.

It was too much. Far too much.

She tried to pull back, but the memories had her locked tight. Time folded around her, crushing and infinite. Her vision went white at the edges.

Somewhere distant, someone called her name.

She couldn't answer. Couldn't move. Could barely remember who she was beneath the avalanche of history and visions.

Then warmth. Solid and real. An anchor point in the chaos.

Joe's voice, low and steady. "Come back, Leanne. Follow my voice. You're in the kitchen at the inn. Come back."

His hand. He'd grabbed her wrist and was pulling her hand away from the box.

The contact should have triggered another vision. Should have flooded her with his memories, his past, his everything.

Instead, it was just Joe. Just the warm, callused grip of someone who was here, now, in the present.

The visions released her all at once.

She gasped and yanked her hand back. The box blurred in her vision, then resolved into something blessedly ordinary. Just wood and carvings. Nothing more.

She was shaking and couldn't stop. Sweat cooled on her forehead. Her breathing came in shallow gasps.

"Easy." Joe's voice stayed calm, grounding. "You're all right. Just breathe."

She tried. Her lungs didn't seem to remember how.

Movement beside her. The scrape of Verena's chair. Then something soft and warm settled around Leanne's shoulders, wrapped snug against the shaking.

A quilt. Verena had grabbed one from

somewhere, and Joe was tucking it around her with gentle, deliberate care. His hands adjusted the fabric at her shoulders, pulled it closed at her chest. Each touch was careful.

"Sorry." Her voice came out ragged. "I'm okay."

Joe crouched beside her chair so they were eye level. "What did you see?"

Everything. Nothing. The end of the world and a riddle she didn't know how to solve.

She pulled the quilt tighter. The fabric smelled like lavender and old cotton, comforting in a way that made her want to cry. She focused on that instead of the lingering echoes of the vision.

"The stone was moved." The words felt clumsy. "The woman—I still couldn't see who she was—took it from this box and hid it somewhere. Somewhere you can see the inn."

Verena leaned forward. "Did you see where?"

"Not exactly." Leanne closed her eyes, tried to sort the jumbled images into something coherent. "She put it inside something. She said..." The words came back to her, clear and strange. "Something born of the grove, yet crafted by hand. Where old magic and new purpose meet."

The kitchen went quiet except for the tick of the clock on the wall and the soft hiss of the kettle's dying heat.

"That's specific and incredibly vague at the

same time." Leanne opened her eyes. "Which seems to be magic's favorite communication style."

Joe smiled. "Wood from the grove that someone made into something."

"Could be anything." Verena tapped her fingers on the table, thinking. "Furniture. A fence post. A thousand different things."

"I saw the inn too." She tried to hold onto the memory before it faded. "But it was very vague, and I couldn't tell exactly where I was looking from. It was more like I sensed the inn was near."

"Nothing more?" Joe asked.

Her head throbbed. The aftershocks of the vision pulsed behind her eyes like a second heartbeat. "There were other things. The stones all pulsing together. Time breaking down. It wasn't just a vision of the past. Some of it was..." She swallowed hard. "A warning, maybe. Of what happens if we don't find it."

Verena reached across the table, almost touching Leanne, but not quite. "Then we find it. You've given us more information than we had an hour ago."

"And nearly given yourself a psychic aneurysm in the process." Joe picked up one of the forgotten mugs and pressed it into her hands. "Drink."

The chamomile was lukewarm now, but she sipped it anyway. The honey was sweet on her tongue, the tea earthy and grounding. Normal things. Real things.

Her hands steadied around the mug.

"We should try to figure out what it means. Search the catalog of the inn's furniture pieces you're making." She looked at Joe.

He pulled out his phone, already scrolling through files. "Give me a few hours to search."

"We don't have hours." But even as she said it, she knew pushing herself right now would be a mistake. The vision had drained her completely. She felt wrung out, hollowed.

"Rest first." Verena stood and began clearing the mugs. "You can't find anything if you collapse from exhaustion. Take the night off. Tomorrow, you and Joe can investigate."

She wanted to argue. But the quilt around her shoulders and the tremor still running through her muscles made protest impossible.

"Fine." She pulled the quilt tighter. "You're probably right."

They discussed logistics for a few minutes. Verena promised to search her records for anything that might give them a clue. Joe would compile his furniture catalog and meet her in the morning.

By the time they stood to leave, Leanne's breathing had returned to normal, though exhaustion almost smothered her.

Joe walked with her toward the main hall. The

inn's familiar warmth wrapped around them, all polished wood and soft rugs and the lingering smell of bread. Through the windows, she could see the gardens stretching toward the tree line.

Somewhere out there—or maybe even inside the inn—the Amber Stone waited to be found.

Three days until the full moon. Three days to solve a riddle and save a town from collapse.

No pressure.

They reached the entrance hall, and Joe paused at the door. "You did good work today."

"I had a vision and nearly passed out. That's not exactly a gold star performance."

"You touched that box knowing it might overwhelm you. That's brave."

Brave. She'd never thought of it that way. Desperate, maybe. Foolish, certainly. But brave?

"Or stupid." She tried for levity. "There's a fine line."

"There is." His hand lifted like he might touch her arm, then fell back to his side. Learning her boundaries even now. "But I don't think you crossed it."

"I'll walk you to the start of the path."

"You sure? You look tired."

"The fresh air will do me good." They headed out onto the porch and down the stairs. She walked with him to the entrance of the maze.

He pulled the quilt tighter around her shoulders

and smiled at her. "Quite a day you've had, but I'm glad I was there with you."

The words settled warmly over her. Before she could figure out how to respond, movement caught her eye.

A woman emerged from the opening of the maze garden, her silver hair catching the morning light. She moved with the unhurried grace of someone who'd never rushed a day in her life. Her eyes, sharp and knowing, fixed on them with an intensity that made Leanne want to step back.

"Leanne McMann." The woman's voice carried that ageless quality that made it impossible to guess if she was sixty or ninety. "And Joe Hall. How lovely to find you both here."

Something about her tone suggested she'd been looking for them specifically.

"And you are?" Leanne asked.

"Zara Bollinger." The woman said it as if that explained what she was doing in the maze as the skies darkened above them.

Joe nodded politely. "Can we help you with something?"

"Oh, I think you're managing quite well on your own." Zara's smile held secrets. Her gaze moved between them, lingering on the quilt still wrapped around Leanne's shoulders, then to Joe's protective stance beside her. "Making good progress, I'd say."

Leanne's spine prickled. "Progress on what?"

"On finding what's lost, of course." Zara stepped closer, and Leanne caught a scent that reminded her of old libraries and older magic. "Though I do have one small piece of advice, if you'll indulge an old woman."

"Of course." Joe's tone stayed polite, but Leanne heard the wariness underneath.

Zara looked directly at Leanne. Her eyes seemed to see straight through skin and bone to something deeper. "Sometimes the oldest things hide in plain sight, waiting for the right hands to reveal their truth."

The words hung in the air between them, cryptic and weighted with meaning Leanne couldn't quite grasp.

"I'll keep that in mind." She pulled the quilt tighter. "Thank you."

"Do." Zara's smile widened. "You'd be surprised what skilled hands can uncover when they know where to look." Her gaze flicked to Joe.

With that, she turned and walked away, down the pathway, humming something under her breath that sounded like a lullaby from another century.

Leanne stared after her. "That was..."

"Weird?" Joe offered.

"I was going to say cryptic, but weird works too." She looked down at her gloved hands, then at Joe's calloused fingers. The right hands to reveal the truth.

A furniture restorer and a psychic. Someone who could analyze wood and someone who could read its history.

"She knows something." Joe watched Zara disappear down the path. "About the stone."

"She definitely knows something. But whether she's being helpful or just enjoying being mysterious is anyone's guess."

"Could be both."

"Could be." She turned and glanced back at the inn. Her bed called to her. "I need to sleep before my brain completely stops working."

"You're right. Go get some rest. I'll see you in the morning."

She started to leave, then paused. The quilt around her shoulders, Joe's steady presence at her back, the mystery waiting in the grove. Everything felt balanced on a knife's edge between terror and something that might, possibly, be hope.

"Joe?" She looked back at him. "Thank you. For before. For pulling me back."

His expression warmed, and he smiled gently. "Always."

*Always.* Like he meant it. Like this partnership they'd stumbled into might extend beyond finding a magical stone and saving a town.

Like maybe, impossibly, she wasn't alone anymore.

She walked back to the porch and climbed the

stairs with the quilt still wrapped around her shoulders. Zara's cryptic words and the words from the woman in her vision intertwined in her mind. *The right hands to reveal the truth. Born of the grove, yet crafted by hand.* Somewhere in those riddles was an answer.

# CHAPTER 12

Joe woke before dawn with Zara Bollinger's words circling through his mind. He'd spent half the night thinking about them, and Leanne's vision, and the cryptic clue the elderly woman had left behind.

He sat up in bed and rubbed his face. His bedroom window showed only darkness, but he knew sunrise couldn't be more than an hour away. Sleep wouldn't return now. It never did when a problem lodged itself in his brain like a stubborn splinter.

He pulled on yesterday's jeans and a flannel shirt, not bothering with socks yet. The cool floorboards beneath his feet helped sharpen his thoughts. His mind worked best in the quiet hours when the rest of Moonlight Springs still slept.

He moved to the kitchen and started coffee, watching the dark liquid drip into the pot while his brain continued working through the puzzle.

*Born of the grove.* Something made from trees, obviously. Wood. His territory.

*Yet crafted by hand.* Not natural, then. Not just a tree or a branch. Something shaped with purpose, with skill.

*Where old magic and new purpose meet.*

He poured coffee into a heavy ceramic mug and leaned against the counter. Steam rose between him and the kitchen window, where the first hint of gray touched the eastern sky. He thought about every piece of antique furniture at the Moonlight Inn. He'd cataloged most of them for Verena and touched nearly all of them during various restoration projects.

The grandfather clock. The writing desk where Leanne had found Elizabeth's letter. The dining room table. The chairs. The armoire in the upstairs hall.

None of them felt right. None of them sang with the kind of significance this riddle demanded.

He sipped his coffee and let his mind wander beyond the inn's interior. Verena's property sprawled across several acres. The building itself. The gardens. The old carriage house behind the inn.

The maze.

He straightened. His thumb rubbed against the mug's handle, feeling the slight imperfection where the glaze had pooled.

The maze. He'd walked its paths dozens of times while working at the inn, sometimes to think, sometimes just to appreciate the careful design of the hedges. And at its entrance, weathered by years and seasons, sat a bench.

Not just any bench.

A massive piece carved from a single fallen oak, its grain still visible beneath layers of patient exposure to sun and rain. He'd admired it countless times, run his hands over its surface, and marveled at the craftsmanship. The way the craftsman had followed the wood's natural curves while shaping something functional and beautiful. The joints that needed no hardware, just perfect understanding of how wood moved and settled.

He set down his coffee cup.

That bench had always drawn his eye and always made him pause. He'd told himself it was professional appreciation and the recognition one craftsman felt for another's exceptional work. But now, standing in his kitchen with dawn breaking outside, another possibility bloomed.

*Born of the grove.* An oak from the old grove that adjoined Verena's property.

*Yet crafted by hand.* Shaped by a woodworker who understood both the material and the magic.

*Where old magic and new purpose meet.* A bench that invited rest, welcomed visitors to the maze, that sat at the threshold between the ordinary garden and the mystical paths within.

He grabbed his boots from beside the door and shoved his feet into them. He didn't bother with more coffee or breakfast. The need to see the bench and examine it properly pulled at him like a grain pattern showing him which direction to cut.

The truck's engine sounded too loud in the pre-dawn quiet. He drove through empty streets, past darkened shops and houses where normal people still slept. The sky had shifted from black to deep purple by the time he pulled into the Moonlight Inn's driveway and parked near the path that led around to the gardens.

He killed the engine and sat for a moment. His breath fogged the windshield. Excitement thrummed through him, the same feeling he used to get before starting a new piece. Not restoration. Creation. The anticipation of discovery, of bringing something into being that hadn't existed before.

Except this already existed. Had existed for decades, probably. Sitting in plain sight while everyone looked past it.

He climbed out of the truck. The cold morning air bit through his flannel shirt, but he barely noticed. Dew soaked the grass as he walked around the inn toward the maze garden. Birds were starting to wake, their first tentative calls punctuating the silence.

The maze rose before him, its entrance marked by an arbor. He entered the maze and turned to his left. There sat the bench, exactly as he remembered.

He approached slowly. The bench sat where it always had, solid against the hedge. Even in the dim light, he could see the quality of its construction. Someone had loved this wood and understood it deeply enough to coax this form from it without violating its essential nature.

He crouched in front of it. The oak's grain flowed in subtle waves across the bench's surface. Weather had silvered it, giving it a soft patina that only time could create. He placed his bare palm against the wood.

Still cool from the night. Slightly damp from dew. But underneath the surface temperature, something else. A warmth. A sense of life that good wood never quite loses, even decades after the tree fell.

He closed his eyes and let his fingertips read the surface. Every craftsman developed their own signature, visible in the tool marks if you knew how to look. The slight variation in a plane's stroke. The angle of a chisel cut. The rhythm of sanding.

This maker had worked with confidence. No hesitation in these cuts. No second-guessing. Just clean, purposeful shaping that honored what the wood wanted to be.

He opened his eyes and shifted position so he could examine the bench's underside. His lower back complained as he bent awkwardly to see beneath the seat. Cobwebs caught the growing light. A spider scurried away from his intrusion.

And there, carved into the wood where weather couldn't reach it, he found what he hadn't quite dared to hope for.

A maker's mark.

He traced the initials with his fingertip, making sure. C.J.H. No mistake.

He knew this mark. Had seen it a thousand times on the wood plane his great-grandfather had made, the same plane he'd handed to Leanne to test her abilities. Three initials intertwined in a specific pattern, elegant in its simplicity. C.J.H.

Charles Joseph Hall.

Joe sat back on his heels. The damp grass soaked through his jeans. The dawn chorus grew louder around him, but he barely heard it.

His great-grandfather had made this bench.

Charles Joseph Hall, who had passed his woodworking tools to his son, who had passed them to Joe's father, who had given them to Joe. Four generations of craftsmen, each learning to read wood like other people read books.

Joe stood slowly. His legs had gone stiff from crouching. He walked around the bench, seeing it with new eyes now. His great-grandfather's hands had shaped this. Charles had chosen this oak, planned the cuts, and fitted each joint.

But why? Charles had been a furniture maker, creating pieces for homes and businesses. This bench sat outside, exposed to the weather, and was situated at the entrance to a maze on property that had belonged to Verena's family even then.

*Where old magic and new purpose meet.*

His great-grandfather had known. Somehow, Charles Hall had understood Moonlight Springs' secrets. Had worked with its magic, not against it. He had crafted this bench from grove wood for a specific purpose.

And no one had told Joe. Not his grandfather, who must have known. Not his father, who surely would have learned the story.

Or maybe they'd planned to tell him. Maybe there was a right time for these revelations, and that time had simply never come before they passed.

Joe placed both hands on the bench's backrest. The wood warmed beneath his palms. He could almost feel his great-grandfather's presence, an echo of the pride and purpose that had gone into this work.

Charles knew. He understood what this town was, what it needed. And he built something to protect it.

The realization settled into his bones like cold on a winter morning. He hadn't realized when he'd moved to Moonlight Springs all those years ago to help out his grandmother that his family wasn't just connected to Moonlight Springs through generations of residency. They were woven into its magical fabric. His great-grandfather had been chosen, just as Leanne had been chosen now.

Just as he himself might be chosen.

The thought should have frightened him. A week ago, it would have sent him retreating to his workshop and the safe, predictable work of restoration. But standing here with his hands on his great-grandfather's work, he felt something different.

Recognition.

He'd spent years convinced the fire was punishment. But Charles hadn't been afraid to make things. Charles had built something that lasted.

What if he'd been wrong about the punishment? What if the opposite was true?

What if creation was exactly what his family had always done? What if making things, ingraining them with purpose and care, was his inheritance?

He lifted his hands from the bench. The sun had

cleared the horizon now, spilling gold across the garden. The maze hedge caught the light, and for just a moment, he could have sworn he saw a faint glow emanating from the bench's center.

He blinked. The glow vanished, if it had ever been there at all.

But he knew what he had to do next.

He turned and strode back toward the parking area. His truck started with a familiar rumble. He needed to get to his workshop and retrieve the wood plane. Leanne had to see this. Had to touch the tool and the bench, use her gift to read what his great-grandfather had known and done.

The drive back to his workshop took only minutes, but his mind raced ahead. What would Leanne see when she touched the plane now, with the bench's existence revealed? Would the visions show her where the Amber Stone lay hidden?

Joe pulled into his workshop's driveway and killed the engine. He sat for a moment, breathing in the familiar scent of wood and varnish that permeated even the truck's interior from years of hauling materials.

*The right hands reveal truth*, Zara had said.

Leanne's hands, which read history through touch.

And his own hands, which carried his great-grandfather's skill and knowledge.

The workshop door swung open beneath his key.

Inside, his tools waited in their careful arrangement. And there, on its special shelf where he kept it safe, sat the antique wood plane that had started all of this.

He lifted it carefully. The handle fit his palm like it had been made for him. Because in a way, it had been. Four generations of the same hands, the same understanding of wood and craft and purpose.

He tucked the plane under his arm and locked the workshop behind him. The sun climbed higher, burning off the last of the dawn mist. Moonlight Springs was waking up. Soon people would fill the streets, going about their ordinary days, unaware that time itself was crumbling around them.

But Joe knew. And Leanne knew. And together, with his great-grandfather's tools and her gift for reading truth, they would find the Amber Stone.

He started the truck and pointed it back toward the Moonlight Inn. Toward Leanne and the bench that held answers.

Toward whatever came next.

His phone showed six forty-five. Early still, but not so early that he'd be waking the entire inn. And this couldn't wait. The full moon was only two days away now. Time was literally running out.

He pressed the accelerator. The truck responded, carrying him back toward magic and mystery and a bench his great-grandfather had crafted from oak more than a century ago.

Whatever his great-grandfather had known, whatever secrets he'd built into that wood, Leanne would uncover them. And Joe would finally understand why his family's craft had been passed down through generations in this particular town, in this particular way.

# CHAPTER 13

The morning sun had cleared the horizon when Joe knocked on Leanne's door, his energy radiating through the wood before she even opened it.

"I found it." He stood in the hallway, hair disheveled like he'd run his hands through it a dozen times, eyes bright with discovery.

"It? What it?"

"The bench. The one at the maze entrance."

Leanne pulled her sweater tighter, her brain still foggy with sleep. "The bench?"

"Born of the grove, yet crafted by hand." He stepped inside without waiting for an invitation, words tumbling out faster than usual. "I went through my catalog of furniture at the inn. Over and over. Then it came to me. The bench is made from oak from the old grove behind the property. And Leanne, there's a maker's mark underneath."

Her pulse quickened despite the early hour. "Whose mark?"

He flipped the wood plane on its side and showed her. "C.J.H. Charles Joseph Hall. My great-grandfather."

The revelation hung between them. Leanne thought of the gentle vision she'd experienced from his wood plane, the craftsman's pride and careful attention to detail. That same man had built something for the Guardians.

"Show me the bench." She grabbed her jacket.

They walked through the still-sleeping inn, past the grandfather clock with its steady tick, through the lobby where early light filtered through lace curtains. The air outside held the crisp promise of winter.

The maze sprawled before them. They entered it and turned left. There it was. She had walked past it hundreds of times without really seeing it. Back when she was a young girl, and since her return. Now she studied the piece with new appreciation.

The wood had aged to a soft gray-brown, its surface worn smooth by decades of guests pausing to rest. Simple in design but beautifully constructed, the bench seemed to grow from the ground itself, as natural as the stones marking the maze paths.

Joe knelt beside it, running his palm along the underside of the seat. "Here. Feel this."

She crouched next to him, their shoulders nearly touching. Even through her gloves, she could trace the carved initials he indicated. C.J.H. The letters had been worked into the wood with the same care she'd felt in the plane, each curve deliberate and sure.

"Your family built this. For the Guardians." She sat back on her heels, considering.

"I think so. And I thought maybe if you touched both pieces, the connection might help."

Smart. Leanne's stomach fluttered with anticipation and dread. Her abilities had been growing stronger, more controlled since she'd started working with Joe. But asking them to bridge more than a century of history, to show her not just memories but purpose and magic...

"No pressure or anything. There's never any pressure," she muttered.

Joe laughed. "You want me to do it first? I could just guess wildly at what my great-grandfather was thinking."

"Your technique needs work." But his attempt at humor steadied her. She pulled off her gloves, tucking them into her pocket. The morning air felt sharp against her bare skin.

He set the antique plane on the bench beside her, within easy reach. Then he settled onto the grass a few feet away, close enough to help if needed but far enough to give her room to work.

Here it was again. The part where she had to actually do something.

A week ago, touching an unknown object would have sent her into a spiral of dread. Now, with Joe watching her with quiet confidence, she felt not quite courage, but maybe its awkward younger sibling. Determination, perhaps. Or stubbornness.

She placed her palm flat against the bench's seat and one on the plane.

The vision slammed into her with the force of a wave.

Moonlight Inn stood before her, but younger. The gardens were newly planted, the maze hedges much shorter. Late afternoon sun painted everything gold. A man knelt where she sat now, his calloused hands working a plane across oak still pale with newness.

*Charles Hall. She recognized him from the earlier vision, though he'd aged since crafting the plane she'd touched. Silver threaded through his dark hair now. His movements carried the same careful precision and the same love for his work.*

*He wasn't alone.*

*A woman stood beside him, tall and elegant despite her simple dress. Dark hair coiled at her nape. She watched Charles work with an expression of profound trust.*

*"This will hold," Charles said, his voice carrying clearly through time. "The seal will keep until it's needed."*

"The lock answers to the moon. Full moon only." The woman's voice held authority worn thin at the edges. "And the stone picks its own moment. We don't get to rush this."

Charles nodded, never pausing in his work. Wood curled away from his blade in pale ribbons. He created a hollow space in the bench's thick seat, hidden beneath a panel so cunningly designed it would be invisible to casual inspection.

The woman crouched beside him. "You're certain about this? Once it's sealed, even you won't be able to access it."

"That's the point." Charles brushed sawdust from the hollow he'd created. "The stone needs to rest. You said the town's magic needs time to settle. This way, it can't be found until it's meant to be."

"Until someone comes looking who can see the past." The woman smiled, sad and knowing. "Until the right hands touch the right object at the right time."

"Your family will watch over it." Charles met her eyes. "And mine will keep the knowledge alive, even if they don't understand why. That's enough."

The woman drew something from her pocket. An amber stone, small enough to fit in her palm but blazing with inner light. Even through the vision, Leanne felt its power. Time itself seemed to bend around it, past and future swirling together.

There. The Amber Stone of Time, after all their searching.

The woman placed it carefully in the hollow Charles had created. The moment it settled into the wood, the stone's light *pulsed once, twice, then dimmed to a soft glow. The temporal energy that had crackled around it eased. Waiting.*

*"Born of the grove," the woman murmured, laying her hand over the stone. "Crafted by hands that honor the old ways. Sealed until the moon calls it forth again."*

*Light blazed from beneath her palm. Not the amber glow of the stone, but something silver-bright. Magic, raw and powerful, flowed from the woman into the wood. The bench seemed to drink it in, the grain darkening and settling as the energy took hold.*

*When the light faded, Charles had already fitted the panel back into place. Leanne couldn't see the seam even knowing it was there. The stone had vanished completely, hidden in plain sight.*

*"Only during the full moon sun." The woman stood, brushing off her skirts. "When moonlight is brightest in the sky. That's when the lock will recognize its Guardian."*

*"And if no one finds it?" Charles gathered his tools.*

*"Then it waits for the next moon. And the next." The woman looked at the bench, then at the maze beyond. "Time is patient. The stone can afford to be the same."*

*They walked away together, leaving the bench in its place.*

The vision should have ended there.

Instead, it lurched forward.

*Seasons flickered past. Rain and snow, summer heat and autumn cold. Guests sat on the bench, laughing and talking, completely unaware of what rested beneath them. Decades compressed into heartbeats.*

*Then the scene steadied.*

*The same woman stood before the bench again. But she'd aged now, her dark hair streaked with silver. She pressed her palm against the wood the way Leanne had, tears streaming down her face.*

*"I'm sorry," the woman whispered. "I'm so sorry I have to leave you like this. But there's no one else. No one I trust to—"*

*Her words cut off. She straightened, composing herself with visible effort. When she spoke again, her voice was steady.*

*"Someone will come. Someone who can see. They'll find you when the time is right, when the town needs you most. Until then, rest. Please, rest."*

*She bent and kissed the bench's arm, a gesture so tender it made Leanne's throat tighten.*

*Then she turned and walked into the maze. The morning light caught her face as she glanced back one last time.*

The vision fractured.

Images cascaded too fast to follow. The bench in snow, in sunlight, in rain. Waiting. Holding its secret.

The connection snapped.

Leanne gasped, her hand jerking away from the wood. She would have fallen if Joe hadn't moved, catching her shoulders and steadying her.

"Easy." His voice came from far away. "I've got you. Just breathe."

She gulped air, her heart hammering. The present world felt thin and insubstantial after the vision. Joe's hands on her shoulders were the only solid thing.

"Did you see it?" She grabbed his wrist, needing the anchor of his warmth. "The stone. It's here. In the bench."

"You're sure?" Joe's face swam into focus beside her, creased with concern.

"Positive." Leanne pushed herself upright, though her head spun. "Your great-grandfather built a hidden compartment. The stone is sealed inside by a lock."

"What kind of lock?"

"The kind that only opens during the full moon." She pressed her free hand to her forehead, trying to organize the cascade of information. "When the brightest moonlight illuminates the sky. That's when the lock will recognize the Guardian and open."

Joe sat back slowly, processing. "The full moon is tomorrow night."

"So we have one chance." Leanne's hand was still wrapped around his wrist. She should probably let go. She didn't want to.

But Joe didn't pull away. Instead, he shifted so he was sitting beside her on the grass, their backs against the bench that held so much history. So much magic. "What else did you see?"

Everything. She had seen everything. Charles's careful craftsmanship. The mysterious woman's blessing. The way the stone had settled into sleep, patient and waiting.

"Your great-grandfather was chosen specifically for this work." She finally released Joe's wrist, though she immediately missed the contact. "The woman who commissioned the bench, she was a Guardian. She needed somewhere safe to hide the stone while the town's magic stabilized after some kind of disturbance."

"A Guardian." Joe's voice held wonder. "My great-grandfather knew about all this. Built furniture for them."

"He understood the responsibility." Leanne touched the bench again, this time just with her gloved hand. No vision came, only the sense of deep peace the wood carried. "He and the Guardian both knew the stone needed to rest. That it would choose its own moment to be found again."

"And that moment is tomorrow night at 11:47."

"Yes." Leanne turned to look at him. "The full moon. When the veil between times is thinnest. That's when someone with the right gift can open the lock and claim the stone."

Someone like her. The woman who could see the past and understand magic. She turned the thought over, not sure what to do with it.

Joe must have seen something in her face because his expression softened. "You don't have to be scared of this."

"I'm terrified of this. What if I can't open it? What if the lock doesn't recognize me as the Guardian?"

"Then we try again during the next full moon." Joe said it like it was simple. "And if that doesn't work, we wait for the next one. But Leanne, I watched you just now. You connected with something more than a century old and pulled out exactly the information we needed. If the stone is choosing its Guardian based on ability, you're the obvious candidate."

"Nothing about my ability feels obvious. Mostly it feels like a very inconvenient way to get overwhelmed in antique shops."

"See, that's your problem right there." He bumped her shoulder gently. "You're thinking about antique shops when you should be thinking about time disturbances and saving the town. Really need to work on your priorities."

A surprised laugh burst out of her. "Did you just make a joke about my existential crisis?"

"Seemed like the right moment." But his smile was kind. "You're not alone in this. You know that, right?"

The words hit deeper than he probably meant them to. She had been alone with her gift for so long that she'd forgotten what trust felt like.

"I know," she said quietly. "I'm starting to know."

They sat in comfortable silence, watching the sun climb higher. The maze stretched before them. Somewhere in the inn, Verena was probably starting breakfast prep. Other guests would be waking soon. The day was beginning.

But here, in this moment, Leanne felt suspended outside normal time. Sitting beside Joe with the knowledge of what tomorrow would bring, she felt something unfamiliar stir inside her.

Hope. Actual, genuine hope.

"There's something else." She pulled the wood plane closer, running her gloved fingers over its smooth surface. "At the end of the vision, I saw the Guardian again. Older this time. She came back to the bench decades after your great-grandfather built it."

"What was she doing?"

"Saying goodbye." Leanne's throat tightened at the memory. "She was leaving. Going somewhere. And she was trusting that the stone would be found when the town needed it most."

"Did you recognize her?" Joe asked. "The Guardian?"

"No, but she looked vaguely familiar. But she couldn't be. It was way before I was born."

Joe was quiet for a long moment. When he spoke again, his voice was thoughtful. "My great-grandfather built this bench knowing it would outlast him. Knowing he'd never see whether the magic worked. That takes a special kind of faith."

"And your whole family has been involved in it. It gives me hope that we'll find the stone for sure tomorrow."

"When did you get so confident?"

"About thirty seconds ago. Could fade at any moment, so let's enjoy it while it lasts."

This time Joe's laugh was full and genuine. The sound wrapped around her like sunlight.

They sat together as morning bloomed into full day, backs against the bench that held the Amber Stone.

The vision had shown her so much. The stone's hiding place. Joe's family legacy. But the thing that stuck with her most wasn't the magic or the history.

It was Charles Hall's hope, the way he'd built something meant to endure, to protect, and serve a purpose greater than himself. He'd trusted that future hands would carry on his work.

And now, more than a century later, here they stood. His descendant and a woman whose gift finally made sense.

"Your great-grandfather would be proud of you," Leanne said. "I felt it in the vision. His love for his craft. His faith in the future."

Joe smiled. "Thank you."

"I'm just the messenger. Though, if we're being honest, I'm a messenger who desperately needs breakfast and possibly a nap. These visions are exhausting."

"You're also a messenger who just solved a century-old mystery and found a magical stone." Joe nodded toward the inn. "I think that earns you pancakes at minimum."

"Pancakes and coffee. Let's not lowball my achievements."

They stood and walked back through the maze entrance together, leaving the bench to keep its secret. When the moon was full, that secret would finally be revealed.

# CHAPTER 14

The scent of sawdust wrapped around Leanne the moment she stepped into Joe's workshop. Morning light filtered through the tall windows, catching particles of wood dust that drifted like golden snow through the air. Her gloved hands relaxed at her sides. This space felt safe in a way few places did.

Joe stood at his workbench, one hand resting on the antique plane while the other traced invisible patterns on the scarred wood surface. He looked up when she entered, and something in his expression made her stomach flutter in a way that had nothing to do with visions.

"I was just thinking about my great-grandfather and everything he built here."

Leanne crossed to the bench where he'd laid out

his sketches of the maze garden. The carving pattern from the bench's hidden compartment occupied the center page, rendered in careful detail. She studied the interweaving lines without touching the paper.

"He was part of something bigger than furniture. All those years, I thought I was just continuing a family trade. But it was never just about the work, was it?"

"No." She leaned closer to the sketches. "Your family helped protect this town. They understood that sometimes the most important things need to be hidden in plain sight."

Joe moved to stand beside her, close enough that she felt his warmth, but not so close that they risked accidental contact. "The full moon is tomorrow night. Are you ready?"

She pulled off one glove, then stopped. The workshop air kissed her bare palm. "I've spent years avoiding moments like this. Being ready feels like a foreign concept."

"You've touched more objects in the past week than you have in years." Joe picked up a clean rag and began wiping invisible dust from his tools, a nervous habit she'd started to recognize. "That counts for something."

"It counts for exhaustion and mild terror. But I suppose that's progress." She managed a bit of a smile.

He set down the rag and turned to face her fully. His brown eyes stayed fixed on her with that steady patience that made her want to believe impossible things. "Watching you face your gift these past days. Seeing you choose to touch objects even when you know they'll hurt. That takes more courage than I've had in a decade."

"Or less sense." She shrugged. "Courage would have been learning control years ago instead of hiding."

"You're learning now. That's what matters."

A comfortable silence settled between them. She studied the sketches again, following the carved patterns with her eyes. Moonlight and oak. Time and protection. Magic woven through wood grain by hands that understood both crafts.

"I still can't believe you figured out the stone was in the bench in Verena's maze and that your great-grandfather made it. He must have been a remarkable man to be trusted with something so important."

"I think he'd like you." Joe smiled, the expression transforming his usually serious face. "He appreciated people who respected history."

"Even people who see too much of it?"

"Especially them."

Leanne's fingers hovered over the sketch. "When we open that compartment in the bench at 11:57 tomorrow night and I touch the Amber

Stone, what if the visions are too much? What if I can't hold on to the present?"

"Then I'll be there to pull you back. Just like before. You don't have to do this alone anymore, Leanne." His voice carried absolute certainty.

The tension inside her that seemed to be her constant companion, loosened slightly. She'd spent so long believing isolation was safety that the idea of partnership still felt a bit unreal. But Joe had proven himself over and over. He didn't treat her like she was broken.

Well, he kind of treated her like she was broken furniture, which was apparently his love language.

That thought made her smile despite her nerves. Leave it to her to finally find someone who understood and have him be a man who thought in terms of wood grain and joinery.

"We should head to the square," Joe said. "I told Verena we'd meet her and Gary around ten."

Leanne pulled her glove back. "To discuss tomorrow's plan?"

"And to check if there have been any more disturbances." Joe gathered his sketches into a worn leather portfolio. "Gary mentioned some strange incidents this morning."

They left the workshop and walked toward the town square. The air carried a chill. The few surviving leaves on the bare trees lining the street drifted down onto the sidewalk like confetti from a celebration no one remembered starting.

"It's beautiful," Leanne murmured. "I'd forgotten how lovely Moonlight Springs is."

"Thirty years is a long time to be away."

"It felt necessary." She watched a leaf swirl past. "Every object here held too many memories. Too many voices I couldn't silence."

"And now?"

"Now I'm wondering if running was the right choice, or if I just wasted three decades being afraid."

"I think we all waste time being afraid." He looked off into the distance for a moment before turning back to her. "The question is whether we're brave enough to stop."

They rounded the corner, and the square spread before them. Verena stood near the gazebo, her silver-streaked hair gleaming. Gary stood beside her in his sheriff's uniform, his posture protective without being overbearing.

"There they are," Joe said.

They crossed the square, passing a young mother pushing a stroller and a young couple walking past, arm-in-arm. Normal life continued, oblivious to the magical crisis building beneath the surface. She envied that ignorance even as she accepted her role in protecting it.

Verena's face brightened when she spotted them. "Perfect timing. I was just telling Gary about tomorrow's plan."

"What do you need from me?" Gary asked. His sheriff's authority radiated calm competence. "Besides keeping people away from the maze after dark?"

"That's the main thing. We can't have anyone wandering around during the retrieval," Verena said.

She opened her mouth to add her thoughts when the air suddenly thickened. The hair on her arms stood up beneath her jacket sleeves. She had learned to recognize that sensation over the past week.

"Something's happening," she said.

The others tensed. Gary stepped closer to Verena, and his hand moved instinctively toward his radio.

The sound came first. A rumbling that grew from distant thunder to immediate danger in heartbeats. Then the image materialized in the middle of the street. A horse-drawn carriage from another era, solid and real, barreling down the modern road with wild-eyed horses and a driver who yanked desperately at the reins.

A car swerved. Brakes squealed. Someone screamed.

The carriage passed through a parked sedan like

smoke, the disruption growing more solid with each second. Leanne's senses flared in response, showing her fragments. A wedding. A runaway team. Terror and determination on the driver's face as he tried to protect his passengers.

Then it faded, dissolving like morning mist, leaving only shocked faces and the smell of something burnt and wrong in the air.

"That's not good." Gary let out a breath. "That's the third one this morning. They're getting worse."

Verena's fingers pressed against her moonstone pendant, and small lines bracketed her mouth. "The Amber Stone's influence is destabilizing. We're running out of time faster than I thought."

"Tomorrow night. We just have to make it to tomorrow night," Joe insisted.

She pressed her gloved hands together. The vision had triggered her gift even without direct contact, showing her pieces of the carriage's history. The boundaries between past and present were dissolving.

"Miss Harrison."

The voice cut through the residual chaos like a blade. Leanne turned to find Blake Denton approaching their group, his expensive suit immaculate despite the morning's strange events. His smile held no warmth.

"Mr. Denton." Verena's tone could have frozen water. "I thought we had nothing left to discuss."

Denton's gaze swept over their group, calculating and sharp. "Oh, I think we have plenty to discuss. Particularly about these unfortunate incidents plaguing your lovely town."

Gary stepped forward slightly. "Unless you're reporting a crime, Mr. Denton, I suggest you move along."

"No crime to report, Sheriff." Denton's smile widened insincerely. "Just a concerned citizen worried about public safety. These strange anomalies are becoming quite dangerous, wouldn't you say?"

Leanne looked at him closely. He knew. He knew exactly what was happening.

"You're running out of time," Denton continued, his attention fixing on Verena and then switching to Leanne. "I'll find this one before you. You'll see. I have eyes everywhere."

Fury sparked inside her, hot and sudden. This man wanted to steal what he didn't understand, to use the town's magic for his own purposes. Every vision she had endured, every moment of courage it had cost her to search for the stone, and he thought he could just take it.

Leanne stepped forward, her gloved hands clenched at her sides. "I won't let you get the stone."

The words emerged before she even consciously decided to speak.

Denton's expression shifted to something uglier. "Brave words from someone who can barely control their own—well—control anything."

"I can control you not finding the stone." She shot the words at him and whirled away.

He reached out. His fingers caught her wrist, skin meeting skin where her sleeve had ridden up.

The vision slammed into her.

*A younger Denton, decades stripped away, standing in a street that looked like Moonlight Springs but older and rougher. A young woman stood beside him, both of them dressed in clothes from the 1800s. They argued about something.*

*Then the vision shifted, showing her more. Denton's face with that same hungry ambition and same grasping need for control.*

Leanne yanked her hand back, gasping. The present snapped into place around her. Denton stood frozen, his eyes wide with shock. He'd felt it too. Seen something through their connection.

He knows what I saw, she realized. Of course, she couldn't have seen a young Blake Denton back in the 1800s. It wasn't possible.

"You," Denton breathed. "You're—"

"Mr. Denton."

The new voice carried layers of meaning Leanne couldn't quite parse. Zara Bollinger approached through the dispersing crowd, her walking stick tapping a measured rhythm on the pavement. She moved with the assured grace of someone much younger than her apparent age.

The tension between Zara and Denton crackled like static electricity. They stared at each other, and Leanne saw recognition in both faces and something older. Deeper. More complicated.

"Still chasing what isn't yours to find?" Zara asked mildly.

"Still pretending to be something you're not?" Denton countered.

"I'm exactly what I've always been." Zara's smile held secrets and sadness. "The question is whether you've learned anything at all."

Leanne looked between them, her mind racing. The vision had shown Denton in the 1800s. Impossible. But she'd also seen the woman at the bench, the Guardian who'd helped hide the Amber Stone, and standing here now, watching Zara's profile catch the morning light...

The resemblance was unmistakable.

Which was ridiculous. Zara couldn't be the same person from her vision any more than Denton could have existed in the 1800s. Even magic had limits.

*Didn't it?*

"We're done here," Gary said, his sheriff's authority filling his voice. "Mr. Denton, I believe you have business elsewhere."

Denton's gaze lingered on Leanne, calculating and cold. Then he turned and walked away, his footsteps measured and unhurried.

She watched him go, her wrist still tingling where he'd touched her. The vision's implications churned through her mind, refusing to settle into anything that made sense.

Zara stepped closer, her expression softening. "You saw something important, dear?"

"I don't know what I saw. Something impossible."

Zara's hand rested on her walking stick. "Impossible is relative in Moonlight Springs. Sometimes the past is closer than we think."

Before Leanne could respond, Zara turned and walked down the sidewalk, leaving them standing in the square with more questions than answers.

Joe's hand touched Leanne's elbow gently. "You okay?"

Was she? Leanne looked at the empty space where Denton had stood, then at the path Zara had taken. Tomorrow, they would open the hidden compartment and retrieve the Amber Stone. Tomorrow, she would have to be strong enough to control whatever visions came.

And after tomorrow, maybe she'd figure out how two people she'd just met had somehow also been in her visions of a time over a century ago.

"I'm fine," she said finally. "Or I will be. After tomorrow."

Verena studied her closely. "What did you see when he touched you?"

"The past." Leanne met her friend's gaze. "And possibly the future. I'm not entirely sure anymore."

"Welcome to Moonlight Springs," Verena said softly. "Where time becomes more suggestion than rule."

Moonlight Inn felt restless.

Leanne sat in the library's worn leather armchair, watching the fire dance in the hearth while the building creaked and sighed around her. Outside the tall windows, the almost-full moon cast scattered silver light across the garden. Tomorrow night, that same moon would be completely full, and she would either find the Amber Stone or watch Moonlight Springs tear itself apart at the seams of time.

The fire popped, sending a spray of sparks against the screen. She jumped. Everything felt charged tonight, like the air before a thunderstorm. The town's magic was unraveling thread by thread, and she could feel it deep inside her.

She'd been feeling it all day. Walking through town that afternoon had been disorienting. The clock in the tower in the square had run backward for ten minutes while they watched. A couple arguing in the coffee shop had suddenly stopped mid-sentence, their faces blank, before continuing their fight with completely different words. Gary had received three calls about people reporting conversations they couldn't quite remember having.

Time itself was coming undone.

The library door opened, and Joe stepped inside, carrying two mugs that smelled of chamomile and honey. He'd learned quickly that she preferred it.

"Thought you could use this," he said, setting one mug on the side table near her chair. His fingers were dusted with sawdust, as always. She'd come to find it oddly comforting.

"Thank you." She pulled one hand from her pocket long enough to accept the mug, wrapping both gloved hands around its warmth. "Did Verena go to bed?"

"I think she headed out to the maze. Said it would calm her." Joe settled into the chair across from hers, his own mug cradled in his capable hands.

"It always was her favorite place." She took a sip of tea, letting the warmth spread through her. The fire crackled again, smaller this time, and she watched the flames twist and curl. "I keep thinking about what Zara said. About the right hands revealing truth."

"Your hands and mine. Strange how this all connects. My great-grandfather built that bench and helped hide the stone. You're able to see it in your vision. And now here we are."

"The universe has a twisted sense of humor." She meant it lightly, but her voice came out thin. "Or maybe the stones just enjoy watching people squirm."

He looked up at her, his brown eyes serious in the firelight. "You're scared."

It wasn't a question. She considered deflecting with another joke, but the truth didn't lie. "Terrified," she admitted. "When I touch that stone tomorrow night, there's no telling what I'll see. Or feel. The visions from the box nearly pulled me under. The stone itself?" She shook her head. "It's pure concentrated time. Every moment it's ever witnessed, every person who's touched it, every—"

"I'll be there."

"I know," she said quietly. "That's the only reason I'm even considering it."

The fire popped again, louder this time. A spark escaped the screen, landing on the rug between them. Joe moved before Leanne could blink, setting down his mug and crossing the space in two strides. He stomped on the ember quickly and efficiently, grinding it out with the heel of his boot.

But he didn't move away. He stood there, staring down at the small scorch mark on the rug, his shoulders suddenly rigid.

"Joe?"

He didn't answer. His gaze had shifted from the rug to the fireplace itself, and something in his expression made her pause. She'd seen grief before. She'd felt it through countless objects, lived through other people's worst moments with a single touch. But watching it move across Joe's face in real time was different. More immediate. More painful.

"It was January," he said, his voice rough. "Twenty-three years ago. I was in my workshop behind my house, working late on a project."

She set down her tea and rose from her chair slowly, not wanting to startle him out of the moment. He needed to say this. She could tell by the way his hands had curled into fists at his sides.

"I was building a cradle," he continued, still staring at the fire. "Walnut, with cherry inlays. The most beautiful piece I'd ever made. I was so proud of it, Leanne. My sister was pregnant with her first child, and I wanted to create something that would last. Something that could be passed down through generations."

He paused, and she waited. The fire crackled softly.

"I got a phone call around midnight. My sister, crying so hard that I could barely understand her.

She was in the hospital. Something was wrong with the baby. She was only seven months along, and—" His voice cracked. He cleared his throat roughly. "I ran out of the workshop to get to the hospital. I was in such a panic that I didn't check the woodstove properly. Didn't make sure the vents were closed."

"Oh, Joe," Leanne whispered.

"By the time I got back the next day, the whole workshop was gone. Burned to the ground." His jaw clenched. "The cradle was just ash. All of it, ash."

She didn't need her gift to feel the pain radiating from him. It filled the room like smoke.

"My niece survived," Joe said, turning away from the fire to face her. He blinked rapidly. "Lindy. She was in the NICU for two months, but she fought through it. She's twenty-three now, healthy and smart and absolutely fearless." A ghost of a smile crossed his face before fading. "But when she was lying in that incubator, tubes everywhere, monitors beeping, I made a deal."

The fire popped again. Neither of them flinched this time.

"A deal?" she asked softly.

"With God, fate, the universe, whomever and whatever was listening." His hands uncurled slowly. "I told myself that my ambition had caused this. That I'd gotten too proud, too focused on creating something perfect. My stupid pride in a *thing*. And in those scary, painful days in the hospital, I made a bargain. I promised that if Lindy lived, I would never create anything new again. Only restore what was already broken. Only fix things, never build them."

Understanding crashed over Leanne like a wave. "You've been keeping that promise for all these years."

"Every single day." He crossed to the window, putting his back to her. His reflection in the glass looked hollow. "I thought the fire was punishment. A sign that I was meant to preserve, not create. And Lindy recovered, so the bargain worked. I couldn't break it. Wouldn't."

"But you wanted to," she said. It wasn't a question.

"Every time I see a piece of beautiful wood," he admitted. "Every time I finish a restoration and remember what it felt like to build something from nothing, something that came from my own mind and hands, I want to so badly it physically hurts."

She moved closer, stopping a few feet behind him. She could see both their reflections now in the dark window.

"You know the fire wasn't punishment," she said gently. "It was an accident. A terrible, tragic accident."

His shoulders slumped. "Maybe. Or maybe I'm just afraid. Afraid to create something I love and lose it again. At least with restoration, the loss already happened. I'm just putting pieces back together. There's no risk of—"

"Of caring too much?" she finished. The words hung between them, and she recognized the truth in them. "Of investing yourself in something new and having it destroyed?"

He turned to face her. "I see it now. Why Verena asked me to help you. Why this whole thing happened the way that it did."

"Because we're the same," she whispered.

"Exactly the same." He took a step closer. "You're so afraid of your gift overwhelming you that you've cut yourself off from everything. Everyone. I'm so afraid of losing what I create that I've stopped creating entirely. We're both just hiding from our own potential."

The fire had burned down to embers now, and the library filled with shadows. "I don't know how to stop hiding."

"Neither do I." He took another step, closing the distance between them until only a few feet remained. "But I think maybe we don't have to figure it out alone."

"I left Moonlight Springs when I was twenty-five," she heard herself say. The words spilled out like water from a cracked dam. "I had a good job lined up in Chicago, far from everyone who knew about my abilities. I thought maybe if I got away from all the history here, all the old objects and memories, I could have a normal life."

He listened without interrupting, his attention steady and patient.

"It didn't work." Her voice felt thick. "Everywhere I went, there were objects with histories. Antiques in shops, heirlooms in people's homes, even just old doorknobs in office buildings. And the visions kept getting stronger and more invasive. I couldn't control them at all."

He waited patiently for her to continue.

"I tried for a while. Really tried. I even dated someone for about six months. Jacob. He was kind and patient and didn't push when I said I wasn't ready for certain things. But eventually, he wanted more. Wanted to hold hands. Wanted to kiss me. Wanted to wake up next to me without me wearing gloves like some kind of eccentric Victorian lady."

A bitter laugh escaped her throat. "So I tried. One evening, I thought maybe if I just pushed through the fear, maybe it wouldn't be as bad as I imagined. I took off my gloves and held his hand and… kissed him."

The memory made her stomach tumble even now. "I saw everything. His childhood trauma. His mother's death. A car accident he'd caused when he was seventeen. Things he'd never told anyone, and private pain that wasn't mine to witness. And he felt it somehow, felt me seeing him, and the look on his face—" She stopped, swallowing hard. "He left that night and never came back. Just walked out."

"Leanne," he said quietly.

"After that, I stopped trying," she finished. "Stopped pretending I could have a normal life. Stopped letting people get close. It was easier to just be alone. Safer." She finally looked up at him, forcing herself to meet his gaze. "I've been alone for a lot of years, Joe. I've convinced myself it's better this way. That I'm protecting people from my gift."

"But you're really protecting yourself," Joe said.

She couldn't argue with that. "Yes," she whispered. "I'm terrified that if I let someone in, if I let myself care, they'll see me the way Jacob did. Like I'm some kind of monster who violates people's privacy just by existing."

He closed the remaining distance between them. He stood close enough that she could smell the sawdust and wood oil that clung to his clothes. "You're not a monster."

"You don't know that." Her voice cracked. "Tomorrow night, when I touch that stone, I might see things that aren't mine to see. Things about you, about Verena, about everyone who's ever been connected to it. And I won't be able to stop it. I'll be drowning in other people's moments, their pain, their secrets, and I—"

"And I'll pull you back." He lifted his hand slowly, telegraphing the movement, and extended it between them. Palm up. An offering. "Just like I did before. However many times it takes."

She stared at his hand. She'd held it before, that day in the workshop when she'd touched his great-grandfather's plane. She'd felt the vision then, but it had been gentle. Controlled. And later, when they'd accidentally touched at the archives, there'd been nothing but warmth. Normal human contact.

But this felt different. This felt like choosing. Like stepping off a cliff and trusting someone to catch her.

"I'm still wearing gloves," she said, her attempt at humor falling flat.

"I know." Joe's hand didn't waver. "But maybe that's okay for now. Maybe we both take one small step at a time."

Leanne pulled her right hand from her pocket. It shook visibly, even through the soft leather glove. She looked at his hand, steady and capable and scarred from years of working with wood. A craftsman's hand. A creator's hand, even if he'd spent years denying that part of himself.

She placed her gloved hand in his palm.

His fingers closed gently around hers, and the world didn't end. No visions slammed into her. No overwhelming flood of memories or emotions. Just the pressure of his hand holding hers, warm even through the barrier of leather.

"I'm scared," Leanne admitted.

"Me too," he said. He gave her hand the gentlest squeeze. "But I'm here. Tomorrow night, when you reach for that stone, I'll be right beside you. And if it tries to pull you under, if the visions get too strong, I'll be your anchor. I promise."

She felt something begin to melt, something that had been frozen solid for decades. Tears burned behind her eyes. "I've spent so long running from this. From my gift, from connection, from anything that might hurt me. I don't know if I remember how to be brave."

"Then we'll figure it out together." His thumb moved slowly across the back of her hand, a small gesture of comfort. "We'll both be brave. You'll touch the stone and trust your gift, and I'll—" He paused, his brow creasing. "I'll start creating again. After this is over, after we've found the stone and saved the town, I'll build something new. Something that matters."

The promise hung between them, fragile and fierce all at once.

"A bargain," she said softly.

He nodded. His brown eyes held hers in the dimming firelight. "We both step into the things that scare us most. We both stop hiding."

She nodded, unable to speak around the lump in her throat. Outside the window, the almost-full moon climbed higher in the sky. Tomorrow night, that moon would shine on the maze entrance where

Charles Joseph Hall's bench waited with its hidden compartment. Tomorrow night, she would put her bare hands on the Amber Stone and let whatever visions came wash over her.

But tonight, she stood in the quiet library with Joe's hand holding hers, and for the first time in thirty years, she didn't feel completely alone.

The fire had burned down to glowing coals. The room had grown cold around them, but neither moved to add more wood. She didn't mind the chill. She could feel Joe's warmth through her glove, steady and real.

"Tell me about the cradle," she said quietly. "What did it look like?"

His expression shifted, surprise flickering across his features. "You want to know?"

"Yes." She squeezed his hand gently. "Tell me about the thing you created. The thing you were most proud of."

He was quiet for a long moment, and she thought he might refuse. But then he began to speak, his voice low and warm in the darkness.

"The headboard and footboard were walnut," he said. "Deep brown, almost chocolate-colored, with this beautiful natural grain that looked like waves. I'd found the wood at a specialty lumber yard three years before and had been saving it for something important."

She listened, watching his face as he talked. The

grief was still there, but something else rose alongside it. Pride. Love. The joy of creation.

"The spindles were cherry," Joe continued, "a lighter wood that contrasted with the walnut. I turned each one by hand on my lathe, getting them as identical as possible. And the inlays—" His free hand moved slightly, sketching the pattern in the air. "Cherry wood inlaid into the walnut headboard in a pattern of stars and moons. It took me weeks to get it right, cutting the channels, fitting each piece perfectly."

"It sounds beautiful."

"It was the best thing I'd ever made. I poured everything I had into it. Every skill I'd learned, every technique I'd mastered. I wanted it to be perfect for Lindy. Wanted her to sleep in something made with love, something that would last her whole life."

"She knows you love her. The cradle burning didn't change that."

"I know." Joe blinked rapidly. "But I think part of me has been punishing myself for twenty-three years. Like if I kept the promise, kept limiting myself to restoration, it would somehow make up for that moment of carelessness where I lost everything. I think the fire was to teach me a lesson. I was so proud of things, possessions. But that night? That night, I realized what really mattered. Family. People I love.

"But it wasn't pride," Leanne said gently. "It was love. You were creating something out of love, and an accident happened. A terrible accident, but not because you loved too much or cared too much. Those things aren't character flaws, Joe."

He looked down at their joined hands. "When did you get so wise?"

"Oh, about five minutes ago." She was rewarded with a small huff of laughter. "I'm a very fast learner when it comes to other people's problems. My own, not so much."

"We're a pair." He shook his head.

"We really are."

The moonlight streaming through the window had shifted. The grandfather clock in the hallway ticked steadily, each second bringing them closer to tomorrow's full moon. To the moment when everything would change.

"We should probably sleep," he said, though he made no move to let go of her hand.

"Probably." She didn't move either.

They stood there for another long moment. Finally, reluctantly, she slipped her hand from his.

"I'll walk you out." She led him to the door and paused. "I'm glad you're here. I'm glad it's you helping me through this."

"Nowhere else I'd rather be." And with that, he slipped out into the night.

# CHAPTER 16

Verena pressed her palm against an oak that stood near the edge of the maze and felt the wrongness pulse through her fingertips. The tree's roots ran deep beneath Moonlight Springs, connecting to the network of magic that threaded through the town like veins through a body. Tonight, those veins felt inflamed.

She pulled her hand away and rubbed her temples. A headache had been building since noon, the kind that sat behind her eyes and made the world feel slightly tilted. The magic was sick. Or maybe she was. After all these years as the town's Guardian, she'd stopped knowing where her own awareness ended and the town's began.

The maze stretched before her in silvery shadows, lit by a moon that was almost, but not quite, full. Tomorrow night it would reach its peak.

Tomorrow night, Leanne would touch the Amber Stone, or they would all watch as time itself came undone in Moonlight Springs.

Verena walked the familiar paths of the maze, her hand trailing along the hedges. The moonflowers opened as she reached them and closed as she passed. The plants whispered to her in a language without words, their distress evident in every leaf. They felt the disturbances too. Everything living in Moonlight Springs did.

She reached the stone bench at the maze's heart and sank onto it. The seat radiated cold through her flowing skirt. Above her, the stars were scattered in their ancient patterns, indifferent to the chaos below. She envied them their distance.

A rustling at the maze entrance made her lift her head. She knew those footsteps.

"Thought I might find you here." Gary emerged from between the hedges, his tall frame blocking the moonlight for a moment before he stepped into the clearing. His leather jacket hung open over a flannel shirt, and his salt-and-pepper hair looked like he'd been running his hands through it. "You left the inn's back door open."

"Did I?" Verena managed a small smile. "How careless of me."

He studied her face, his blue eyes missing nothing. "How bad is it?"

She considered lying. Considered brushing it off

with her usual humor. But exhaustion had worn her defenses thin, and Gary had always seen through her deflections anyway.

"I feel like I'm coming apart," she admitted. "Like someone's pulling a thread, and I'm unraveling."

He crossed the distance between them and lowered himself onto the bench beside her. The cold stone suddenly felt warmer with him there. He sat close enough that their shoulders almost touched.

"The disturbances?"

"They're everywhere now. Mrs. Wilson called an hour ago because her kitchen keeps flickering between 1965 and now. She made dinner in her old avocado-green appliances, then blinked and found herself at her current stove with the pasta burned. She thought she was losing her mind." Verena's hands twisted in her lap. "I told her it was a gas leak. That the fumes can cause hallucinations."

"She believed you?"

"No." Verena laughed, but it came out brittle. "She's lived here her whole life. She knows something's wrong with the town itself."

He shifted, angling toward her. "What about you? Are you safe?"

"I don't know." The admission cost her. She'd spent decades being the one with answers and the steady presence others relied on. "I can feel the magic destabilizing. It's like... have you ever had a fever so high that you couldn't tell what was real and what was a dream?"

"Once or twice."

"It feels like that. I'll be making breakfast, and suddenly I'm also pouring tea for guests who checked out in 1987. I can see both versions of the dining room at once. Hear conversations from different decades overlapping." She pressed her fingers to her temples again. "I'm not sure how much longer I can hold the boundaries."

The confession hung in the night air between them. She braced herself for the worry she'd see in his face, the protective instinct that would make him want to solve this for her.

Instead, his hand found hers. His fingers, warm and calloused, closed around her cold ones.

"I'm right here with you. Whatever's coming, you're not facing it alone."

She looked down at their joined hands, hers pale in the moonlight, his tanned and scarred from years of work. They'd held hands countless times forty years ago, but this felt different. Steadier. Earned.

"You don't have to fix this," he continued. "I'm not asking you to have all the answers. I'm just saying I'm here."

"Gary." His name came out rough. "If the magic breaks tomorrow night—"

"We'll figure it out."

"You don't understand. If Leanne can't claim the stone, if something goes wrong—"

"Then we'll handle it. Together." He squeezed her hand. "You've been carrying this town on your shoulders for four decades, Vee. Maybe it's time you let someone help share that burden."

"But I chose this. When you asked me to leave all those years ago, I chose to stay. To be the Guardian. I don't get to complain about it now."

"Choosing something doesn't mean it's not heavy. And you were twenty-two. You made the choice you needed to make then. But you're not that young woman anymore, and I'm not the angry kid who left. We're allowed to be different now."

She turned to look at him properly. The moonlight silvered his features, softening the lines around his eyes but emphasizing the strength in his jaw. He'd grown into himself over the years away, becoming someone solid and sure in ways he hadn't been at twenty-two.

"When did you get so smart?" she asked.

"Around year fifteen of missing you." He smiled. "Turns out leaving the woman you love doesn't actually make the love go away. It just makes you stupid and stubborn in a different location."

A laugh surprised its way out of her. "That's the most romantic thing anyone's ever said to me."

"My timing was always terrible." But warmth softened the humor in his expression. "I left when you needed me to stay. Came back forty years too late to court you properly."

"You're here now." The words felt monumental. She shifted on the bench so she could face him fully, their knees touching. "That matters."

"Does it?" Something vulnerable flickered across his features. "Because I've been back for months, and we've been circling each other like we're afraid to land. I pour you coffee every morning. You save me the good pastries. We talk about everything except what's actually between us."

"I don't know how to do this, Gary. I haven't let myself want anything beyond protecting this town for so long. I'm not sure I remember how to just be a woman who—" She faltered.

"Who what?"

"Who still loves you. Who never stopped."

Gary's eyes widened. "Vee."

"I know it's complicated. I know the timing is terrible, with everything happening tomorrow night. But you're here, and I'm tired of pretending my heart doesn't jump every time you walk into a room." She squeezed his hand. "I'm tired of being alone when you're right here."

For a moment, he just looked at her. Then he raised his free hand and cradled her face, his palm warm against her cheek. His thumb brushed just beneath her eye, gentle as a whisper.

"You're not alone," he said. "Not anymore. Not ever again if I have anything to say about it."

The headache that had plagued her all evening faded. The wrongness in the magic still simmered in the garden, but it felt bearable now. Manageable.

"We should probably talk about what this means," he murmured. "Talk about us."

"We should. But maybe not tonight. Tonight I just want to sit here with you."

"I can do that." He shifted on the bench, drawing her closer. She settled into the warmth of him, her head finding the hollow of his shoulder like it had always belonged there.

They sat in the almost-full moonlight, the maze silent around them except for the rustle of the wind through the hedges. Above, the stars twinkled in the night sky.

Tonight, for the first time in forty years, Verena Harrison let herself just be a woman sitting in a garden with the man she loved. The magic could wait. The town could wait.

"Thank you," she said quietly.

"For what?"

"For coming back. For being patient with me. For still being here after everything."

Gary pressed a kiss to the top of her head. "Vee, of course I'm here. I just wish I'd always been here for you."

The next morning, Leanne walked from one end of Joe's workshop to the other, her hands clasped behind her back. Thirteen steps to the window. Turn. Thirteen steps to the door. Turn. Repeat.

"You know," Joe said from his position at the workbench, where he was ostensibly sanding a chair leg, "if you keep that up, you're going to wear a groove in my floor."

"At least I'd be contributing something useful." She reached the window again and pivoted. "A nice worn path. Very rustic. Very authentic. Future psychics could touch it and experience the thrilling memory of an anxious woman slowly losing her mind."

He set down his sandpaper. "Leanne."

"Fourteen more hours." She continued her

circuit. "Fourteen hours until we find out if I can actually do this, or if the town gets erased from existence because I panicked and couldn't hold on long enough to claim the stone properly."

"You're not going to panic."

"You don't know that." She stopped at the window, staring out at the quiet street beyond. A woman walked past with a golden retriever. Two kids on bikes raced toward the park. Normal life. Normal morning in Moonlight Springs. "What if I touch it and everything just… ends?"

Joe crossed the workshop in four long strides. He didn't touch her, but he stood close enough that she could smell sawdust and the faint scent of coffee on his breath. "That's not going to happen."

She wanted to believe him. The rational part of her brain, the part that had spent years cataloging historical trivia from accidental touches, knew he was probably right. But the rest of her, the wounded part that remembered every overwhelming vision and every person who'd walked away, whispered that she was fooling herself.

"What if the visions show me something about you?" The question came out before she could stop it. "Something you don't want me to see?"

Joe's expression didn't change. "Then you'll see it. And we'll deal with it. My past isn't going anywhere, Leanne. It's already happened."

"That's pretty philosophical for a guy whose

secrets might get invaded by someone's magic hands." She tried for humor, but her voice cracked on the last word.

"Gifted hands." He returned to his workbench and picked up the sandpaper again.

"Tell that to my gifted hands at eleven forty-seven tonight."

The morning crawled forward like honey in winter. Joe tried to distract her with stories about various restoration projects. She learned more about wood grain and joinery techniques than she'd ever imagined existed. He showed her the differences between quartersawn and plainsawn oak. He explained the intricacies of French polishing versus modern finishes. He demonstrated how to identify wood species by scent alone, holding up different samples for her to smell.

Cedar, sharp and clean. Walnut, rich and slightly sweet. Cherry, with its subtle almond undertone.

"You're trying very hard to distract me," she said around noon when he produced sandwiches from somewhere and set them on a cleared corner of his workbench.

"Is it working?"

"Not even a little." She picked up her sandwich and took a bite. Turkey and swiss on wheat bread. She chewed slowly, tasting nothing. "But I appreciate the effort."

By two o'clock, she'd memorized every tool on his pegboard. By four, she could have drawn a map of his workshop from memory, including the old coffee can full of bent nails he kept meaning to throw away but never did. By six, when the light was fading outside the windows, she thought she might actually vibrate out of her skin.

"This is torture," she announced, resuming her pacing circuit. "This is worse than waiting for biopsy results. This is worse than waiting for the dentist. This is worse than—"

"Worse than listening to someone describe how terrible waiting is?" His tone was mild, but she caught the hint of amusement underneath.

"Mock me all you want. When this is over and the town is a smoking crater in space-time, you'll regret not being more sympathetic to my very reasonable anxiety."

"The town is not going to become a smoking crater."

"You don't know that. Nobody knows that. For all we know, the Amber Stone could explode the moment I touch it. Boom. No more Moonlight Springs. Just a big old hole where a charming historic town used to be."

He set down the plane he'd been adjusting for the last twenty minutes. He hadn't actually been working on anything. She'd noticed. He was just giving his hands something to do, the same way she needed her feet to keep moving.

"Come here," he said.

"Why?"

"Because I'm asking you to."

She stopped pacing and crossed to his workbench. He reached into a drawer and pulled out a smooth piece of wood, pale and pristine, about the size of his palm. He set it on the workbench between them.

"What's that?"

"Maple. From a tree that was cut down last month over on Sycamore Street. The Watson place. You remember Mrs. Watson?"

"Vaguely. She used to make cookies shaped like cats."

"She died last year. Her kids sold the house, and the new owners wanted the tree gone." Joe ran his finger along the wood's surface. "I bought some of the lumber. This piece has no history, Leanne. It's too new. Nothing's been done to it except cutting and planing. No memories attached."

She stared at the pale wood, understanding what he was offering. "You want me to touch it."

"I want you to practice. We've got five hours until we need to leave. You said yourself that the wood plane and the bench gave you clearer visions than usual. Maybe working with wood specifically, with me nearby, that's your control point. Your anchor."

"Or maybe I'll touch it and still see nothing useful, and we'll have wasted time I could have spent pacing productively."

"Leanne."

She pulled off her right glove. Her fingers looked long and thin, with nails cut short and practical. So many years since she'd let people see her bare hands.

Joe had seen them, of course. But this felt different. More deliberate. More vulnerable.

She reached out and pressed her palm flat against the maple.

Nothing happened.

No visions. No overwhelming cascade of memories. Just the smooth coolness of wood against her skin and the faint sensation of grain beneath her fingertips.

"It's just wood," she whispered.

"It's just wood," he agreed. "New wood. Clean wood. No ghosts attached."

She left her hand there for another moment, marveling at the simple normalcy of it. Then she pulled back and tugged her glove on again, her fingers shaking slightly as she worked the leather into place.

"Thank you," she said.

"For what?"

"For reminding me that not everything has to hurt."

The sky outside darkened. Joe made more coffee. Leanne resumed pacing, but slower now, less frantic. At nine-thirty, he locked up the workshop, and they walked together through the quiet streets of the town, heading toward Moonlight Inn.

The town felt hushed, expectant. Lights glowed in windows. A cat darted across their path and disappeared into a hedge. Somewhere nearby, someone was playing piano, the notes drifting soft and melancholy through the evening air.

"Do you think Denton knows?" Leanne asked. "About tonight?"

"I don't see how he could. We've been careful."

"But you said he's been watching the inn. And he grabbed my wrist yesterday. What if he—"

"Leanne." His voice was steady, grounding. "We can only control what we can control. The rest, we handle as it comes."

She wanted to argue. Her anxiety wanted to spin out every possible disaster scenario, examine each one from every angle, and prepare for catastrophes that might never happen. But Joe's calm presence beside her and the solid reality of his footsteps matching hers on the sidewalk pulled her back to the moment.

One step. Then another. That's all she had to do.

They reached the inn a little after ten. Gary's patrol car sat in the parking lot, and they found him standing near the entrance to the maze, a flashlight in his hand.

"Evening," he said, his voice low. "Everything's quiet. Too quiet, honestly. We had three more disturbances this afternoon, all minor. Sounds from the past bleeding through. Jenny Gilbert heard her mother calling her name, and her mother's been dead for fifteen years. But for the last hour? Nothing. It's like the whole town is holding its breath."

"Maybe the magic knows," Leanne said. "Maybe it's waiting."

Gary studied her for a long moment, his sheriff's eyes taking in her gloved hands, the tension in her shoulders, and the way she stood slightly behind Joe as if he were a shield she could duck behind if needed.

"Verena has faith in you," he said finally. "That's good enough for me. If you need anything, I'll be patrolling nearby. Just yell."

"If something goes wrong, you should probably run in the opposite direction," she said. "Fair warning."

Gary's smile was small but genuine. "I've been running toward trouble my whole career. Not about to stop now." He tipped his head in a brief nod and walked back toward his car, the flashlight beam bobbing through the darkness.

Joe led the way into the maze. Leanne had been here many times before, but at night, with only the moon and Joe's flashlight to guide them, the hedge walls felt taller and more imposing.

They entered the maze and went to the left. The bench sat exactly where it had been, weathered oak gleaming faintly in the moonlight. Above them, the moon hung heavy and round. Another hour and forty minutes until it reached its peak.

Another hour and forty minutes until she had to touch the Amber Stone and either save the town or watch it crumble into nothing.

"Well," she said brightly, "at least I can pace here just as expertly as back in your workshop. Look at me. Already a professional maze pacer. I could put that on a resume."

Joe settled onto the bench, careful to sit at the far end, away from where the hidden compartment waited. He patted the space beside him.

"Sit. You'll wear yourself out."

"I'm already worn out. At this point, I'm running on anxiety and stubbornness."

"Then sit and be anxious and stubborn from a more comfortable position."

She sat, leaving a careful foot of space between them. The bench was solid beneath her, and she tried not to think about the fact that Joe's great-grandfather had built it, had hidden the Amber Stone inside with the help of a Guardian who looked mysteriously like Zara Bollinger. Tried not to think about the fact that in less than two hours, she'd have to reach into that hidden compartment and touch something that had been sealed away for over a century.

Time crawled. Joe pulled out his phone and checked it. 10:45.

"Tell me something," Leanne said, needing to fill the silence before her thoughts grew too loud. "When you build something, when you create it from scratch, what does that feel like?"

Joe was quiet for a moment, and she worried she'd asked the wrong question. Then he said, "It feels like hope, I guess. Like taking all these separate pieces, wood and glue and time, and making them into something that didn't exist before. Something that might last. Something someone might love."

"You should do it again. After tonight. Win or lose, promise me you'll create something new."

"I promise." He checked his phone again. 11:10. "What about you? What will you do?"

"Assuming I survive and the town survives and we're not all trapped in some nightmare time loop? I don't know. Maybe I'll actually take my gloves off sometimes. Maybe I'll shake someone's hand without having a panic attack first. Small steps."

"Those aren't small steps, Leanne."

"They feel pretty small compared to saving an entire town from magical destruction."

11:15. 11:23. The minutes stretched like taffy, each one longer than the last. She stood and resumed pacing, walking the perimeter of the small clearing. Five steps to the hedge wall. Turn. Seven steps to the gap in the path. Turn. Six steps to—

Footsteps.

She froze, her hand halfway to the hedge. Joe stood up from the bench, moving to place himself slightly in front of her.

Blake Denton stepped into the clearing with another man just behind him. In the moonlight, Denton looked different. Sharper. Older somehow, though his face hadn't changed.

"You thought you could get the stone? I think not. I'm more clever than you." Denton's voice was smooth, amused. "Conrad, deal with this."

The man—Conrad—pulled out a gun. He gestured with it, a small, economical motion. "Back away from the bench."

Her heart pounded. Joe didn't move, and she found herself gripping the back of his shirt, her gloved fingers twisting in the fabric.

"How did you know?" Joe asked, his voice steady despite the gun pointed their way.

Denton laughed, the sound wrong in the quiet garden. "I put a bug in your workshop three days ago. It was almost too easy. You talked through the whole thing. The bench, the time lock, the full moon. I should thank you, really. You did all the hard work for me."

"You can't use the stone," Leanne said, and her voice came out stronger than she'd expected. "It chooses its Guardian. The magic won't work for you."

"Then I suppose we'll find out, won't we?" Denton checked his watch. "Eleven fifty-four. Three more minutes."

They stood frozen. Conrad with his gun. Denton, watching the bench with hungry eyes. Joe, solid and unmoving as one of his own wooden creations. And Leanne, her mind racing through possibilities, all of them bad.

She could rush Denton. Probably get shot. She could try to reach the stone first. Definitely get shot. She could run for help. Leave Joe here alone with a gun pointed at him. Not an option.

"Two minutes," Denton said.

The moon seemed brighter now, the light taking on an almost liquid quality. The air felt thick, charged.

"One minute."

She pulled off her gloves. Joe glanced back at her, a question in his eyes. She shook her head slightly. She didn't have a plan. But if the compartment opened, if the stone was there, maybe she could touch it before Denton. Maybe the visions would tell her what to do. Maybe she'd just die trying, but at least she'd have tried.

"Thirty seconds."

The moonlight intensified, pouring down like honey, like water, like time itself made visible. It pooled on the bench, highlighting the carved oak, and Leanne saw the exact moment the time lock released.

A seam appeared in the wood where none had been before. The hidden compartment revealed itself at last.

Denton lunged forward. His hand reached into the opening.

And the world exploded.

Not with sound or fire, but with time. With history and future and present all colliding at once, all trying to exist in the same space at the same moment.

*The maze fractured into a thousand overlapping versions of itself. The hedge walls were young and green, ancient and overgrown, burned to nothing, blooming with impossible flowers. The moon multiplied across the sky, a dozen moons, a hundred, each one showing a different phase.*

*Leanne saw the town burning. Frozen in ice. Empty, buildings crumbling, streets overgrown. She saw it thriving, its lights bright against the darkness, but wrong somehow, twisted. Then it was just gone, nothing left but an empty space where Moonlight Springs used to be, where memory used to exist.*

The visions slammed into her one after another, too fast to process, too many to hold. Past and present and future, all the possible timelines, all the ways this could end. She couldn't breathe. Couldn't think. Couldn't—

Joe's hand closed around hers.

The visions didn't stop, but they slowed. Steadied. Like someone had taken a thousand spinning threads and braided them into something she could hold. She gasped air into her lungs and focused on Joe's calloused palm against hers, his fingers interlaced with hers, the only thing that felt real.

Through the fractured madness, she saw Denton. He was still reaching into the compartment, but time was moving strangely around him. His movements stuttered, jumped forward, jumped back. He was old, then young, then something else entirely, something that flickered between ages like a bad television signal.

The Amber Stone pulsed in the hidden compartment, throwing off waves of energy that bent reality like heat shimmer on pavement. It was beautiful. Terrible. Alive with power that had been locked away for over a century, and now, released too soon, by the wrong person, it was tearing everything apart.

Then Denton had it in his hand. *His* hand. Not *her* hand.

# CHAPTER 18

Joe's lungs burned as he pulled in air thick with energy. The maze around them flickered like a damaged film reel, with shadows stretching and retracting across stone paths that couldn't decide which decade they belonged to.

Denton and Conrad's footsteps faded into the darkness beyond the hedge wall. Gone. The stone with them.

Joe's hands shook. Not from fear. From the raw fury of standing helpless while everything shattered.

The bench sat ten feet away, its hidden compartment blown open by the magical explosion. Except now the wood had fused. The grain ran in impossible directions, swirling like water frozen mid-current. He'd worked with damaged pieces for thirty years and had never seen anything like it.

Gary appeared by his side. His radio crackled.

The sheriff spoke in clipped tones, calling for backup that wouldn't arrive in time. They all knew it.

Then Joe wasn't looking at the bench anymore. Leanne stood with her back to him, shoulders curved inward like she was trying to fold herself small enough to disappear.

"Leanne." His voice came out rougher than he meant.

She didn't turn.

Gary finished his radio call and moved past them back toward the maze entrance. His hand touched Joe's shoulder briefly. A silent message to take care of her.

Then they were alone with the broken bench and the smell of scorched earth that had nothing to do with actual fire.

His feet carried him forward. Three steps. Five. Close enough to see her hands trembling.

"It's not your fault." The words felt clumsy in his mouth. He was better at speaking with his hands, with the careful restoration of broken things. But Leanne wasn't a chair with a split leg or a table with water damage. She was a woman who'd just watched her worst fear materialize.

"I saw it." She whispered the words, her voice raw with pain. "In the visions. I saw time breaking apart. I should have known. Should have warned you all that he'd come. That he'd take it."

"You couldn't have known Denton would bug the workshop."

She laughed. The sound had sharp edges that cut. "My gift is supposed to show me the past. The present. Pieces of what might come. And I saw nothing useful. Nothing that mattered."

His heart beat slightly off-rhythm. Not the quick panic of his fire nightmares but something slower. The feeling of watching something precious slip through his fingers while he stood frozen.

"You saw the bench. You saw my great-grandfather building the compartment. The Guardian hiding the stone. You gave us a fighting chance." He kept his voice steady. Practical.

"A chance we lost."

She finally turned. Her face in the moonlight looked carved from pale wood. Smooth. Expressionless. But her eyes gave her away. They held the same look he'd seen in his own mirror for twenty-three years. The look of someone who'd made a bargain with fate and come up empty.

"I'm not a Guardian. I can't be. A Guardian protects. A Guardian keeps the magic safe. All I did was lead Denton straight to the stone he wanted."

"That's not true."

"Isn't it?" Her voice rose. Not quite a shout, but close. "Everything I touch breaks, Joe. Every connection I make causes pain. I spent years avoiding people because my gift hurts them. Hurts me. And the one time I think maybe it's different, maybe I can use it for something good, this happens."

She gestured at the bench. At the maze. At the space where reality still shimmered wrong at the edges.

His hands curled into fists. He wanted to reach for her. Wanted to close the three feet between them and prove with touch what words couldn't seem to convey. But she'd taken a step back, putting distance between them deliberately.

"You're exhausted." He tried for calm. For the steady presence he'd given her in his workshop a dozen times over the past week. "You've been using your gift nonstop. Let's get you inside. Some tea. Some rest. Then we'll figure out what comes next."

She yanked on her gloves. The motion was abrupt. Angry. "There is no next. Don't you see? I thought I was finally learning control. I thought that with you there to ground me, I could handle the visions without falling apart. But tonight proved I was wrong. The second the real crisis hit, I couldn't function. I froze. And because I froze, Denton won."

"Leanne—"

She held up a hand. "I need to be alone." She looked at him then. Really looked. Her eyes were wet, but no tears fell. "I'm sorry, Joe. You've been so patient. So kind. But my power doesn't bring anything but disaster. It always has. Tonight just made it impossible to pretend otherwise."

Every word landed like a hammer blow.

Joe thought of the cradle. Of the fire that had consumed six months of careful work and transformed his life into a series of restoration projects. Of the promise he'd made to never create again because creation meant risk and risk meant loss.

Standing in the moonlit maze, watching Leanne pull away from him, he finally understood what Verena had been trying to tell him when she'd given him her first piece of furniture to restore. She'd said, "Sometimes the broken things teach us more than the perfect ones ever could."

He'd thought she meant furniture.

But broken wasn't the same as unfixable. Broken was just another word for something that needed the right hands and enough patience.

"You're wrong." He said it quietly. Firmly. The same tone he used when evaluating a piece other restorers had given up on. "Your gift didn't cause this. Denton did. He's been hunting these stones since before you arrived. He would have found a way to the bench with or without us."

"But I led him right to it."

"You gave us the only real chance we had." Joe took a step closer. She didn't back away this time, but her posture screamed *don't touch*. "Without your visions, that stone would have stayed hidden until the magic tore the town apart. At least now we know where it is. Who has it. That's more than we had a week ago."

She shook her head. Hair fell across her face, and she didn't brush it back. "You don't understand."

"Then help me understand."

"I can't keep doing this." Her voice cracked. "I can't keep hoping I'm more than my worst moments. I did that once. Thirty years ago. I let someone in. I took off the gloves, and I tried so hard to control the visions. But I couldn't. And I hurt him. I broke something in him, and it broke something in me, and I swore I'd never do it again."

"I'm not him."

"I know. That's what makes this worse. You're steady and patient, and you see my gift as something other than a curse. But I don't want to be the reason you lose something you care about. I don't want to be another fire that destroys what you're trying to build."

The comparison hit harder than she probably meant it to.

He looked at his hands. At the calluses and scars from years of working with wood. With broken things. He'd spent over two decades believing creation was dangerous. That making something new invited disaster. That the only safe path was restoration.

But standing here watching Leanne fold in on herself, he saw the truth he'd been avoiding.

Restoration was just another word for hiding. He'd been too afraid to build anything that mattered because things that mattered could burn.

Leanne mattered.

The realization settled in his chest. Solid. Something to build on.

"I spent twenty-three years refusing to create anything new," he said. "I told myself it was penance. That I'd made a bargain and had to keep it. But I was just afraid. Afraid that anything I made would be destroyed. That caring about something new meant inviting loss."

She looked up at him. Confusion flickered across her face.

He looked directly at her. "You're the bravest person I know."

"I'm not."

"You came back to a town you left years ago. You agreed to use the gift that terrifies you. You've touched objects that flood you with centuries of pain and memory. And every single time, you got back up and tried again." He took another step, close enough to touch now, but he kept his hands at his sides. "That's not weakness, Leanne. That's courage."

"It doesn't feel like courage." Her voice was small. "It feels like failure."

"Failure is giving up." The words came easier now. "Failure is letting fear make your choices. You haven't failed. You've just hit a setback. And setbacks are part of building anything worth keeping."

She studied his face, looking for something. He didn't know if she found it.

"I need time," she said finally. "I need to think. To figure out what comes next without you watching me like I'm about to shatter."

His heart lurched. The old familiar grief rose up. The certainty that he was watching something precious slip away because he wasn't enough to hold it together.

"All right." He nodded once. "Take the time you need. But I'm not going anywhere. When you're ready to fight for the stone, I'll be there."

She opened her mouth, closed it, then turned and walked toward the inn's back entrance.

Joe watched her go. Every instinct screamed to follow, to fix this, to find the right words that would restore what had broken between them.

But he knew broken things. Knew them in his bones.

And sometimes the kindest thing you could do was give them space to settle before you started the repair.

He looked at the bench. At the empty compartment that had once held the Amber Stone.

This wasn't over. Denton had the stone, but he didn't understand it. Didn't have someone who could read its history or a craftsman who understood how protection was built into the very grain of things. And he didn't have Leanne's gift.

Leanne sat on the bed in her room with her back against the headboard and her knees pulled to her chest. The position probably looked childish, but no one was here to see it.

Morning light filtered through lace curtains. She'd watched the sun rise an hour ago. Or maybe two. Time felt slippery after last night's disaster.

Her gloved hands rested on her knees. She studied them. Soft gray cotton. Thick enough to block most casual contact. Thin enough to let her function in the world.

The nightstand held a water glass, a small lamp, and a wooden coaster. She looked at the coaster and thought about touching it. About letting the visions come. About drowning in the cascade of memories from every person who'd ever set a cup on its surface.

She didn't reach for it.

Her stomach growled. She ignored it. The idea of going downstairs and facing Verena, Joe, or anyone made her skin crawl. They'd look at her with pity or disappointment or, worse, understanding. She didn't deserve understanding.

A knock sounded at the door.

Leanne closed her eyes. "I'm fine. Just tired."

"I brought tea." Verena's voice carried through the wood. Warm but firm. "And I'm coming in whether you want me to or not."

The door opened before Leanne could protest.

Verena entered carrying a tray. She wore a deep blue cardigan over a cream blouse, and her hair was twisted up in a casual style. She looked exactly like herself. Completely unshaken by the fact that time itself was dissolving around them.

She set the tray on the dresser and turned to study Leanne.

She braced for the lecture. For the gentle insistence that she try again, or the reminder that the town needed her, or the reassurance that it wasn't her fault. All the things people said when they wanted you to feel better but really just wanted you to stop being inconvenient.

Verena pulled the desk chair over to the bed and sat. She poured two cups of tea from a ceramic pot painted with tiny moons. The scent of chamomile and honey filled the room.

"I failed once." Verena handed Leanne a cup. "Catastrophically. Nearly destroyed everything my family had protected for generations."

Leanne blinked. That wasn't what she'd expected.

Verena settled back in the chair with her own tea cradled in both hands. "I was twenty-eight or so. Young and convinced that I understood the magic better than I actually did. There was a man trying to buy properties in town. Not Denton. This was forty years ago. Different threat, same greed."

Steam rose from Verena's cup. She stared into it like she was reading something written in the vapor.

"I thought I could handle it alone. My grandmother was giving me more Guardian responsibilities, preparing me. I thought I knew… everything. I felt capable. Powerful." Verena's mouth curved into something that wasn't quite a smile. "I felt invincible."

Leanne's fingers tightened on her cup. The tea inside rippled.

"The man found one of the stones. The Opal." Verena looked up. Her brown eyes held old pain that had been worn smooth by time. "He touched it, and the magic responded the way magic always responds to someone with the wrong intentions."

"What happened?"

"Every memory in Moonlight Springs became visible. Not just impressions or visions. Actual, physical manifestations of moments from the past." Verena set her cup on the nightstand. "People walked down the street and saw their dead relatives having conversations from twenty years ago. Children watched their parents' worst arguments play out in their living rooms. The town's entire history became a museum that no one asked to visit."

She tried to imagine it the chaos and the pain. "How did you stop it?"

"I didn't. Not alone." Verena leaned forward. Her hands rested on her knees. "I had to admit I'd made mistakes. Had to ask for help from people I'd been trying to protect. Had to trust that the magic would respond to collective effort instead of individual power."

"You're trying to make me feel better. Trying to show me that failure isn't the end."

"I'm trying to show you that Guardians don't get to quit." Verena's tone didn't change. Still warm. Still firm. "We fail. We make terrible choices. We watch things we love break apart. And then we get up and keep going because that's what the job requires."

Leanne set her cup down harder than she meant to. Tea sloshed over the rim. "I'm not a Guardian. I'm just someone who sees things she can't control and causes disasters wherever she goes."

"You saw Denton's intentions last night." Verena

stood and walked to the window. She looked out at the garden below. "When you touched the stone's hiding place. When the visions hit you. What did you see?"

She didn't want to remember. Didn't want to relive those fractured images of timelines collapsing and the town burning and freezing and simply ceasing to exist. "I saw everything falling apart."

"No." Verena turned. Light from the window framed her. "You saw what would happen if the wrong person claimed the stone. Your gift gave us a warning."

"A warning I couldn't use."

"A warning that's still active." Verena moved back to the chair. She sat on its edge. "Denton has the stone now. But he doesn't understand it. He thinks it's a tool he can wield for power or profit or whatever drives men like him. What happens when he tries to use it?"

She thought about the visions. About the way time had splintered the moment Denton's hand closed around the amber. "It'll destroy him."

"Maybe. Or maybe it'll destroy the town first." Verena's voice stayed level and matter-of-fact. "The stones aren't just objects. They're amplifiers. They take what's in the user's heart and magnify it. Make it real. A person filled with greed touches the Stone of Time, and time itself becomes greedy. Consuming. Devouring everything in reach."

"Then we've already lost."

"We've lost the first battle. The war isn't over. Denton has the stone, but we have something he doesn't. We have you."

She looked away, then back at Verena.

"Your visions aren't a curse. They're a warning system. A way to see what's coming and prepare for it. You've been treating your gift like a disease that needs to be contained. But it's not. It's a tool. One that could save everything if you'd stop being afraid of it."

"I hurt people. Every time I let someone close, my gift destroys something. You don't know what it's like to touch another person and get buried in their worst memories. Their traumas. Their secrets. To have all of that flood into you like you're drowning."

"You're right. I don't know what that's like." Verena sat back. "My gift is different. I see possibilities. Futures that might happen. Paths that could unfold. And for forty years, I've watched every possible future where I chose love over duty. Where I left town with Gary and built a different life."

Her voice stayed steady, but something in her expression shifted and became more raw.

"I know what it costs to put your gift first. To choose the magic over the connections you want. I know how it feels to watch other people build lives while you stand guard over something that might not even need protecting in your lifetime." Verena folded her hands in her lap. "And I know what it's like to wonder if the sacrifice was worth it."

She stared at this woman who'd always seemed unshakeable. "Was it?"

"I don't know yet." Verena's mouth lifted in a small smile. "Ask me again when this is over."

Despite everything, Leanne felt her lips tilt upward. Not quite a smile, but close. "So what happened to the Opal Stone?"

"My grandmother retrieved it and placed it somewhere safe."

"Do you know where she put it?"

"I do not. It was her secret. Her way of protecting the stone. She knew when the time came, the right Guardian would find it." Verena stood and moved to the tray. She picked up a cloth napkin and unfolded it. Inside were two scones. She offered one to Leanne.

She took it. The scone was still warm. Probably from a batch Verena had baked at dawn while the rest of them were still processing the disaster.

"I can't do this alone," Leanned sighed. "I thought I could. Thought if I just pushed hard enough, controlled the visions enough, I could be what the town needed. But I can't."

"Good." Verena bit into her scone. "Guardians who try to work alone always fail. I learned that the hard way. You're learning it now. The difference is you have people who already understand what's at stake. Joe. Gary. Me. The others who found their stones. You're not alone unless you choose to be."

Leanne broke off a piece of scone, and it crumbled in her fingers. "Joe thinks I'm brave."

"He's right."

"He doesn't know what I'm really like. How much I want to run. How every instinct I have is screaming at me to leave this room, leave this town, and go back to my careful, controlled life where I never touch anything that matters." She put the scone piece in her mouth. Blueberry. Perfectly sweet.

"Bravery isn't about not being scared. You're terrified, and you're still sitting here. That counts."

"What do I do now?" She looked at Verena. "Denton has the stone. He's probably already trying to use it. The town is falling apart, and I'm sitting in a guest room eating baked goods and feeling sorry for myself."

"First, you finish that scone. Then you take a shower. Get dressed. Come downstairs." Verena collected the cups and put them back on the tray. "Then we start planning. Because Denton might have the stone, but he doesn't have what we have, someone who can track its history. He doesn't have a craftsman who understands how protective magic gets built into objects. And he definitely doesn't have a network of people who love this town enough to fight for it."

She picked up the tray and moved toward the door.

"Verena." Leanne paused. "What if I fail again?"

Verena's expression softened. Not with pity. With something closer to recognition. "Then you fail. And you get up. And you try again. That's what Guardians do. That's what living does."

She left, closing the door quietly behind her.

Leanne sat on the bed with half a scone in her hand, and morning light warming her face. Peaceful. Like nothing terrible had happened just hours ago.

She finished the scone. Then she stood and walked to the small bathroom attached to the guest room.

The mirror showed her a woman with tangled hair and shadows under her eyes. She looked exhausted. Defeated. Like someone who'd just watched her worst fear materialize.

She peeled off her gloves and set them on the counter. She turned on the tap and let water run over her fingers.

The pipes were old. Over a century, probably. But the water coming through was new, fresh, untouched by history.

She washed her face. The cold shocked her system awake. Made her feel present in her body instead of floating somewhere above it.

Verena was right. Guardians didn't get to quit.

And maybe she wasn't ready to claim that title. Maybe she'd never be ready. But she could show up. Could use her gift even though it terrified her. Could stand with Joe, Verena, and Gary and face whatever came next.

She dried her face and looked at her reflection again.

Still exhausted. Still afraid.

But no longer defeated.

# CHAPTER 20

The staircase felt longer than it should. Each step required its own small act of courage, which would have been funny if Leanne's legs weren't trembling. She'd faced the chaos of time and armed thieves in the last twenty-four hours, but descending to the library where Verena waited for her felt like walking into a jury box.

Her gloves were firmly in place. Old habits.

Voices drifted from the library as she reached the bottom floor. Feminine voices layered with the particular warmth of women who knew each other well. Leanne paused outside the doorway, smoothing her hands over her jacket even though it didn't need smoothing.

*Just walk in. You've already decided. No going back now.*

She stepped through the doorway.

Five women turned to look at her. Verena stood by the fireplace. The others sat in a loose semicircle, and even though Leanne had never met them, she recognized them from around town. The antique dealer. The baker. The bookshop owner. The artist.

The stone-finders. The Guardians.

Verena held out a hand. "Leanne, come sit. Everyone, this is my dear friend Leanne McMann."

"We've heard about you." The woman with auburn hair and paint-stained fingers stood first. "I'm Quincy. And before you feel weird about it, we've all been exactly where you are right now."

"Lost and convinced we'd ruined everything?" She tried for lightness but didn't quite succeed.

"That's the one." A blonde woman with flour dusting her sleeve gestured to an empty chair. "I'm Ivy. I run the bakery. When I found my stone, I accidentally sent half the town into time slips through my lemon cookies. So believe me, you're in good company for magical disasters."

Despite everything, Leanne felt a smile tug at her lips. "That's either horrifying or impressive."

"Little of both." Ivy's grin was unrepentant.

The other women introduced themselves. Maura, who'd inherited Starlight Antiques and had nearly lost it to Denton's schemes. Hazel, whose bookshop was a cozy haven that Leanne had passed twice already without going inside. Each of them watched her with understanding rather than judgment.

It helped. More than she wanted to admit.

"Verena said you needed us." Maura leaned forward, her dark eyes sharp with intelligence. "And that it had to do with the Amber Stone."

"Denton has it." The words tasted bitter. "He took it last night. Grabbed it right out of the compartment before I could stop him."

"We know." Quincy's voice softened. "The whole town's feeling it. Time's getting slippery again."

"I led him straight to it. If I hadn't used my abilities, hadn't touched everything trying to find it—"

"You'd never have found it at all," Hazel interrupted quietly. "And Denton would still be searching. At least now we know what we're dealing with."

"A wealthy sociopath with control over time itself?" Leanne's laugh held no humor. "Fantastic. Really narrows it down."

Verena moved from the fireplace, settling into the chair beside Leanne's. "That's why I asked everyone to come today. And why I asked them to bring their stones."

For the first time, Leanne noticed the objects sitting on the coffee table. An amethyst that caught the light like purple fire. A sapphire that seemed to hold entire oceans in its depths. A ruby that pulsed with warmth even from a distance. An emerald that made her eyes want to water if she looked at it too long.

Four of the six stones. Right there within arm's reach.

"You want me to touch them." It wasn't a question.

"I want you to work with them," Verena corrected. "Each stone chose its Guardian for a reason. Each one amplifies a specific kind of magic. And you, Leanne, have a gift that might be able to connect with all of them."

She stared at the stones. "You think my… gift… will interact with their power?"

"I think you're meant to be a bridge. Your gift isn't just about seeing the past. It's about understanding the story an object carries. And these stones? They each carry a piece of this town's deepest magic." Verena's voice held absolute certainty.

Maura picked up the amethyst, holding it loosely in her palm. "This one's the Stone of Protection. It taught me how to shield myself and others, how to set boundaries that actually hold."

"The Sapphire is Memory." Ivy cradled the blue stone like something precious and fragile. "It helped me focus on specific moments instead of being overwhelmed by all of them at once."

"Ruby is Stories." Hazel's fingers traced the facets of the red stone. "It showed me how to read the story in objects and places. How to understand what they're trying to tell me."

"And Emerald is Vision." Quincy lifted the green stone, and it seemed to glow brighter in response. "It helped me learn to direct what I saw instead of just receiving whatever came through."

Four stones. Four kinds of magic. Four women who'd already walked the path she was stumbling down.

Leanne frowned. "But I don't understand. How is touching them supposed to help find Denton?"

"Because your gift isn't like ours." Verena leaned forward, her brown eyes intent. "Each of us connects to one specific aspect of magic. But you, Leanne? You read the essence of things. If you can connect with each stone, let them teach you what they taught their Guardians, you might be able to do what none of us can alone."

"Which is?"

"Use the stones to see past Denton's plans and find the weakness in whatever he's trying to do." Verena's words hung in the air like a dare.

Leanne looked at the four stones gleaming on the table. Her hands ached to touch them and recoiled from the idea in equal measure. Years of training herself to avoid contact, and now she was supposed to deliberately reach for objects literally made of magic.

This was insane. This was absolutely insane.

And yet, she looked at each of the women, paused, then pulled off her gloves. She stretched her fingers, then curled them as anxiety spiked in her chest.

"Okay." Her voice steadied. "Okay. Tell me what to do."

Maura moved first, kneeling beside Leanne's chair with the amethyst cradled in both hands. "Start with Protection. It'll help you build a foundation, keep you from getting lost."

She held out the stone.

Leanne reached for it, her hand trembling. The moment she made contact, power rushed through her like a wave of purple light. But instead of chaos, instead of the usual overwhelming flood of images, she felt... structure. Boundaries forming in her mind like walls around a garden. The amethyst's magic showed her how to create space, how to control what came in and what stayed out.

*You don't have to let everything through*, the stone seemed to whisper. *You choose.*

"Oh." The word came out breathless. "Oh, that's—"

"Good?" Maura's smile was knowing.

"Different." Her fingers tightened on the amethyst. "It's teaching me. How is it teaching me?"

"Because that's what they do." Verena's voice held quiet satisfaction. "They respond to genuine need. And right now, you need every tool you can get."

Leanne released the amethyst reluctantly, already feeling the loss of its clarifying presence. Ivy moved forward next with the sapphire.

"This one's trickier," Ivy warned. "Memory can pull you deep if you're not careful."

The sapphire was cool against Leanne's palm, smooth as water. The moment she touched it, time expanded. She could feel layers of moments stacked like pages in a book, each one distinct and accessible. The stone showed her how to flip between them, how to focus on one specific instant without being dragged through the entire cascade of history.

*Not all at once*, it told her. *One moment. Then another. You control the pace.*

"It's like..." She struggled for words. "Like learning to read instead of just staring at random letters."

"Exactly." Ivy's grin was triumphant. "That's exactly what it is."

Hazel brought the ruby next, and this time Leanne reached for it with less hesitation. The red stone vibrated with warmth and stories being told and retold across generations. It showed her how objects held narrative, how they collected meaning through the lives they touched.

*Listen to what they're trying to tell you. Every object has intent.*

And finally, Quincy placed the emerald in Leanne's hands. This one blazed green fire across her vision, but instead of overwhelming her, it sharpened everything. Suddenly, she could direct her sight, point her gift like a lens at exactly what she needed to see.

*You're not a victim of your visions. You're their master.*

When Leanne finally released the emerald, she sat back in her chair, breathing hard. Her hands were bare and tingling with residual magic. The four stones gleamed on the table like they were waiting for something.

For her to put it all together.

"I need to see what Denton's planning." She looked at Verena. "If I touch all four at once, use what they taught me, I think I can direct my gift to show me his intentions."

Verena nodded toward the stones.

She took a breath and reached for the stones. All four of them, her fingers making contact simultaneously. Power exploded through her like lightning.

She used the amethyst's walls to contain it. The sapphire's focus to direct it. The ruby's narrative sense to read the story unfolding. The emerald's vision to see exactly what she needed.

And then she was inside Denton's mind.

The vision swirled her through his thoughts. She saw him in a modern office tower that didn't exist in Moonlight Springs, saw blueprints spread across a massive desk. The Amber Stone sat in a glass case, pulsing with golden light. Denton stood before it, his hands pressed against the glass, his face transformed by greed and hunger.

She could hear his thoughts. *Rewrite it, he was thinking. Rewrite the whole thing. My family should have owned this land from the beginning. Should have been the founders, the power behind everything.*

Time itself began to unravel like a pulled thread.

*The town around him shimmered and changed. Victorian buildings became modern glass towers. Quaint shops became corporate franchises. The boardwalk vanished beneath a parking structure. And at the center of it all, a gleaming headquarters with "Denton Industries" emblazoned across its face.*

*He was trying to rewrite history so that his family had always owned Moonlight Springs. So that the original founders never existed. So that the town's magic, its heart, its very identity was erased and replaced with his vision of power and profit.*

*She saw him wielding his power for profit, twisting it toward something ugly and evil.*

*The vision shifted again. She was standing in a forest, and a spring was a spring, ancient and aware, waiting patiently. Energy and magic swirled and sparkled in the small clearing.*

*She sensed that the spring had its own magic and rules. Its own sense of who deserved its power and who didn't.*

Leanne gasped and released the stones. Five women stared at her with matching expressions of concern and hope.

"He's trying… trying to erase Moonlight Springs. The town in my vision was all gleaming modern buildings. The fountain was gone. None of the old historic buildings. There was no riverwalk. It was just all… gone. Like it never even existed."

"And what else?" Quincy asked.

"Nothing else. It didn't show me any way to stop him."

Verena looked at her closely. "There was nothing more?"

"Well, there was a spring in the forest. It was beautiful. But I don't know how that can help me."

"The Hidden Spring." Maura nodded.

"What hidden spring? I know there are springs scattered around town, but I don't know of any deep in the forest."

"Hence the name, Hidden Spring," Ivy grinned. "But it's there."

"It only reveals itself to people whom it chooses

to see it. If you saw the spring clearly, that means it's calling you," Quincy added.

"She's right. The spring showed itself to you in the vision. It wants you to find it." Verena stood. "I think you should go find the spring. And I think you should take Joe with you."

"But how do we find it?"

Hazel smiled. "You don't exactly find it... It finds you."

# CHAPTER 21

Leanne found Joe in the maze garden, kneeling beside the oak bench where everything had gone wrong. Morning light filtered through the hedge walls. The air smelled fresh and filled with dew, a gentle contrast to the chaos of the previous night.

His hands moved across the bench's surface carefully. They were covered in a fine layer of pale sawdust that caught the light. He'd brought his entire restoration kit. Tools lay arranged on a canvas cloth beside him with the methodical care she'd come to recognize as distinctly Joe. Chisels, files, brushes, and small jars of what might have been oil or wax.

The bench looked worse in daylight. A jagged crack ran through the center of the seat. The hidden compartment gaped open, violated and empty. The wood around it had splintered, revealing pale grain beneath the weathered surface.

She'd spent the morning with the other Guardians, learning to control her gift through their stones, discovering she wasn't as broken as she'd believed. But standing here, watching Joe try to repair what Denton's greed had shattered, the guilt came flooding back.

"Verena told me I'd find you here."

He glanced up. Sawdust clung to his flannel shirt and dusted his forearms. His brown eyes showed no accusation, only that steady calm that somehow made her feel both safer and more vulnerable at once.

"Couldn't sleep." He returned his attention to the bench, running his thumb along the crack with the focused tenderness he might show an injured animal. "Figured I might as well do something useful."

She stepped closer, gravel crunching beneath her boots. The gloves felt heavier than usual on her hands. After touching four magical stones and surviving visions that should have shattered her mind, soft leather shouldn't feel like armor anymore. Yet old habits held tight.

She forced herself to meet his gaze. "About last night. When I said I needed to be alone. When I pushed you away."

"You were overwhelmed." He picked up a small brush, sweeping sawdust from the crack with gentle strokes. "You'd just watched someone steal what you were meant to protect. Anyone would need space after that."

"That's generous. Most people would say I panicked. Ran away. Proved I was exactly as broken as I always feared."

"Most people didn't watch time splinter into a thousand possible futures." He set down the brush and looked at her fully. "You're here now. That's what matters."

The simple acceptance in his voice did something strange to her breathing. She'd spent years expecting judgment, building walls against it, and here was Joe dismantling them with basic decency.

"I'm sorry." The words felt clumsy, insufficient. "You've been nothing but patient and kind, and I repaid that by shutting you out when things got hard. You deserved better."

He stood, brushing sawdust from his jeans. The motion was practical and unhurried. When he stepped closer, she caught the scent of wood and the faint sweetness of the finishing oil he used.

"Leanne." Her name in his voice sounded like something solid, real. "You spent decades protecting yourself the only way you knew how. One breakthrough with some magical stones doesn't undo years of survival instinct. I'm not angry. I understand better than you might think."

Right. The fire. The cradle. His own decades of hiding behind restoration work instead of creation. They were both experts at building cages from their fears.

"Well, you're officially more emotionally mature than I am." She tried for lightness, that deflective humor that had served her so long. "That's mildly embarrassing for a woman my age."

The corner of his mouth twitched, almost a smile.

She gestured to the bench, redirecting to safer ground. "What are you doing exactly? Can it be fixed?"

He knelt again, picking up what looked like a thin wooden shim. "I'm trying to stabilize it. But it's more complicated than normal restoration."

"Complicated how?"

He pressed the shim carefully into the crack, testing the fit. "After you went upstairs last night, Verena and I examined the damage. This bench isn't just furniture. It's connected to the town's magic somehow."

She crouched beside him, careful to keep her gloved hands away from the wood. "Connected how?"

"Your vision showed my great-grandfather

building the compartment with a Guardian, right? They weren't just hiding the stone. They were anchoring it. The bench became part of the magical structure holding Moonlight Springs together."

She studied the crack with new understanding. The splintered wood suddenly looked less like simple damage and more like a wound in something living.

"So when Denton took the stone and all that energy let loose..."

"He damaged the anchor. The timeline was already unstable from the stone being awakened. Now it's actively unraveling."

"That explains the disturbances." She thought of Mrs. Wilson trapped between present and past, and the ghostly carriage nearly causing accidents. "It's getting worse because the anchor is broken."

"And will keep getting worse until either the stone is returned to its rightful Guardian or the damage is repaired." He fitted the shim into place and applied gentle pressure. The wood accepted it with a soft creak. "Possibly both."

She watched him work, his hands steady despite discussing the time apocalypse. There was something deeply reassuring about his methodical approach. Crisis or calm, Joe apparently addressed problems the same way, one careful step at a time.

"Can you repair it?"

"I can stabilize the physical damage. Whether that's enough to restore the magical anchor, I don't know. This is beyond my experience with furniture."

"Welcome to my entire existence." The dry comment slipped out before she could stop it. "Nothing in my life has ever been within normal experience."

He glanced at her, and this time he definitely smiled. "Fair point. Though you're handling magical chaos better than most people would."

"Oh yes, my recent panic attack was very impressive." She settled more comfortably beside him, tucking her knees up. "Very calm. Very mature. Definitely Guardian material."

"You came back. That's what matters."

She'd spent the morning learning the same lesson from Verena and the other Guardians, but hearing it from Joe felt different. More personal.

More true.

"I learned something this morning from the other Guardians. About my gift."

His hands stilled on the bench. He gave her his full attention, patient as always, waiting for her to find the words.

"It's not a curse. It's a warning system. A way of reading history so we can protect the future. The stones showed me how to control it, how to set boundaries, and direct the visions instead of just drowning in them."

"That's good." Simple words, but his voice carried genuine relief. "That's really good, Leanne."

"It is." She pulled her knees closer. "It's also terrifying. Because if my gift has purpose, if it's meant to protect things, then I've wasted thirty years hiding from it. And now, when it matters most, when the town actually needs a Guardian, I led the wrong person straight to the stone."

"At least  you found the stone."

"Speaking of which." She took a breath. Time to share the rest. "I had a vision. After you left. The other Guardians helped me use their stones to track Denton."

His hands paused again. "What did you see?"

"Denton is trying to… change things." The memory of the vision sent a cold river of ice trailing down her spine. "He wants to rewrite history itself. Go back to Moonlight Springs' founding and change everything. Erase what actually happened and replace it with a timeline where his family controlled the town from the beginning."

"That's... That's not possible… is it?"

"Apparently, with the Amber Stone of Time, it might be. If he succeeds, everything we know disappears. The town, the magic, the Guardians. All of it gets replaced with whatever corporate empire he imagines. We cease to exist in any meaningful way."

Joe turned to face her fully, his expression more serious than she'd ever seen. "We can't let that happen."

"No." Simple agreement, though nothing about the situation was simple. "We can't."

Silence settled between them, heavy with implication, while all around, the world looked… normal. Everything looked so beautifully, impossibly normal.

"There's more." Leanne made herself continue. Might as well share all the impossible news at once. "The vision showed me something else. A hidden spring in the forest. Ancient, powerful. Verena says it only reveals itself to specific people, and since it appeared in my vision, it's calling to me."

His eyebrows rose. "A hidden spring."

"I know how it sounds. Magical stones, time chaos, and now mystical water features. It's like someone wrote a particularly ambitious fantasy novel and forgot to check if any of it made sense."

"What does Verena think you should do?"

"Find it. She thinks the spring might have answers about how to stop Denton. Or at least guidance about what to do next. Something about it being a source of the town's magic, older than the stones themselves."

"Then we should go find it." Joe's matter-of-fact

tone made it sound like he'd just suggested getting coffee.

"We?" She hadn't asked him to go with her… at least not yet.

"You didn't think I'd let you go alone?" He started gathering his tools, returning each to its proper place. "After everything we've been through?"

"It could be dangerous." The warning felt necessary even though her heart was already lifting at his casual assumption that they'd face this together. "Denton is still out there. Conrad too. And we don't know what the spring will show me or demand. My visions could become overwhelming again."

Joe secured his tackle box and stood, offering her his hand. She took it automatically, her gloved fingers closing around his hand as he pulled her to her feet.

"All the more reason for backup." He didn't release her hand immediately. Instead, he held it gently for a moment. "Besides, you've touched enough terrifying magical objects lately. Time for someone else to share the burden."

The casual contact, the steady warmth of his hand around hers, sent an entirely different kind of flutter through her. Not psychic, not visionary. Just human connection.

And she didn't pull away.

"You know this is probably a terrible idea." She tried for humor again, that old defense mechanism. "Following cryptic guidance from magical sources. Wandering into an enchanted forest. It has a very beginning-of-a-cautionary-fairy-tale energy, doesn't it?"

"Most worthwhile things are terrible ideas at first. Creating original furniture after swearing never to. Touching magical stones that could shatter your mind. Trusting people after years of isolation. All terrible ideas. All worth doing."

She laughed, surprising herself. When had laughter become possible again? When had anything felt possible?

"You're annoyingly wise for a man who talks to furniture."

"I *listen* to furniture. Important distinction."

"Of course. My mistake."

He held out his hand again, an invitation. "So let's go find it."

She started at his outstretched hand and slowly took off her gloves. She knew what he was offering, what he was asking. Trust. Partnership. And the fact that taking his hand might simply bring… connection.

She took his offered hand. His palm was warm. His fingers closed around hers with gentle certainty.

"No visions?" Joe asked.

"No visions." She tightened her grip, holding on. "Just you."

"Then we should go find this hidden spring." Joe's words echoed her earlier statement, completing the circle. His hand stayed steady in hers. "Together."

"Together," she agreed.

The forest beyond the Moonlight Inn's maze stretched dense and wild, untouched by the tidy gardens Verena maintained closer to the building. Leanne stood at the edge where cultivated land gave way to wilderness.

"Ready?" Joe stood beside her, his voice steady as always.

*Ready to find a magical spring that only appeared to chosen people? Ready to potentially stop a man from unraveling the entire timeline? Sure. Completely ready. Piece of cake.*

"Absolutely," she said instead.

The trees ahead formed an impenetrable wall of oak and maple, their bare branches knitted together so tightly that morning sunlight barely penetrated. No path. No trail markers. Nothing remotely resembling an invitation to enter.

She closed her eyes and reached for that new awareness the Guardians had helped her develop. Her gift hummed beneath her skin, no longer wild and uncontrollable, but something she could *almost* touch with intention. The spring was out there. She'd seen it in her vision. Felt it calling.

"I don't see a path." She opened her eyes and studied the dense undergrowth. Brambles twisted between tree trunks. Ivy climbed in cheerful abundance. The forest had clearly never heard of welcoming committees.

"Maybe it's like the spring itself." Joe moved closer. "The path only appears to certain people."

"Or maybe my vision was just wishful thinking, and we're about to get thoroughly lost in the woods. That's also a possibility."

He bit back a grin, but the sparkle in his eyes gave him away. "Your optimism is inspiring."

"I try."

He held out his hand. Not pushing, not demanding. Just offering. The morning sun caught the fine sawdust still clinging to his flannel sleeve despite his attempts to brush it off. His palm bore the familiar calluses of his work and the slight stain of wood finish he never quite managed to wash away completely.

Just days ago, touching anyone would have flooded her with their memories, their emotions, everyone they'd ever touched. Now Joe's hand just felt like a hand. Warm. Calloused. Normal. She'd forgotten how good normal felt.

She laced her fingers through his.

The forest shimmered.

Between one heartbeat and the next, the impenetrable wall of vegetation simply melted aside. The trees remained exactly where they'd stood. But now a path wound between them, narrow and inviting, carpeted with moss that glowed emerald in the filtered sunlight.

She stared at the impossible trail. "Well, that's new."

"The spring knows you're coming." He squeezed her hand gently.

"Let's hope it's rolling out the welcome mat and not leading us into some fairy tale where we get turned into trees or something equally inconvenient."

They stepped onto the moss path together.

The forest closed around them, but not oppressively. Birds chattered above them, filtered through the canopy, cheerful and ordinary. As they walked, the trees burst alive with leaves on their branches, seemingly unaware it was almost winter. Sunlight dappled the trail ahead, playing across tree bark and highlighting tiny wildflowers that bloomed in impossible shades of blue and violet, also unaware of the season. The air smelled of earth and growing things, rich and alive.

Her gift hummed louder with each step. Not overwhelming, but present. Aware. The forest itself carried memory in its roots and bark, centuries of growth and change, but the information remained at a gentle distance. Available if she reached for it, but not forcing itself on her consciousness.

"This is incredible." Joe's attention moved from tree to tree, his craftsman's eye appreciating the massive oaks that must have stood for hundreds of years. "I've never seen growth like this so close to town."

"Magic has a way of preserving things." She studied a particularly ancient oak, its trunk wider than both of them together. "Or maybe time works differently here. I'm still getting used to the rules being more like suggestions."

The path curved deeper into the woods, following some logic she couldn't quite grasp. Not random, but not straightforward either. They walked for what felt like ten minutes, or possibly an hour. Her normal sense of time seemed to slip sideways and become unreliable.

"Do you feel that?" She paused. The air had changed around them, growing thicker. But this wasn't threatening. It felt old. Patient. Aware. "We're close."

They rounded a bend where an enormous fallen log forced the path to split and rejoin. Beyond it, the forest opened into a clearing that stole every coherent thought from her mind.

She gasped.

The spring lay in the clearing's heart, fed by water that bubbled up from some hidden source and gathered in a pool no larger than Verena's library. But calling it a pool felt inadequate. The water glowed with soft silver light, reflecting the sky above while somehow maintaining its own luminescence. Delicate wisps of light curled from its surface.

Trees ringed the clearing, ancient beyond measure. Their trunks bore the character of centuries, bark deeply grooved and hung with moss that draped like ceremonial cloth. Wildflowers Leanne had no names for bloomed in profusion, their colors too vivid to be entirely natural. The whole clearing hummed with magic so profound it felt like standing inside a heartbeat.

"Oh." The word came out barely above a whisper.

Joe's hand tightened around hers. "Yeah."

She walked forward as if pulled by invisible threads. The clearing welcomed her, the magic parting like curtains to let her pass. Her boots sank into grass softer than any carpet.

The spring drew her to its edge.

She knelt on the smooth stones that ringed the water, smooth as glass and warm beneath her knees. This close, the silver glow painted her hands and arms and reflected in Joe's face as he crouched beside her. The water's surface held perfect clarity despite its light, revealing a bottom covered in stones that glittered like stars.

Magic thrummed against her senses, vast and deep and utterly unlike anything she'd experienced. Not the specific memories locked in objects, but something older. Something that existed before memory began and would continue long after.

"It's beautiful." Her voice came out hushed, instinctively respectful.

The spring seemed to respond. The water's glow brightened, welcoming and acknowledging.

She reached toward the surface, drawn by an impulse she didn't fully understand. Her fingertips hovered an inch above the water.

The air shattered.

Not physically, but perceptually. Reality twisted sideways, shimmering like heat waves rising from summer pavement. The clearing flickered, layers of time suddenly visible all at once. The trees flickered between saplings and ancient giants, cycling through centuries in seconds. The stones beneath her knees were new, then weathered, then covered in moss, then new again.

Her gift screamed a warning.

She spun around, already knowing what she'd find.

Blake Denton stood at the clearing's edge.

The developer looked remarkably composed for someone who'd triggered a time-warp catastrophe less than twenty-four hours ago. His expression showed smug satisfaction as he surveyed the spring, the clearing, and Leanne herself.

Her stomach dropped. "How did you get here?" She rose to her feet.

Denton smiled. Not pleasantly. "That's easy."

He pulled the Amber Stone from his pocket.

The stone pulsed with chaotic golden light, its glow feverish and wrong. Power leaked from it in waves that made the air shimmer and twist. In Denton's hand, the stone's magic felt corrupt. Sick. Like an infected wound spreading poison through healthy tissue.

"The stone wants you." Denton stepped into the clearing, his movements casual despite the way reality buckled around him. Past and present overlapped with each step, showing the clearing as it had been decades ago, centuries ago, as it might be in the future. "It led the way to you, and I just followed it."

Devastation crashed through her. She'd led him here. To this secret place. This sacred source of Moonlight Springs' magic. Her attempt to save the town had instead delivered its heart directly to the man trying to destroy it.

Some Guardian she'd turned out to be. She'd handed him exactly what he wanted.

Joe rose to stand between her and Denton, his body language shifting into protective mode. "You need to leave. Now."

"I don't think so." Denton's attention fixed on the spring, hunger naked in his expression. "Do you have any idea how long I've searched for this? The source of it all. Raw, unfiltered magic."

He stepped closer to the water's edge.

The clearing reacted immediately. The shimmer in the air intensified, becoming almost solid. Trees aged and grew young in rapid succession, their leaves budding and falling and budding again. The ground beneath her feet felt unstable, as if the earth itself couldn't decide which moment to exist in.

"Stop." She held out her hands. "You don't understand what you're doing."

"I understand perfectly."

Denton held the Amber Stone over the spring. The stone's chaotic pulse synchronized with the water's silver glow, creating an echo that made Leanne's teeth ache. Magic answered magic, but wrong. Discordant. Like forcing two melodies together that were never meant to harmonize.

# CHAPTER 23

The Amber Stone pulsed in Denton's hand, its light strobing between golden and a sickly cream color. The air in the clearing compressed, becoming thick and difficult to breathe. Leanne's gift shrieked a warning half a second before Denton's smile widened into something vicious.

"Let me show you what real power looks like."

He thrust the stone forward.

Reality shattered.

The clearing vanished. The spring, the ancient trees, and Joe standing protectively beside her were all ripped away like pages torn from a book. Memories hit her, one after another, too fast to block.

*She was young again, reaching for her mother's hand at her grandmother's funeral. The instant their skin touched, visions exploded through her mind. Her mother's grief, yes, but also every secret resentment, every moment of regret, every private darkness a parent never wanted their child to witness. Her mother had jerked away, eyes wide with violation. "What did you see?"*

The memory dissolved. Another took its place.

*She was back with her boyfriend, Daniel, finally brave enough to kiss him. His warm lips had met hers. For one perfect heartbeat, she had felt normal. Then the visions came. His father's violence. His brother's overdose. His own suicidal thoughts at seventeen. She'd gasped and pulled back, but too late. He'd seen the horror in her face. "What's wrong with you?"*

Wrong with her. Always what was wrong with her.

The memories came faster. Every failed relationship. Every friendship that withered when people realized touching her meant nothing casual, nothing simple. The colleague who'd shaken her hand and then avoided her for months after she'd flinched from his dead marriage and dying dreams. The child at the grocery store who'd grabbed her arm and left her sobbing in the parking lot from the innocent chaos of a six-year-old's unfiltered joy and terror.

Her apartment. Alone. Always alone. Gloves in every room. Layers of fabric between her and the world. Years of careful isolation because connection hurt too much, cost too much, revealed too much.

The visions wouldn't stop. Couldn't stop. They poured through her mind like water through a shattered dam. Every painful moment she'd ever lived, every time her gift had destroyed something precious, every reminder that she was broken, wrong, cursed.

Her knees hit stone. The clearing. She was still in the clearing, but she couldn't see it through the cascade of memory. Couldn't breathe through the weight of decades of loneliness and failure pressing against her chest.

Through the chaos, she heard Joe cry out.

The sound cut through her spiral. She dragged her awareness toward it, fighting against the current of her own history. Her vision cleared fractionally.

Joe had collapsed beside her. His hands clawed at the grass like he was trying to hold onto something that wasn't there.

"The fire." His voice came out strangled, desperate. "The workshop. The smoke. I can smell it. Lindy. Lindy's in the hospital. The cradle. Everything's burning."

He was there. Twenty-three years ago, living his worst moment again. The trauma that had broken something fundamental inside him and convinced him that creating anything new was too dangerous, too costly.

Denton laughed. The sound echoed across impossible distances, coming from everywhere and nowhere. "This is what you get for interfering. Your past, on repeat. Forever."

The stone's chaotic pulse intensified. More visions slammed into Leanne. Her first vision at age seven, touching her grandfather's watch and experiencing his death. The teacher who'd called her disturbed when she'd tried to explain her gift. The therapist who'd suggested medication for hallucinations.

No.

No, this wasn't who she was anymore. She'd learned better. The Guardians had taught her better.

She forced her mind to still. To remember.

Maura's Amethyst had taught her about boundaries and building walls that protected without completely shutting everything out. Ivy's Sapphire had shown her how to control the pace, to slow the flood to a manageable stream. Hazel's Ruby had revealed how to read narrative instead of drowning in raw emotion. Quincy's Emerald had demonstrated directing her sight with precision.

She grabbed hold of those lessons like lifelines.

The visions kept coming, but she held them at arm's length. Watched them instead of drowning in them. Not blocking them completely. Acknowledging them. Yes, those things happened. Yes, they hurt. But they were past, not present. Memory, not reality.

The chaos filtered. Slowed.

She could breathe again.

Joe was still trapped in his fire, his face contorted. She reached for him, her bare hand finding his wrist. His skin burned fever-hot.

"Joe. Listen to me. It's not real. It's memory, not now. Come back."

He didn't respond. His eyes stared at something only he could see, trapped in his personal nightmare on repeat.

Denton stood at the spring's edge, the Amber Stone raised high. "You can't fight it. The past has its hooks in you both. You'll relive your failures until you break."

Wrong. He was wrong. The revelation crystallized in her mind with perfect clarity.

This wasn't the stone's true power. This corruption, this weaponization of memory was Denton's intention, poisoning the magic. The stone amplified the user's heart, Verena had said. Denton's greed and hunger for control had twisted the Amber Stone's gift into something cruel.

But the spring water still glowed with pure silver light, untouched by Denton's corruption. Ancient. Patient. Waiting.

For her.

The realization struck with the force of physical impact. The spring had called her here. Not

Denton. Her. She was meant to find this place and meant to understand what it offered.

She released Joe's wrist and turned to the water's edge. Her vision still flickered with unwanted memories, but her barriers held firm. The techniques the Guardians had taught her created a framework her gift could work within instead of overwhelming her completely.

Denton's attention snapped to her. "Don't."

She ignored him. Her hand extended toward the glowing water. The silver light painted her fingers, warm and welcoming.

"I said don't!" Denton thrust the Amber Stone toward her. Its chaotic pulse struck like a bolt of lightning.

Fresh visions slammed through her. Every object she'd ever touched. Every history she'd ever witnessed. The accumulated memory of thousands of artifacts cascaded through her consciousness in a tsunami of information. Too much. Far too much. No human mind could process this volume of time and experience without shattering.

Her boundaries cracked. Her control splintered.

She fell forward. Her palm struck the spring's surface.

The water's touch detonated through her entire being.

But this wasn't chaos. Wasn't corruption. Wasn't the sick pulse of Denton's twisted magic.

This was everything.

The spring's magic flooded through her like light through a prism, refracting into infinite colors. She saw time, but not as a weapon. As a gift. A story. An interconnected history that stretched back to the moment the first human settlement took root in this valley.

She saw the grove planted by the town's founders, six trees for six stones. Saw the careful magic woven into root and branch, protection and memory growing together. Saw the Hidden Spring bubble up from ancient bedrock, drawn by the intentions of those who understood that some places were meant to be sanctuaries.

The vision expanded. Centuries unfolded like pages in an infinite book. She saw Moonlight Springs grow from a handful of buildings to a thriving community. Saw the six stones hidden throughout the town, each one a focal point for the magic that made this place special. Saw Guardians through the generations, ordinary people who chose to protect something extraordinary.

She saw the oak grove mature. Saw Charles Joseph Hall—Joe's great-grandfather—select a tree with reverent care, understanding he was working with living magic. Saw him craft the bench that would hide the Amber Stone, his hands guided by something larger than individual skill.

The vision spiraled wider. She saw how it

connected. Verena staying when Gary left. Joe's great-grandfather choosing which tree to cut. Small decisions that kept the magic alive for the next person to find.

She saw Verena as a young woman, making the agonizing choice to stay when Gary left. Saw how that decision preserved the town's magic through a crucial moment when it might have faded completely. Saw Gary return forty years later, not by chance, but because some stories weren't finished yet.

She saw herself arriving at the inn. Saw Joe in his workshop, hands moving over wood with unconscious grace. Saw the moment their paths intersected, two people carrying wounds they'd chosen to define themselves by. Saw the fragile beginning of trust between them, the possibility of healing through connection rather than isolation.

The spring showed her all of this not as a warning or a weapon, but as context. As understanding. This was the Amber Stone's true gift —not the power to rewrite history, but the wisdom to understand it. To see how past moments created present opportunities. To recognize that time wasn't a prison but a foundation.

All the painful memories she carried weren't failures. They were lessons. They were the path that brought her here, to this moment, to this choice.

The realization struck with gentle force. She'd

spent years running from her gift because she'd seen it as a curse. But what if it had always been exactly what she needed? What if understanding the past was how you learned to build a better future?

Her awareness expanded further. She felt Joe's presence beside her, still trapped in his burning workshop. His trauma played on repeat because he'd never forgiven himself for a choice made in panic and grief. He'd locked himself in the past, refusing to create anything new because he was terrified of loss.

But loss was part of life. Part of growth. The spring showed her that clearly. The ancient oaks in this grove had weathered storms, fires, and droughts. Some branches had died. Some trees had fallen. But the grove continued, adapting, persisting, always growing toward the future.

She understood what Joe needed to hear. What she needed to tell him.

Her consciousness pulled back from the vast expanse of the spring's magic. The clearing came into focus around her. She knelt at the water's edge, her hand still pressed to the glowing surface. Joe sprawled beside her, trembling. Denton stood frozen, the Amber Stone clutched in white-knuckled fingers.

The spring's magic still flowed through her, strong and steady. She knew what to say.

"Joe!" Her voice rang across the clearing,

cutting through the chaos of corrupted magic. "It's not about changing the past. It's about what you build for the future!"

The fire consumed everything.

Joe's hands clawed at grass that felt like ash. His workshop burned around him, flames licking up the walls with terrible hunger. The heat pressed against his face, stealing oxygen, leaving nothing but smoke and the smell of burning wood. His wood. His work. Years of careful craftsmanship turned to char and ember.

The cradle sat in the center of the inferno, flames caressing the walnut headboard he'd shaped with such care. The cherry inlays blackened. The joints he'd fitted so carefully together separated under the heat's assault. His masterpiece. His gift for his sister's unborn child. His pride and joy, and his greatest creation.

All of it burning because he'd been careless. Stupid. In too much of a hurry.

The vision shifted without warning. He stood in a hospital corridor, fluorescent lights humming overhead. His sister clutched his arm, her fingers digging into his flesh hard enough to leave bruises. Her face had gone white. Her whole body shook.

"She's so small." His sister's voice cracked. "They said her lungs aren't developed. They don't know if she'll make it through the night."

Through the nursery window, an impossibly tiny infant lay in an incubator. Lindy. His niece. Tubes and wires covered her fragile body. Machines beeped and hissed, breathing for her because she couldn't breathe on her own. She weighed less than four pounds, the nurse had said. Born too early.

The doctors whispered in the corner, their voices low but carrying sentence fragments laced with words like complications and prepare yourself.

Please. The word formed in his mind, desperate and raw. Please let her live. I'll do anything. I'll never create again. I'll only fix what's broken, never risk something new. Just please let her live.

The hospital dissolved. The fire roared back to life. His workshop collapsed in on itself, sending up a column of sparks that disappeared into the night sky. Every piece he'd ever made, every tool he'd inherited from his great-grandfather, everything that defined him as a craftsman.

Gone.

The heat intensified. His lungs burned. He tried

to move, to escape, but his body wouldn't respond. Trapped. He was trapped in this moment, forced to watch his life's work destroy itself over and over in an endless loop of failure and loss.

Through the roar of flames, a voice cut like a blade.

"Joe!"

Leanne's voice. Present, not memory. Real, not vision.

"It's not about changing the past. It's about what you build for the future!"

The words struck deep inside him. The fire flickered. Just for a heartbeat, the flames wavered, and through them, he saw something else.

A bench. Weathered oak, joints fitted with exquisite precision. His great-grandfather's work. The piece that had hidden the Amber Stone for over a century, protecting the town's magic through threats.

Charles Joseph Hall hadn't been afraid to create. He'd understood that building something new was an act of faith. A declaration that the future mattered. That beauty, function, and purpose deserved to exist in the world, regardless of what might happen to them later.

The bench hadn't survived unscathed. Weather had worn its surface. Time had weathered its wood. But it had endured. It had served its purpose. And that purpose was more important than its creator's fear of eventual decay. And when the bench finally gave way to time, would that make its creation meaningless? Would its eventual end negate the decades it had served?

No.

The realization broke through the smoke choking his thoughts. The fire hadn't destroyed his worth as a craftsman. The fire had been an accident, a moment of tragedy, but he'd let it become a prison. He'd convinced himself that creating invited disaster, that making something new was tempting fate. Because he'd made the bargain so Lindy would live.

She had lived. She'd survived that terrible night and grown into a healthy, happy young woman who called him every Sunday and sent him photos of her college classes. Her survival wasn't because of a bargain he'd struck with the universe. It was medicine, luck, and her own fierce will to exist.

The workshop fire faded. The hospital corridor dimmed. He knelt in the clearing beside the Hidden Spring, his hands pressed against cool grass. His lungs pulled in air that tasted of earth and growing things. Real air. Present moment. Not trapped in the past.

Leanne knelt at the spring's edge, her hand glowing with silver light where it touched the water. Her face held fierce concentration. Whatever magic she'd connected with had pulled her beyond

Denton's reach, beyond his corruption of the Amber Stone.

Denton stood frozen, the stone clutched in his hand. His face twisted with concentration as he tried to force the magic to his will. The chaotic golden pulse struck toward Leanne in waves, trying to overwhelm her, trying to shatter her control.

She held steady, but Joe could see the strain in her shoulders and the tension in her jaw. She couldn't maintain this forever. The spring's magic protected her for now, but Denton had the Amber Stone. He could wait. He could attack again and again until her defenses finally crumbled.

Joe's hands curled into fists. His craftsman's hands, scarred from decades of work. Stained with wood finish and marked with the occasional slip of a chisel. Strong hands that knew how to shape, smooth, and join.

His great-grandfather's bench had been an act of creation that protected Moonlight Springs. What if that was the answer? He wasn't here to fix anything, but to create something new.

The thought terrified him. Every instinct screamed against it. He'd made a promise. A vow. Never again.

But that vow had been born from fear and guilt, not wisdom. It had kept him from his true gift. Kept him from being the craftsman his great-grandfather had trained him to become.

Leanne had faced her fear. She'd chosen growth over safety.

Could he do the same?

Movement caught his eye. A fallen branch lay near his knee, oak from one of the ancient trees ringing the clearing. Not dead wood, but fresh. Storm-broken perhaps, or shed naturally as the tree grew. Or possibly the magic had placed it there. The wood grain caught the spring's silver light, golden and rich and full of potential.

His hand reached for it before conscious thought caught up.

The moment his fingers closed around the branch, rightness flooded through him. This was oak from the grove, from trees planted by the town's founders. The same trees his great-grandfather had worked with. The same wood that had hidden and protected the Amber Stone.

The branch fit his palm perfectly, smooth and solid. About as thick as his wrist and long as his forearm. Good weight. Good grain. Workable.

His other hand dropped to his belt, finding the small folding knife he always carried. A craftsman's habit, keeping a blade handy for marking measurements or cleaning joints. The knife felt familiar in his grip, an extension of his hand.

Denton's attention was fixed entirely on Leanne, trying to break through her connection to the spring. He hadn't noticed Joe's movement. Hadn't seen the branch or the knife.

Joe's hands began to move.

Twenty-three years fell away like dried leaves. His fingers remembered what his mind had tried to forget. How to read grain. How to find the shape hidden inside raw wood. How to work with the material instead of forcing it.

The knife's blade bit into the oak's surface. A curl of pale wood spiraled away. Then another. His hands moved faster, guided by instinct and decades of experience. Not restoration now. Creation. Pure and terrifying creation.

Denton had corrupted the Amber Stone with his greed and his hunger for control. He'd twisted time magic into a weapon, using memory as torture. His intentions poisoned everything he touched.

But creation itself was pure. The act of making something new that hadn't existed before, something born from hope rather than fear. His grandfather had called it listening to the wood. Joe had thought it was just an old man's way of talking. Now he wasn't sure.

The branch transformed under his hands. The shape emerged as if it had always been there, just waiting for someone to reveal it. A crescent moon, simple and elegant. The symbol that marked the town, that hung above the inn's door, that appeared on the fountain in Crescent Park.

The symbol of Moonlight Springs itself.

His hands moved faster still, smoothing and refining. The knife whispered against wood, each cut deliberate. Sawdust clung to his fingers and dusted his jeans. The familiar smell of fresh-cut oak filled his nose, rich and alive and achingly missed.

He'd forgotten this. The joy of creation. The satisfaction of bringing something new into existence. The connection between craftsman and material.

How had he survived all these years without this?

The crescent moon took its final form in his hands, no larger than his palm. Simple, but clean. Honest work, reflecting his skill without showing off. The kind of piece his great-grandfather would have approved of.

The kind of piece meant to serve a purpose.

Joe looked at the spring. At Leanne, still holding her connection to its magic. At Denton and the Amber Stone blazing with chaotic light as he attacked again.

At the choice in front of him.

He could keep this carving. His first original creation in twenty-three years. Proof that he'd finally broken free from his self-imposed prison. A tangible reminder that he could create again.

Or he could offer it. Give it freely. Let it go

without knowing if the gesture would matter, without any guarantee of outcome.

Creation without attachment to the result. Making something beautiful for its own sake, not for what you could keep or control or protect.

That was the lesson he'd refused to learn. That was the fear that had caged him.

Leanne had touched the spring and found understanding. She'd faced her past and found strength in it. She'd embraced her gift fully for the first time.

Now it was his turn.

Joe stood. His legs felt steady beneath him, solid and sure. The crescent moon rested in his palm, warm from his hands and the friction of shaping. Perfect. Complete. Ready.

He drew his arm back and threw the carving into the spring's glowing water.

The wooden moon arced through the air, spinning slowly. Silver light reflected off its smooth curves. For a heartbeat, it seemed to hang suspended, caught between earth and water, between past and future.

Then it struck the surface.

The spring's magic poured outward with absolute authority. Pure silver light exploded from where the carving entered the water, expanding in waves that washed across the clearing. The light carried intention. Carried purpose.

The chaotic golden pulse from the Amber Stone disappeared in wisps into the air.

Denton cried out. The stone in his hand blazed white-hot, rejecting his corrupted intentions. His fingers spasmed open.

The Amber Stone fell from his hand and hit the grass at his feet.

He reached for it immediately, his face twisted with fury and desperation. His fingers closed around the stone.

It jumped from his grip as if alive, skittering across the ground away from him. He lunged after it, grabbed it again with both hands this time.

The stone moved in his grip, thrashing like a living thing. Light poured from between his fingers, pure golden. The magic refused him now. Rejected him. The stone had tasted pure creation and wanted no part of Denton's selfish destruction.

His hands opened involuntarily. The Amber Stone tumbled free and rolled toward the spring, toward Leanne, toward the person it had been trying to reach all along.

The Amber Stone rolled across the grass toward her, trailing golden light like a comet.

Leanne's hand lifted from the spring's glowing surface. Water droplets clung to her fingers, each one catching silver light and holding it. The spring's magic still flowed through her awareness, vast and patient and utterly calm.

The stone stopped rolling an inch from her knee.

She waited for the flinch, the urge to pull back and avoid touching something with so much history. But the spring's wisdom still flowed through her thoughts, steady as a heartbeat. The past wasn't a weapon. Understanding wasn't a curse. Her gift had brought her here precisely because she could do what needed doing.

She reached forward.

Her bare fingers closed around the Amber Stone.

Power slammed into her like a river breaking through a dam.

Every time distortion that had plagued Moonlight Springs flooded through her awareness at once. The mailman stepping into 1891. Mrs. Wilson's kitchen flickering between decades. The harvest festival that had terrified the town square. The clock running backward. Conversations that erased themselves. The maze aging and growing young again in heartbeats.

All of it poured through her, a torrent of temporal chaos that should have torn her mind apart.

But the spring had taught her better.

She didn't fight the flood. Didn't try to dam it, redirect it, or shut it out completely. She'd learned that lesson. Suppression only made things worse. Control came from acceptance, understanding, and working with the current instead of against it.

She opened herself to the stone's magic and let it fill every corner of her awareness.

The torrent transformed. Not chaos, but information. Not a weapon, but a gift.

The Amber Stone showed her time itself.

She saw time as a whole. A vast interconnected web where every moment touched every other moment. She saw Moonlight Springs not as a town moving through time, but as a place where time gathered, pooled, and eddied.

The six stones were anchors. Focal points. Places where the flow of time could be observed and understood, and when necessary, gently guided back into healthy patterns.

The Amber Stone's true purpose crystallized in her mind with perfect clarity. Not to rewrite history. Not to change what had been. But to understand how past moments created present possibilities, and how present choices shaped future outcomes.

Denton had tried to corrupt that gift into a weapon. Had tried to force the stone to bend time to his will and rewrite reality according to his greed. No wonder the magic had twisted into something sick and chaotic. He'd been using it backward, trying to control instead of understand.

But in her hands, held by someone whose entire gift was built on reading history and honoring what had been, the stone settled into its natural rhythm.

The spring's magic still flowed through her from where she'd touched the water. The Amber Stone blazed in her palm. Two sources of power, two types of understanding, meeting in her and waiting for direction.

She understood what she needed to do.

Still holding the Amber Stone in one hand, she pressed her free hand back against the spring's surface and closed her eyes.

The stone's power flowed through her like light through glass. She didn't direct it so much as allow it to find its proper path. The spring's ancient magic recognized the stone's energy, welcomed it, grounded it. Pure power cycling from stone to spring to earth, finding balance.

She felt peace settle across the town as the magic reached it. The knots loosened. The tangled moments separated back into their proper places. Past settling into the past. Present solidifying into the present. The boundaries between them growing strong and clear again.

Mrs. Wilson's kitchen stopped flickering and stayed firmly in the current decade. The town square released its grip on the harvest festival from years ago. Every clock in Moonlight Springs found its proper rhythm. Conversations stayed in memory instead of erasing themselves.

Time healed. The chaos settled into order.

The magic poured through her in waves, each one carrying another distortion back to stability. Her whole body hummed like a plucked string. Not painful, but intense. More power than any human was meant to channel alone.

But she wasn't alone. The spring supported her. The stone trusted her. And somewhere behind her, Joe's presence anchored her to the physical world even as her consciousness expanded across the entire town.

The last distortion unraveled. The final knot smoothed. Moonlight Springs settled into stability with an almost audible sigh of relief.

She opened her eyes.

The clearing looked exactly as it had before, with ancient trees ringing the glowing spring. Wildflowers bloomed in impossible colors. Morning sunlight filtered through leaves that shouldn't exist in winter. Magic gently hung in the air, contentedly, like a held breath finally released.

She turned her head, still kneeling at the water's edge.

Denton was gone.

The grass where he'd stood showed no trace of him. No footprints, no disturbed earth, no indication anyone had been there at all. Had the spring expelled him? Had the stone's rejection sent him somewhere else? Had he simply run when his weapon was taken away?

She didn't know. Couldn't sense him anywhere in the clearing or the forest beyond. Part of her should probably worry about that, should wonder if he'd return with some new scheme. But exhaustion pulled at her, and the spring's wisdom suggested some battles didn't need fighting twice. Denton had lost his chance. The stone had chosen. That door had closed.

Her attention dropped to her palm.

The Amber Stone rested there, no larger than a

robin's egg. In the clearing's soft light, it glowed with warm golden luminescence. Not the chaotic, sickly pulse it had shown in Denton's grip, but something steady and beautiful. Light moved through its depths, slow and rich. The surface felt smooth under her thumb, worn by centuries.

Power still coursed through it as vast as the ocean. But contained. Controlled. Waiting patiently for whenever it might be needed again.

She'd done it. Actually done it. Found the stone, claimed it, and used it to heal the town's chaos. The woman who'd spent thirty years afraid to touch anything had just channeled enough magical power to stabilize reality itself.

The thought should have been triumphant. Victorious. Instead, it felt surreal. Like something that had happened to someone else, in some other life.

Footsteps crunched on grass behind her.

Joe dropped to his knees beside her, his shoulder pressing against hers. Solid. Warm. Real. His chest rose and fell quickly, breath still catching from whatever he'd experienced in his own visions. His hands bore a small cut that hadn't been there before.

"You did it." His voice cracked. "The stone. You found it. You claimed it."

"We did it." She looked at him, really looked. His

face had gone pale, and his eyes looked older than they had an hour ago. He'd been forced to relive his worst trauma, trapped in the burning workshop and the hospital corridor while his infant niece fought for her life. "Your carving broke Denton's hold. The spring responded to that, to pure creation offered freely. I couldn't have reached the stone without you."

"Leanne." Her name on his lips sounded like a prayer, a question, and a declaration all at once.

His arms came around her, pulling her close.

She turned into the embrace, the Amber Stone still clutched in her hand. Her forehead pressed against his shoulder. His heart beat steadily against her ear, grounding her in the present moment.

His hand came up to cradle the back of her head, fingers gentle in her hair. Not possessive, not demanding. Just holding her. Offering comfort and receiving it.

"I was so scared." The words escaped before she could stop them. "Not of the magic, exactly. But of failing. Of proving everyone right who ever said my gift was a curse. Of being the reason Moonlight Springs fell apart."

"You didn't fail." His arms tightened fractionally. "You were extraordinary."

Her throat tried to close around her tangled emotions. Relief, maybe. Gratitude. Wonder. The bone-deep exhaustion that came after holding yourself together through something that should have broken you.

So she just held on. Let herself be held. For someone who'd spent decades avoiding physical contact, being held should have felt strange. It didn't.

After a moment, she became aware of the stone in her hand, still pressed between their bodies. Its warmth pulsed against her palm. Not demanding attention, but present. Patient.

She pulled back enough to look at Joe. "The stone. I think it wants something."

His eyebrows rose slightly. "Wants something? It has opinions now?"

"Everything magical in this town seems to have opinions. Why should the stone be different?"

The ghost of a smile touched his mouth despite the lingering shadows in his eyes.

She opened her hand, revealing the Amber Stone resting on her palm. Golden light played across its surface, beautiful and mesmerizing. Joe's attention fixed on it, his craftsman's eye appreciating the way light moved through the stone's depths.

"I think it wants you to touch it."

His hands came up to cover the stone resting on her palm.

The Amber Stone's glow brightened.

Understanding flooded through her, through them, through the connection of their joined hands.

The stone shared its peace, its vast perspective. All those centuries of witnessing Moonlight Springs grow and change, of watching Guardians come and go, of serving its purpose with patient dedication.

Time wasn't something to fear. Change wasn't something to fight against. The past had shaped them both, yes, had carved wounds that needed healing. But those wounds didn't define them. Didn't limit what they could become.

The walls between them crumbled like sand.

She saw herself through his eyes for a heartbeat. Her courage in facing her gift. Her dry humor that made him smile despite everything. Her fierce determination to protect people even when she was terrified. The way her presence had somehow convinced him that he could create again.

The stone's magic faded back to a gentle hum, its message delivered. Peace settled over the clearing like a blanket.

Joe's hands remained cupped around hers, steady and sure. His eyes held hers, warm and utterly present. No more barriers. No more careful distance. Just two people seeing each other completely and choosing not to look away.

"That was remarkable. I felt everything. Saw everything. You're remarkable."

Heat climbed into her cheeks. "The stone did most of the work."

"The stone showed me what was already there."

She couldn't hold his gaze any longer without her face catching fire. Her attention dropped back to the Amber Stone, still glowing contentedly in their joined hands. "We should probably get this to Verena. Tell her what happened. Make sure the town is actually stable and not about to experience some new disaster."

Joe's hands squeezed hers gently before pulling back. "Probably smart. Though I'm not entirely sure how to explain any of this."

"Hi Verena, we found the stone, channeled ancient magic, and fixed the town. Possibly scared off the bad guy. That about covers the highlights." She smiled as she pushed herself to her feet.

Her legs wobbled alarmingly. Every muscle in her body ached as if she'd run a marathon. The magical work had drained her more thoroughly than she'd realized. Black spots danced at the edges of her vision.

Joe caught her elbow, his grip firm and stabilizing. "Easy. When's the last time you ate anything?"

"Define ate anything."

"That's what I thought." He shook his head, but his mouth curved into a small smile. "We'll get you fed once we reach the inn. Verena probably has something baked and ready to go. She always does."

# CHAPTER 26

Leanne's legs threatened to give out halfway up the stairs to the inn. Only Joe's steady hand at her elbow kept her upright. The Amber Stone rested in her other palm, warm and quiet now, its chaotic energy settled into a gentle pulse that matched her heartbeat.

"Almost there." Joe's voice rumbled close to her ear.

She nodded, not trusting herself to speak. Everything felt distant and cotton-soft, as if she'd used up every bit of herself at the spring and only an echo remained. Her fingers still tingled with residual magic. Her mind still spun with the visions the stone had shared.

The inn's kitchen door glowed with welcoming light. Voices drifted through the half-open window, low and anxious.

Joe pushed the door open, and warmth rushed out to meet them. The scent of fresh coffee and something cinnamony wrapped around her. Her knees wobbled again.

"Easy." Joe's arm circled her waist, taking more of her weight.

They stepped into the kitchen together. Verena stood at the counter, her hands wrapped around a mug. She turned at the sound of their entrance, her expression shifting from worry to relief.

"Thank the stars." Verena set down her mug and crossed to them in three quick strides. Her gaze moved from Leanne's face to the stone in her hand and back again. "You found it."

"She found it." Joe's correction came quietly. "She claimed it."

Verena's eyes brightened with something that looked suspiciously like pride. She reached out as if to touch Leanne's shoulder, then hesitated, her hand hovering in the space between them.

Right. The gloves. Leanne glanced down at her bare hands and felt a flutter of panic. She'd taken off her gloves at the spring and never put them back on. Now she stood in Verena's kitchen, exposed and vulnerable, with no barriers between her skin and the world.

"Everyone's in the parlor." Verena let her hand fall. "Gary's been coordinating with his deputies. The others have been waiting for news."

The others. The Guardians. Leanne's stomach twisted. They would want to hear everything, and she would have to find words for experiences that defied language. How did you explain what it felt like to channel pure time magic? How did you describe touching the Hidden Spring and seeing the entire history of a town unfold in your mind?

"I should find my gloves first." Her voice came out rough and thin.

"Later." Verena gestured toward the hallway. "Come. They need to see you're safe."

Joe's hand moved to the small of her back, a gentle pressure that both steadied and guided her forward. She let him lead her through the familiar hallway toward the parlor. Each step felt like moving through water.

The parlor doors stood open. Light spilled out into the dim hallway, and Leanne could see figures moving inside. Voices rose and fell, tense with worry.

Then Verena called out, "They're back."

The voices stopped. Footsteps rushed toward the doorway. Leanne's instinct screamed at her to step back, to protect herself, to find her gloves and build her walls. But Joe's steady presence at her back kept her rooted.

Ivy appeared first, her flour-dusted apron still tied around her waist. Behind her came Maura, then Hazel, then Quincy. The four Guardians crowded into the doorway, their faces reflecting the same mixture of relief and concern that Verena had shown.

"Oh, thank goodness." Ivy pressed a hand to her chest. "When Gary said there was some kind of magical disturbance in the forest, we were so worried."

Gary emerged from the parlor, his sheriff's uniform rumpled and his expression weary. He nodded at Joe, then turned his attention to Leanne. "I guess you had quite an adventure."

"You could say that." The words came out more sardonic than she'd intended. Old habits. Use humor to deflect and keep people at a safe distance. Except she didn't want distance anymore.

"Come sit before you fall down." Maura moved to Leanne's other side, mirroring Joe's supportive stance without actually touching her. "You look exhausted."

They ushered her into the parlor, a gentle tide of concern and care. Someone pressed her into the overstuffed armchair by the fireplace. Someone else draped a soft throw blanket over her lap. Ivy disappeared and returned with a steaming mug of tea.

Leanne wrapped her still-bare hands around the mug and let the warmth seep into her palms. The Amber Stone rested in her lap now, its golden surface catching the firelight.

Gary settled into the chair across from her while the others found seats on the sofa and scattered chairs. Joe remained standing behind her chair, close enough that she could feel his presence like a shield at her back.

"Blake Denton was found about an hour ago." Gary's voice carried the professional tone he probably used for witness statements. "He was wandering the forest service road two miles south of here. Disoriented. Angry. Kept insisting he'd been robbed."

"Robbed." She rolled her eyes. "That's rich."

"He couldn't explain what was stolen or who took it. Couldn't remember how he got to the forest or why he was there." Gary smiled. "I, of course, didn't clue him in."

"But I'm sure we haven't seen the last of him. The man is determined, I'll give him that," Maura said, frowning.

Leanne thought of Denton's face at the spring, twisted with greed and rage as he'd tried to force the Amber Stone to his will. She thought of the corrupted magic he'd unleashed and the way it had ripped through time itself. Part of her had hoped the spring would simply unmake him, erase him from existence like a mistake rubbed out.

"I'm sorry the magic didn't just *poof* him away." She took a sip of tea and let the honey coat her throat. "Would have been tidier."

Hazel laughed, surprised and genuine. "I had the same thought when Denton tried to steal the Ruby Stone. Unfortunately, magic seems to prefer complicated solutions."

"Magic has a terrible sense of drama." Quincy grinned as she tucked her legs under her on the sofa. "Everything has to be a production."

The casual humor eased the tightness inside her. These women understood. They'd all faced their own trials and their own moments of crisis when everything hung in the balance. They'd all wondered if they were enough.

"Tell us what happened." Verena had claimed the chair nearest the fire, her moonstone pendant catching the light. "If you're able."

She glanced at Joe. He gave her an encouraging nod.

So she told them. About the path through the forest that only revealed itself when she and Joe held hands. About the Hidden Spring in its impossible clearing, blooming with life in the winter. About Denton appearing with the corrupted stone, about the time loops, and the trapped memories.

Her voice steadied as she spoke. The story wanted to be told, and these people deserved to hear it.

"The spring showed me everything." She stared into her tea, watching steam curl upward. "The founding of Moonlight Springs. Generations of

Guardians. How every choice and every moment ripples forward through time."

"And Denton?" Gary leaned forward, his elbows on his knees.

"The spring rejected him. Or the stone did. Maybe both." She shook her head. "When Joe made his offering, when he created something new and released it without attachment, the magic responded. It broke Denton's hold on the stone."

She felt Joe's hand settle on her shoulder, a brief touch of acknowledgment and support.

"The stone chose Leanne. Just like Verena said it would." His voice carried quiet certainty.

She looked down at the Amber Stone in her lap. In the firelight, its depths seemed to shift and swirl, holding millennia of gathered time. It had chosen her. The woman who'd spent years running from her gift had been chosen to guard the stone that governed time itself.

The irony wasn't lost on her.

Maura stood and crossed to Leanne's chair. "May I?"

Leanne tensed, old instincts screaming warnings. Maura stood close enough to touch. If she reached out, if skin met skin, Leanne would be flooded with visions. Decades of memories, painful and intimate and overwhelming.

Except.

The thought came quietly, gently. The spring

had shown her so much. The stones had taught her control. Maybe, just maybe, things had changed.

"Okay." The word came out barely above a whisper.

Maura bent and wrapped her arms around Leanne in a firm, warm hug.

She braced herself for the onslaught of visions. She prepared for the chaos, the tumbling cascade of other people's memories that always came with physical contact. Then the look that would be in Maura's eyes, knowing her deepest secrets had been revealed.

Instead, she felt only Maura's arms, the softness of her sweater, and the faint scent of vanilla and old books clinging to her clothes. The simple, human warmth of another person's embrace.

No visions. No psychic overflow. Just a hug.

Her hands came up automatically to return the embrace, and still nothing happened. No windows into Maura's past. No flood of emotions and experiences that weren't her own.

Maura pulled back, blinking quickly. "Welcome to the family."

"I didn't." She stared at her own hands as if they belonged to someone else. "I didn't see anything."

"What?" Ivy sat up straighter.

"No visions." The words tumbled out faster now,

edged with wonder and disbelief. "I touched her and got no visions."

Quincy rose from the sofa. "Try me."

She held out her hand. Leanne reached up slowly, her heart hammering against her ribs. Their fingers met. Quincy's hand felt small and warm in hers.

No visions.

"Wow..." That was the only word she could think to say.

"Me three." Hazel bounced over and grabbed Leanne's other hand. "This is amazing."

Still nothing. Just the pressure of Hazel's fingers, enthusiastic and solid and absolutely, blissfully normal.

Ivy joined them, and then the four Guardians stood in a circle around Leanne's chair, all of them touching her, all of them grinning like they'd discovered buried treasure.

She wanted to laugh. She wanted to cry. She wanted to grab them all and never let go, to make up for years of isolation in this single moment of connection.

"Maybe because we're all Guardians? That allows me to touch you?"

"Try Gary then," Ivy urged.

"Gary." Her voice came out rough. "Would you mind?"

The sheriff looked surprised but stood and

offered his hand. She took it, ready for the visions to take hold this time. His palm felt warm and calloused, his grip careful and respectful.

No visions. Nothing. Just a handshake.

"Well." Gary released her hand, his expression thoughtful. "That's interesting."

She reached for the end table beside her chair and picked up a small ceramic figurine of a cat. The moment her skin touched the cool porcelain, visions flooded her mind. A gift shop in Portland, a woman's hands wrapping it in tissue paper, Verena unwrapping it years later and setting it on the table with a smile.

"Still works on objects." She set the cat down carefully.

Verena rose from her chair with the grace of someone who'd been waiting for this exact moment for years. She crossed to Leanne and held out both hands.

"May I?"

She stood on shaking legs and let Verena pull her into an embrace. Her friend's arms wrapped around her, and she felt herself crumple slightly, leaning into a hug from her best friend, something she hadn't allowed for so many years.

"I think," Verena said quietly, her voice pitched for Leanne's ears alone, "that you're safe with Guardians and those entrusted with protecting the stones. The magic recognizes its own."

She pulled back to look at Verena's face. "The magic recognizes its own," she repeated slowly.

The implications settled over her like snow. The Guardians she could touch safely. Gary, who knew the town's secrets and protected its people. Anyone truly invested in Moonlight Springs' magical heart.

Her gaze found Joe, still standing behind the chair where she'd left him. He watched her closely. "Maybe that's why I don't get visions from you."

Joe went very still. The entire room seemed to hold its breath.

Then he stepped forward, closing the distance between them. His hand rose slowly, giving her every chance to pull away. His fingers brushed her cheek, feather-light and questioning.

No visions. Just the warmth of his touch, the slight roughness of his calluses, and the way his thumb traced the line of her cheekbone with infinite gentleness.

She covered his hand with her own, pressing it more firmly against her face, feeling skin on skin and the tenderness of his touch. Joe finally pulled his hand away.

Ivy smiled at them. "You were always meant to be a Guardian, you know."

"The worst Guardian in history." Her attempt at humor wavered. "I led Denton right to the spring."

"You stopped him," Maura spoke from behind

her. "You claimed the stone. That's what Guardians do."

"We all make mistakes." Hazel settled back onto the sofa. "I got literally sucked into a book and had to be rescued. You're in good company."

"I accidentally time-slipped half the town." Ivy raised her hand.

"I painted potential disasters that almost came true." Quincy shrugged, then grinned. "Repeatedly."

Despite everything, Leanne laughed. These women understood. They'd all stumbled, all questioned, all wondered if they were enough.

And they'd all found their way through.

Verena moved closer to Leanne. "You came back to Moonlight Springs afraid of your own hands."

Leanne wanted to look away but found she couldn't.

"And look at you now." Verena's hand squeezed gently. "You found the Amber Stone and claimed it as its rightful Guardian. You saved us all."

The words settled over her, solid and true. She had done those things. Terrified and uncertain and sure she would fail, she'd done them anyway.

"I had help." She glanced around the room at the gathered faces. "A lot of help."

"That's what we do." Maura smiled. "We help each other."

Verena's expression shifted, something formal and ceremonial entering her bearing. She straightened her shoulders and lifted her chin, and suddenly she looked less like a kindly innkeeper and more like what she truly was: a Guardian descended from a long line of protectors, the keeper of Moonlight Springs' deepest secrets.

Then Verena's face transformed with a smile that could have lit the entire room. She pulled Leanne into another embrace, this one celebratory and fierce.

"Welcome, Guardian." She pressed a kiss to Leanne's temple. "Welcome home."

The other Guardians surged forward, wrapping them both in a group embrace that should have been suffocating but instead felt like safety. Like belonging. Like everything she had convinced herself she could never have.

When they finally pulled back, Ivy was wiping her eyes. "We should celebrate. I'll make something special."

"Coffee cake," Hazel suggested. "The good kind, with the crumb topping."

"At this time of night?" Maura laughed. "Why not? We're all too wound up to sleep anyway."

They dispersed in a flurry of plans and friendly arguments about recipes. Gary followed them toward the kitchen, probably to make sure someone started an actual pot of coffee. Verena paused in the doorway, looking back at Leanne with pride still glowing on her face.

Then she, too, disappeared, leaving Leanne and Joe alone in the parlor.

The fire crackled quietly. Joe moved to stand in front of her. "How do you feel?"

"I'm not sure." The honest answer came easily now. "Exhausted. Grateful. Confused." She looked down at the Amber Stone.

His hand found hers, their fingers threading together. "You were extraordinary."

"I was scared out of my mind."

"Bravery and fear aren't opposites." His thumb traced circles on the back of her hand. "You taught me that."

Leanne remembered the oak branch he'd carved at the spring, his first act of creation in twenty-three years. She remembered the way his hands had moved, sure and skilled despite his fear. "We taught each other."

He tugged gently on her hand, drawing her closer. She went willingly, closing the distance until she could rest her forehead against his chest. His heart beat steady and strong beneath her ear. His arms came around her carefully, as if she might break.

"You can hold tighter." She wrapped her own arms around his waist. "I won't shatter."

His embrace tightened, solid and warm, and

everything she'd denied herself for decades. No visions intruded. No cascade of memories. Just Joe, present and real, holding her like she mattered.

She pulled back enough to look up at him. In the firelight, his face looked softer, younger, hope smoothing away the lines that worry had carved. "What happens now?"

"Now?" He smiled, small and wondering. "Now we figure it out together."

Together. She wasn't alone anymore. Wasn't broken.

She was a Guardian of Moonlight Springs, surrounded by people who understood, protected by magic that recognized her as its own. She was a woman who could hold someone's hand without fear, who could accept an embrace without armor.

She was home.

Laughter drifted from the kitchen, followed by the rich scent of brewing coffee. Leanne took Joe's hand and led him toward the sound and the family she'd found in the most unexpected place.

CHAPTER 27

Aweek after claiming the Amber Stone, Leanne stood in the doorway of her room at the Moonlight Inn and stared at her collection of gloves laid out across the bed. Leather ones, cotton ones, silk ones for summer, and wool ones for winter. An entire wardrobe dedicated to avoidance.

She picked up a pair of soft gray cotton gloves and slipped one on her right hand. The familiar fabric settled against her skin. Then she pulled it off again and dropped it back onto the bed.

Old habits. Time to break them.

Her bare hands felt strange and exposed as she made her way downstairs. The bannister called to her with its accumulated history, but she ignored the temptation. Small steps. That's what Verena had advised. Learn your new limits before you push them.

The morning sun poured through the windows, turning the kitchen into a cozy haven. Coffee and cinnamon scented the air. Verena stood at the kitchen counter kneading bread dough, her movements rhythmic and sure.

"Morning." Leanne poured herself a cup of coffee from the pot on the stove.

"Sleep well?" Verena shaped the dough into a smooth ball.

"Better than I have in years." She wrapped both hands around the warm mug. The ceramic held only the faintest whisper of history. Nothing overwhelming. Nothing she couldn't handle. "Turns out saving the world from a time chaos collapse is exhausting."

Verena's laugh rippled soft and knowing. "I've found that to be true, yes."

An envelope rested against the sugar bowl, her name written across the front in strong, practical handwriting. She recognized Joe's script from the notes he'd made in his furniture catalog.

"That came for you about an hour ago." Verena covered the dough with a cloth. "Hand delivered."

She set down her coffee and picked up the envelope. The paper felt crisp and new under her fingers. No visions. Just paper and ink and possibility.

She opened it and pulled out a single card.

*Meet me in the maze at the bench at ten? I have something to show you.*

The words were simple and direct. Pure Joe. She folded the note and slipped it into her pocket before she could overthink it.

"Good news, I hope?" Verena's eyes sparkled with what could only be described as matchmaking satisfaction.

"Yes. Good news." She smiled as she said it.

She spent the next hour trying to decide what to wear, which was ridiculous. She'd spent decades avoiding human contact, and now she was worried about whether her blouse looked better tucked in or left out. Finally, she settled on dark jeans and a soft blue sweater that Joe had once mentioned he liked.

When had she started choosing her clothes based on what he might notice?

Somewhere between the grandfather clock and the Hidden Spring, apparently. Somewhere between terror and trust.

At ten o'clock precisely, she made her way toward the maze entrance. The maze rose before her, its hedges thick, green, and neatly trimmed. She'd walked these paths as a girl, racing Verena to the center and back. The memory sat gently in her mind, sweet and unthreatening.

She stepped into the maze's entrance and turned left. Joe stood waiting by the oak bench. He wore jeans and a flannel shirt rolled to his elbows. His hair looked slightly disheveled. In the morning light, he looked younger. Nervous. Hopeful.

"Hi." He smiled, and warmth spread through her chest.

"Hi yourself." She crossed to stand in front of him. "I got your note."

"I noticed." His smile widened. "You came."

"Well, you did say you had something to show me. I'm curious by nature." She gestured toward the bench. "Should I be worried? Did you find another secret compartment with another impossible task?"

"No more impossible tasks. I promise." He turned and picked up something from the bench's seat. A wooden box, roughly the size of a large jewelry case, crafted from golden oak that glowed in the dappled sunlight.

Her hands rose automatically, drawn to the piece. "Joe. Did you make this?"

"Finished it this morning." He held it out to her. "It's for you."

She took the box carefully, her bare fingers touching wood that sang with newness. No visions flooded her mind. Just the warmth of recently worked wood and the faint scent of oil and polish.

The craftsmanship was extraordinary. The joints fit together seamlessly. The grain flowed in beautiful patterns across the lid. A crescent moon had been carved into the top, each curve precise and elegant.

"This is beautiful." She traced the moon with one fingertip. "I mean it. This is exceptional work."

"Open it." He watched her with an expression of pride mixed with a touch of vulnerability.

She found the small brass clasp and lifted the lid. Inside, the box was lined with soft velvet the color of midnight.

"There's a secret compartment for the Amber Stone."

A secret compartment. Just like the bench. Just like his great-grandfather's work.

"There's a trick to it." Joe reached over and pressed two spots on the box's side simultaneously. A small drawer slid open, revealing a second compartment beneath the first, just large enough for the Amber Stone.

"You made a secret compartment." Wonder softened her voice. "Your first new piece in twenty-three years has a secret compartment."

"Seemed appropriate." He ducked his head, almost bashful. "Given the circumstances."

She closed the box and held it against her chest, feeling the solid reality of it. Joe had created this. He'd chosen wood, shaped it, joined it, and finished it. He'd broken his long exile from creation to make something beautiful for her.

"Thank you." The words felt inadequate for what she meant. "This is the most thoughtful gift anyone has ever given me."

"And I've been sketching." He pulled a small notebook from his back pocket and opened it to show her pages filled with furniture designs. Tables and chairs and cabinets, all rendered in careful detail. "New pieces. Things I haven't made before."

She studied the drawings, seeing his vision take shape in pencil lines. "These are wonderful. You should make them."

"I'm going to." He closed the notebook and met her eyes. "I decided I'm done hiding behind other people's work. Time to create again."

She set the box carefully on the bench and took his hand, threading their fingers together. "I'm so glad."

"What about you?" He squeezed her hand gently. "How are you managing?"

"Learning." She looked down at their joined hands. Still strange. Still miraculous. "I've been practicing with small things. Touching objects just long enough to get impressions without being overwhelmed."

"Is it working?"

"Mostly." She thought of the milk glass vase she'd tested herself with that morning. The brief flash of its history, clear and manageable. "I'm starting to understand the boundaries. With Guardians and people connected to the town's magic, I'm safe. With objects, I can control the flow if I'm careful. With strangers..." She shrugged. "I don't know yet. Haven't been brave enough to test it."

"That's fair." He pulled her closer, until barely a foot of space separated them. "You've been plenty brave already."

The maze around them felt cozy and protective. Somewhere overhead, a robin sang its territorial claim. The sun warmed her shoulders.

Joe's thumb traced circles on the back of her hand, the gesture absent and affectionate. "So what comes next?"

"Next?" She raised her eyebrows. "I just saved the town from annihilation. I was hoping for a break before the next crisis."

His laugh rumbled low and genuine. "I meant for you. Now that you're a Guardian. Now that you've found what you came for."

Oh. The real question hiding behind the casual words. She heard it clearly. *Are you staying?*

Her heart picked up speed. This mattered. How she answered this mattered more than anything had mattered in a long time.

"Well." She kept her tone light, conversational. "I suppose I should figure out where I'm going to live. Can't stay at the inn forever, though Verena's been incredibly generous."

"There are some nice places in town." Joe's voice matched her casual tone, but his hand tightened slightly on hers. "The apartment above the old Five and Dime just opened up. Good light. Lots of space."

"I saw that listing." She looked up at him through her lashes. "Of course, I'd need a reason to stay in Moonlight Springs. I'm hoping someone will ask me."

Joe went very still. The playful pretense dropped away, leaving only hope in his expression. "Leanne."

"I've become kind of attached to this town." She let her own mask slip, letting him see the truth she'd been holding close. "And the people in it."

"The town needs its Guardian." His voice came out rougher now. "The Amber Stone belongs here. You should stay."

"Should I?" She tilted her head, watching him. "Is the Stone the only reason?"

"No." The word came swift and certain. "No, that's not the only reason."

"What's the other reason?"

Joe released her hand and brought both of his up to frame her face. His palms felt warm against her cheeks, his calluses rough and real and perfect. "There's a man here who cares very deeply for you. He'd like you to stay in Moonlight Springs."

"Would he?"

"Yes." Joe's eyes searched hers. "Very much."

"Then I should probably stay." The words came easily, as natural as breathing. "Since I care very deeply for him too."

He grinned. Actually grinned, like a kid. "Yeah?"

"Yeah." She covered his hands with her own, holding him there. "Absolutely yes."

He stepped closer, erasing the last bit of distance between them. She could feel the warmth radiating from him, see the fine lines around his eyes, and the silver threading his hair. She could smell sawdust and coffee and the subtle scent of the oil he used on his woodwork.

His gaze dropped to her mouth, then rose back to her eyes. A question.

Fear spiked through her anticipation. She wanted this. Wanted him. But the memory of Daniel rose like a ghost between them.

Years ago, she'd tried this. She had removed her gloves for a man she thought she loved. At first, the kiss had been sweet and gentle and normal. The next moment it had opened the floodgates. She'd been swept into his memories, drowning in his past traumas and fears and regrets. The psychic connection had been so intense, so invasive, that he'd pushed her away in horror.

Would that happen with Joe? Was a kiss one touch too far?

"Leanne?" He must have seen something in her expression. "We don't have to—"

"I want to." She cut him off. "I just don't know what will happen."

Understanding dawned in his eyes. "You mean visions."

"A kiss is more... intimate than a touch. A closer connection. When I kissed Daniel, it was fine at first. Then suddenly it wasn't. He couldn't forgive me for seeing inside him like that."

"I'm not Daniel." Joe's voice stayed steady and sure.

"I know." She did know. Joe was different. He wasn't Daniel. She'd known that for weeks. Knowing it and trusting it were different problems.

"We can wait." His thumbs stroked gently along her cheekbones. "However long you need."

"I don't want to wait." The words burst out of her. "I'm so tired of being afraid. I'm so tired of denying myself every normal human connection because of what might happen."

"Then trust the magic." He smiled, soft and encouraging. "It's protected you so far."

He was right. The magic had changed things. It had given her boundaries, control, and safety she'd never had before. She could touch the Guardians without consequence. Could touch Joe and feel only warmth.

Why should a kiss be different?

"Okay." She rose on her toes, bringing her mouth closer to his. "Okay. Yes."

Joe closed the remaining distance slowly, giving

her every chance to pull back. His lips brushed hers once, feather-light and questioning.

No visions came. Just the soft pressure of his mouth, the warmth of his breath, the gentle way he held her face like she was something precious.

Relief and joy flooded through her. She pressed closer, deepening the kiss, and still no psychic overflow threatened. Just sensation. Just connection. Just Joe.

When they finally pulled apart, both breathing harder, she laughed. The sound burst out of her, bright and disbelieving and full of wonder.

"What?" Joe's smile matched her own.

"Nothing." She shook her head, feeling giddy. "Everything. I can kiss you. I can actually kiss you without my brain exploding."

"Good to know." His eyes crinkled with humor. "I was planning on doing it again."

"You should probably do it soon." She looped her arms around his neck. "Before I start overthinking things."

"Can't have that." He leaned down and captured her mouth again.

This kiss lasted longer and grew deeper. She lost herself in the kiss, no longer thinking about visions or anything really. Only his lips.

When they broke apart this time, Joe rested his forehead against hers. "I love you."

Her eyes widened. "What?"

"I love you." He repeated it like it was easy, like it didn't represent everything she'd convinced herself she couldn't have. "I'm pretty sure I started falling for you the moment you walked into the library and tried to hide that you were terrified."

"No, I was very good at hiding it." Her voice came out shaky.

"You were terrible at hiding it." He pressed a kiss to her forehead. "But you were brave anyway. That's what got me."

Tears filled her eyes. Happy tears. Grateful tears. She blinked them back and smiled up at him. "I love you too. In case that wasn't clear from the excessive kissing."

His laugh vibrated through his chest into hers. "I hoped. But it's nice to hear."

"I'm probably going to say it a lot." The admission came easily. "I've got years of not saying things to make up for."

"Say it as much as you want." His hand came up to tuck a strand of hair behind her ear, the gesture casual and intimate. "I won't get tired of hearing it."

She caught his hand and pressed a kiss to his palm. "I love you. And I'm grateful I can touch you."

"Touch me anytime you want." His eyes sparkled with affection. "I'm not going anywhere."

"Anytime?" She raised an eyebrow. "That's a dangerous promise."

"I'm a brave man." He grinned. "And you're worth the risk."

"Keep talking like that, and I'm going to kiss you again."

"Please do." He bent his head toward hers. "I'm counting on it."

So she did. She kissed him in the maze where his great-grandfather's bench guarded its secrets. She kissed him with decades of loneliness transforming into hope. She kissed him until the sun climbed higher and the moonflowers opened up as if signaling their approval.

# CHAPTER 28

Verena walked the familiar paths of her maze, her hand tucked comfortably into the crook of Gary's arm. The evening air held the crisp bite of winter. Not that it stopped the moonflowers from unfurling as they passed by, their white petals luminous in the fading light.

"This never gets old." Gary's voice rumbled low and content beside her. "Walking here with you."

She smiled and squeezed his arm. They'd walked these paths forty years ago, certain about everything. Now she wasn't certain about much, except that she wanted him beside her.

"I've walked these paths alone for a long time." The admission came easily. No walls between them anymore. No careful distance. "It's better with company."

"I'm not going anywhere. You're stuck with me now."

"Promise?" She glanced up at him, watching the way the last rays of sunlight caught in his silver hair.

"Cross my heart." He made the gesture with his free hand, solemn as a child making a vow.

They turned left at the next junction, following the spiral path toward the maze's center. The stone bench waited there, weathered and solid. She'd sat on that bench through every season of her life. Through joy and grief. Through decades of choosing duty over desire.

She wasn't choosing anymore. She was allowing herself both.

Gary settled onto the bench and tugged her down beside him. She went willingly, tucking herself against his side. His arm came around her shoulders, solid and sure.

"Do you regret it?" The question slipped out before she could stop it. "Coming back here? All this chaos you escaped when you left?"

He turned to look at her fully, his eyes serious. "Vee. Not even a little bit."

"But it's been one crisis after another since you arrived. Time disturbances and missing stones, and Blake Denton causing trouble." She picked at a thread on her skirt. "You could have stayed away. Had a peaceful retirement somewhere quiet."

"Peaceful retirement." He snorted. "That sounds boring."

Despite herself, she laughed. "Most people find peace appealing."

"Most people aren't close with the Guardian of a magical town." His hand came up to tilt her face toward his. "I came back because this is where I belong. Because you're here. Because I wasted forty years trying to convince myself I could build a life somewhere else."

She swallowed hard against the surge of emotion. "Gary."

"I have one regret." His thumb traced along her jaw, tender and careful. "Just one."

"What's that?"

"That I didn't understand all this back then. That I asked you to leave instead of finding a way to stay." His eyes held shadows of old pain. "If I'd been less stubborn, less certain that I knew what was best, maybe we wouldn't have lost all those years."

She covered his hand with hers, pressing it more firmly against her cheek. "We both made choices. I could have explained better. Could have trusted you with more of the truth."

"I'm not sure I would have been ready to believe you back then." He shook his head. "You were twenty-two and carrying the weight of protecting an entire town. I was twenty-two and thought love should be simple. That you just decided what you wanted and everything else fell into place."

"We were young." She turned her head to press a kiss to his palm. "And foolish. And so certain we had all the time in the world."

"And now we're old and hopefully wiser." He smiled. "And we know exactly how precious time is."

"Not that old." She raised an eyebrow. "Speak for yourself."

His laugh rolled through the maze. "Fair enough. Seasoned. Experienced. Distinguished."

"Better." She settled back against him, watching the moonflowers. "I keep thinking about how close we came to missing this. This chance."

"What do you mean?"

"If you hadn't come back. If you'd decided Moonlight Springs was part of your past and stayed away." Her fingers found his and threaded through them. "If I'd been too stubborn or too scared to let you in again."

"But we didn't miss it." He squeezed her hand. "I came back. You let me stay. We found our way here."

"Barely. I fought it so hard at first. Convinced myself we'd already had our chance and lost it. That second chances were fairy tales."

"Are you sorry I pushed?" His voice held a note of uncertainty she rarely heard from him.

"No." She twisted to face him more fully. "I'm grateful. So grateful you were stubborn enough for both of us."

"Stubbornness is one of my best qualities." His smile returned, warm and self-deprecating. "That and my devastating good looks."

She laughed and swatted his shoulder. "Your humility is also notable."

"I'm a complicated man." He caught her hand and brought it to his lips. "But my feelings about you are pretty simple. And I thank whatever powers brought me back here."

"It was probably my magical powers." She smiled at him.

Then a voice spoke from directly behind them. "How lovely."

Verena jerked upright. Gary was on his feet in an instant, standing between Verena and the voice.

Zara Bollinger stood three feet away, her silver hair gleaming in the twilight. She wore her customary flowing dress, this one the color of storm clouds. Her ageless face held an expression of serene amusement.

"Zara." Verena pressed a hand to her chest, willing her pulse to slow. "You startled me."

"My apologies." Zara didn't sound particularly apologetic. "I didn't mean to interrupt."

"How did you get in here?" Gary's sheriff

instincts had kicked in, his body still tense and alert. "We didn't hear you approach."

"That sometimes happens." Zara's smile suggested mysteries she had no intention of explaining. "The maze and I are old friends."

Verena stood slowly, smoothing her skirt. Something in Zara's manner set her Guardian senses humming. This wasn't a social call. "Is something wrong?"

"Wrong? No." Zara's gaze moved between them, measuring and knowing. "I came to offer congratulations. The fifth stone has been secured. Leanne has claimed her role as Guardian of the Amber Stone."

Verena studied the other woman's face, looking for clues. "Your riddles pointed them in the right direction."

"I merely offered suggestions." Zara's expression remained unreadable. "The work was theirs."

Gary had relaxed slightly but still watched Zara with the careful attention he gave to anything he didn't fully understand. "Five down, one to go."

"Indeed." Zara turned her full attention to him. "Five stones create a foundation. But only the final stone, the Opal of Unity, can build the house."

The words fell into the quiet evening like pebbles into still water, rippling outward with meaning. The Opal. The final stone.

"The Opal." Gary looked at Verena, then back at Zara. "That's the last one. The Unity stone."

"Yes." Zara's gaze locked onto Verena's face, intent and knowing. "And it will require the greatest unity of all."

The air between them seemed to thicken. Verena felt the certainty settle into her bones. This was it. The moment she'd been both dreading and anticipating her whole life. As each Guardian found their stone, she'd known her own time was approaching.

"Unity." She repeated the word slowly, tasting its implications. "Between the Guardians?"

"Among other things." Zara's smile turned cryptic.

She looked pointedly at Verena, then at Gary, then back to Verena. The message couldn't have been clearer if she'd written it in skywriting.

Gary's hand found Verena's, his fingers threading through hers. "What exactly are you saying?"

"I'm saying that some stones require not just one Guardian but two." Zara's voice gentled slightly. "I'm saying that love and duty need not be separate paths. I'm saying that the Opal has been waiting a very long time for both of you to be ready."

The words hung in the air like a benediction. Or a challenge. Verena wasn't entirely sure which.

"Both of us." Gary's grip on her hand tightened. "You mean Verena and me. Together."

"The Stone of Unity tends to favor unity, yes." Zara's eyes sparkled with something that might have been humor. "Fitting, don't you think?"

Before Verena could formulate a response, Zara stepped backward into the shadows between the hedges. One moment she was there, solid and real. The next, she had melted into the darkness as if she'd never existed at all.

"Wait." Verena stepped forward, but the space where Zara had stood held only empty air and moonflower petals.

Gary moved to her side, peering into the shadows. "Did she just disappear?"

"She does that." Verena released a shaky breath. "I still haven't figured out how."

"Add it to the list of things about this town that don't make sense." He turned to face her fully. "Vee. The last stone. The Opal."

She met his eyes and saw understanding dawning there. "Yes."

"It's your stone. You're the Guardian of the Opal." Not a question. A statement of fact delivered with quiet certainty.

She nodded, her throat too tight for words.

"How long have you known?"

"I'm not sure. At some point, I just knew." She shrugged. "Years ago. It was right before you left."

His eyes widened. "That's why you couldn't leave. Not just the inn. Not just the town. You were protecting the final stone."

"I was Guardian of all six, technically." She looked down at their joined hands. "My family has been for generations."

"Do you know where the Opal is?"

"No, but I'm certain it will reveal itself when it's ready."

"And you think it's nearing that time now?"

"Five stones have been found. Five Guardians have claimed their roles." She turned back toward the bench and sank onto it, suddenly weary. "The pattern is clear. The Opal is the final piece."

Gary sat beside her and circled an arm around her shoulders. "What does that mean? For you? For us?"

"I don't know." Honest uncertainty. "Zara said it would require unity. That it needs both of us."

"Both of us." He turned the words over carefully. "She was pretty clear about that."

"She was." Verena looked up at the first stars beginning to appear in the darkening sky. "The Opal Stone of Unity. It makes a certain poetic sense that it would require two Guardians working together."

"Two Guardians." Gary's arm came around her shoulders, drawing her close. "Or one Guardian and one stubborn sheriff."

Despite the uncertainty churning inside her, she smiled. "The second one."

"I can work with that." He squeezed her shoulder. "Whatever you need. Whatever it takes. I'm with you."

"It could be dangerous." She had to warn him. Had to make sure he understood. "All the stones have tested their Guardians. Required them to face their fears and grow past their limitations."

"Then we'll face it together. That's what unity means, isn't it? Not doing it alone."

She looked up at the stars before looking back at him. "I've been alone with this for so long."

"Not anymore. You're stuck with me, remember? For whatever comes next."

She pulled back enough to look at him properly. In the gathering darkness, his face looked younger. Softer. Full of the same determination she'd fallen in love with decades ago.

"What do we need to do?" He brushed a lock of her hair away from her cheek.

"I don't know yet." The admission came hard. She'd spent her life knowing, planning, protecting. This felt different. Bigger. "Wait for the sign. Prepare ourselves. Trust that we'll know when the moment comes."

"That's not very specific." A hint of his dry humor colored the words.

"Magic rarely is." She smiled despite her nerves. "It prefers drama and mystery to clear instruction."

"Inconvenient." He smoothed his thumbs along her cheekbones. "But I suppose that's part of the charm."

She studied his face, looking for signs of fear or doubt. "You're taking this remarkably well. Most people would be terrified."

"Most people aren't dating the Guardian of Moonlight Springs." His smile warmed her from the inside out. "I knew what I was signing up for when I came back."

"Did you?" She raised an eyebrow. "Really?"

"Okay, maybe not the specific details." He laughed softly. "Okay, I had no idea what I was walking into."

"And you came back anyway."

"I came back because of… you."

Her heart felt too full for her chest. She wrapped her arms around his neck and held on, letting herself lean into his strength. "I'm glad."

"Me too. So what now?"

"Now?" She pulled back and stood, tugging him to his feet. "Now we go inside and have some tea. Maybe some of that lemon cake Ivy brought over this afternoon. And we wait."

"Wait for the Opal to call to you."

"Something like that." She took his hand and led him toward the maze's exit. "The stones have a way of making themselves known when they're ready."

They emerged from the maze. Lights glowed in the windows, warm and welcoming. Home. Her home. The place she'd chosen over everything else.

Except now she didn't have to choose. She had both. The inn and the magic and the man walking beside her.

Above them, the moon rose higher, full and bright. Somewhere in town, the five stones rested with their chosen protectors. And somewhere, hidden and waiting, the Opal Stone of Unity prepared to reveal itself.

Verena took Gary's hand. The porch steps creaked under their weight, just as they had for a hundred years.

# CHAPTER 29

Zara emerged from the maze's shadow paths and stopped at the wooden bench, her hand resting briefly on the weathered oak. The wood felt cool beneath her palm, familiar as an old friend. More than an old friend, really. A keeper of secrets she'd helped create.

She pressed her fingers more firmly against the bench's surface, feeling the grain of the wood. Charles Joseph Hall had built this piece with such care. She could still see him in her mind's eye, his skilled hands planing and sanding, his brow creased in concentration.

The wood remembered Charles Hall's hands. The careful way he'd shaped each joint, the precision of his tools, the quiet pride he'd taken in creating something meant to last.

The wood remembered her too. The day she'd stood here watching Charles finish his work, her heart caught between hope and dread. The day she'd placed the Amber Stone in its hidden compartment and sealed it away from the world.

From Blake Denton.

She drew her hand back and tucked it into the folds of her dress. Even after all these years, thinking of his name created an ache behind her ribs. The ache wasn't sharp anymore. Time had dulled the edge. But the scar remained, a reminder of choices made and prices paid.

The moon climbed higher, spilling silver light across the maze. She'd walked these paths in every season, watched them grow from tender shoots to towering hedges. Watched generations of Guardians tend them, each adding their own touch to Verena's family legacy.

Old soul. That's what the legends called people like her, but most folks considered that a poetic metaphor rather than a literal truth. People who shouldn't exist. People who watched centuries pass like most people watched seasons pass. They didn't imagine someone like her who had quit counting her birthdays when she turned one hundred and fifty.

And the legends never mentioned the loneliness.

She settled onto the bench and looked up at the stars. The same stars she'd watched the night everything changed. The night she'd first held all six stones, their combined magic singing through her blood. The night their power had transformed her into something more than human and less than whole.

She'd told herself it was protection. The stones needed someone. She'd made herself that someone. Someone had to be their keeper, their Guardian across the years. Someone had to make sure they were divided and hidden before Blake could claim them.

Before he could use them to reshape the world according to his vision.

Even now, she couldn't think about what he'd wanted without feeling the betrayal slice fresh and new. He'd stood in her parlor, his eyes bright with ambition, and explained his plans. How the stones could grant him power. How together they could rule. How love was simply another form of control if you knew how to wield it properly.

She'd loved him. That was the cruel truth. She'd loved Blake Denton with everything she had, believed in the goodness she'd glimpsed beneath his hunger for more. Convinced herself that love could transform him, gentle him, teach him that power meant nothing without compassion.

She'd been spectacularly wrong.

Zara stood and walked the perimeter of the bench, her fingers trailing along the wood. Charles had crafted this piece from grove oak, the same trees that sheltered the Hidden Spring. The magic in the wood called to the magic that flowed through her, a quiet conversation that never quite stopped.

She'd come back to this bench decades later, when her hair had silvered, and her face had lined with age that would never progress further. Had sat here and said goodbye to the stone, knowing it wasn't time yet. The town needed to settle. The magic needed to stabilize. Blake needed to believe the stones were lost forever.

Only they weren't lost. They'd simply been waiting.

She pressed her palm flat against the place where the hidden compartment rested. Empty now. Leanne had claimed the Amber Stone, had done exactly what she was meant to do despite her fears. Despite Blake's interference.

Blake. Always Blake, circling back like a predator who'd never stopped hunting.

The shudder that moved through her had nothing to do with the evening chill. He'd come so close. Had held the stone in his hands, had tried to bend it to his will just like he'd tried to bend her all those years ago. The thought of him possessing the Amber Stone's power sent a shiver through her.

But he'd failed. The stone had rejected him. The spring had rejected him. And yet, she was certain he wouldn't quit trying.

Blake hadn't learned. Even with centuries to reflect, to grow, to become something better than his worst impulses, he'd chosen greed over growth. Had convinced himself that power was the only thing worth pursuing.

She rose slowly and left the maze. Five stones safe now. Five Guardians who'd faced their fears and claimed their power. Five pieces of a puzzle that had taken lifetimes to arrange.

One more to go.

The Opal Stone of Unity. The most important stone. The one that bound all the others together, that created harmony from separate notes. The one meant for Verena.

She smiled despite the ache in her chest. Verena would be spectacular. Was already spectacular. The woman had shouldered an impossible burden with grace and strength, had protected this town and its magic for decades without asking for recognition or relief.

Now she would have both. Gary would make sure of that.

She had watched them find their way back to each other with something close to envy. Not because she wanted what they had. She'd made her peace with solitude long ago. But because they'd been given what she and Blake had destroyed. A second chance. A choice to do things differently.

Unity required two people willing to stand together. To trust despite fear.

She and Blake had failed that test. Verena and Gary wouldn't.

Zara paused, looking back at the maze walls that held so many secrets. The time capsule had changed her. The stones had marked her. And Blake's betrayal had taught her that some wounds never fully healed, no matter how many years you had to recover.

She pulled her shawl tighter and headed down the path. The night embraced her like an old friend. She'd walked through centuries of nights, and she was tired. Bone-deep tired, the kind that had nothing to do with sleep. But soon Verena would try to claim the final stone. The work of all these years might finally mean something.

And perhaps, when the last stone found its Guardian, she might finally find something she'd stopped believing in centuries ago—rest.

Dear Reader, I hope you enjoyed Leanne's story. Now, are you ready for the final book in the series, *Hidden Springs?* Yes, Verena finally gets her own book!

And if you missed the beginning of Verena and Gary's story, you can sign up for my newsletter and get *Where it Begins: Verena and Gary's Story*. Watch for an email to confirm your signup and then an email with the download link.

Thank you for spending time in the world of Moonlight Springs with me. I hope it left a little bit of magic in your heart and your life. *~Lula*

Find more information on all my books at
***LulaWardAuthor.com***

**MOONLIGHT SPRINGS ~ THE SERIES**
Starlight Antiques - Book One
Sweet Memories Bakery - Book Two
Enchanted Bookshop - Book Three
Painted Visions - Book Four
Moonlight Inn - Book Five
Hidden Springs - Book Six

Thank you for reading my story. I hope you enjoyed it.

Want to be the first to know about exclusive promotions, news, giveaways, and new releases? You can sign up on my website:

https://lulawardauthor.com/newsletter-sign-up/

Visit my website:

https://LulaWardAuthor.com/

## MOONLIGHT SPRINGS ~ THE SERIES

Starlight Antiques - Book One

Sweet Memories Bakery - Book Two

Enchanted Bookshop - Book Three

Painted Visions - Book Four

Moonlight Inn - Book Five

Hidden Springs - Book Six

Meet Lula Ward:

Hi, I'm Lula—lover of soft magic, small towns, and stories where the heart always finds its way home. I write cozy fantasy for women who crave a little wonder, a little warmth, and just enough enchantment to make you believe in the impossible again.

My books are filled with gentle spells, old secrets, and strong, heartfelt characters—often with a cup of tea in hand and a second chance just around the bend.

The *Moonlight Springs* series is my love letter to magical places that feel like home. If you enjoy women's fiction with a touch of romance and a sprinkle of everyday magic, you're in the right place.

Learn more about me and my books at
LulaWardAuthor.com

While you're there, sign up for my newsletter to hear about new releases, sales, and giveaways.

facebook.com/LulaWardAuthor
instagram.com/LulaWardAuthor
pinterest.com/LulaWardAuthor